A TASTE OF SIN

Books by Fiona Zedde

BLISS

A TASTE OF SIN

Published by Kensington Publishing Corporation

A TASTE OF SIN

Fiona Zedde

KENSINGTON BOOKS
http://www.kensingtonbooks.com

KENSINGTON BOOKS are published by

Kensington Publishing Corp.
850 Third Avenue
New York, NY 10022

All Kensington titles, imprints and distributed lines are available at special quantity discounts for bulk purchases for sales promotion, premiums, fund raising, educational or institutional use.

Special book excerpts or customized printings can also be created to fit specific needs. For details, write or phone the office of the Kensington Special Sales Manager: Kensington Publishing Corp., 850 Third Avenue, New York, NY 10022. Attn. Special Sales Department. Phone: 1-800-221-2647.

Kensington and the K logo Reg. U.S. Pat. & TM Off.

ISBN 0-7582-0920-7

First Kensington Trade Paperback Printing: July 2006
10 9 8 7 6 5 4 3 2 1

Printed in the United States of America

A TASTE OF SIN

Chapter 1

"Excuse me?"

Ruben flinched at the sharply hissed words but didn't stop stuffing clothes into his duffel bag. "I said I'm leaving. Caitlyn is waiting for me in the car."

Dez backed up and crossed her arms, a precaution against the sudden urge toward violence that bubbled up inside. He was leaving her. For another woman. If this wasn't some surreal, fucked-up shit. She focused on her anger. It kept her attention away from the pain that started a few seconds ago when she had walked in on him dragging clothes out of the closet and flinging them into his bag.

Their argument yesterday hadn't prepared her for any of this. He was spending too much time with that girl, the stranger they picked up in Santa Fe a week ago on a whim. Yesterday, nothing was said about leaving, about dumping Dez in the middle of the desert like trash. This was coming way the fuck out of nowhere. Wasn't it just three days ago that they were trading body fluids on the stairs leading up to this very room, their hands tight over each other's mouths to stop their noises from waking the people down the hall? The whole time when they were fucking was he thinking about the other one—Caitlyn—as his dick moved inside her, as Dez's fingers moved inside him, making him shudder and quake and almost bite her fingers off when he came?

She took a deep breath and fought for calm. "Why are you doing this to me, Ru?"

"Dez, what we had was casual. Neither of us wanted anything permanent so I'm not doing anything to you. I'm just giving you the room you need."

"Room? Are you fucking kidding me? For two years you were ten feet up my ass looking like you wanted to stay there for life and now you're talking about *room*."

"She doesn't know." That, too, came out of nowhere. He made his voice soft as if Caitlyn could hear him through the walls.

"Doesn't know what? That you're as much of a queer as I am? That I fuck your ass every night and you love it? Shit." Her voice rose in a wail, dragging out the last word until she clamped her lips shut over it.

He didn't have anything to say. Dez watched him finish up, zip the bag closed, then rush into the bathroom for something that sounded like his toothbrush and the oversize Ziploc bag full of condoms. The bag that Dez had just filled. He came back into the room and looked at her briefly, his eyes skittering over her stone face.

"Sorry." Then he was gone.

She squeezed the bridge of her nose. Fisted her stinging eyes. Breathing deeply, she tightened her eyelids until dark spots danced behind them, but when she opened them the pain was still there. Beyond the window, the taillights of Caitlyn's powder blue Ford Thunderbird flashed to life. Ruben jumped into the convertible and they coasted down the drive.

Dez turned away from the window in disgust. There was no point in staring after them like some lovesick little bitch. There were things to be done. But when her gaze raked the room, she couldn't think of a single fucking thing that she wanted to do. Not one. At the desk near the door lay a scattered heap of letters she'd gotten from the mailbox in

Albuquerque earlier that day. With relief she grabbed the one with her mother's handwriting, the rectangular business-sized envelope with the pink valentine stamp. She ripped open the letter, needing comfort badly. She glanced at the sheets of paper with their flowing green script, then blinked when the print blurred before her eyes. Shit. Dez flung the letter down and grabbed her jacket. She had to get out of here. As she tugged the jacket on and headed for the door, her cell phone rang.

"Hello?"

"Ms. Desiree Nichols?"

"Yes. Can I help you?"

The official-sounding voice on the other end asked politely if she knew where her mother was. She battled her impatience long enough to be courteous in return and kept walking. Then the woman mentioned a biopsy and test results and Dez stopped walking. All thoughts of Ruben and his red-headed fucktoy disintegrated and blew away on the breeze like ashes. She paused in the middle of the hallway. Her hand lifted and fell against the pink and green floral wallpaper. The hardwood floor seemed to stretch out for miles beyond her feet and suddenly the white banister leading downstairs seemed very necessary for her to stay upright. Dez cleared her throat. She pressed the phone to her ear, listening carefully for anything that would tell that this was some sort of stupid prank, that she was on *Punk'd* or something. The voice continued. No one jumped out from behind the wallpaper to tell her that it was all a joke. The woman wanted to change Claudia's appointment and needed confirmation that she would be there. She wasn't answering any of her numbers in Miami, and Dez was listed as next of kin on her forms. It was very important that Claudia show up for the appointment. Could Dez guarantee her presence? Through the pounding in her ears, she said yes, finessing more information out of the woman until all she could do was hold the phone against her ear and stare at the closed door at the end of the hallway. Ovarian cancer. As soon as the woman hung up the phone, Dez called home.

"Ma, your doctor's office just called. They need you to come in on the second of next month instead of the eighteenth." She stumbled over the rest, unable to maintain coherence with the unresponsive voice mail. After she hung up, Dez turned abruptly back to her room to start packing.

Chapter 2

Claudia wasn't home. Dez stood in the middle of her mother's house feeling another flood of panic. She glanced at her watch: 2:47 A.M. Barely three minutes since the last time she looked at it. *Where was Claudia? Was she back in the hospital? Had Derrick even tried to reach her?* Her mother's Audi TT sat in the garage, the engine cold and silent. The kitchen was equally quiet, with only the hum of the refrigerator to distract Dez from her panic. Fear turned her fingers cold.

The kitchen was spotless, with everything neatly ordered and put away. Copper pots winked at her from their place above the kitchen island. Nothing was out of place. Dez focused on that with desperation. If Claudia had gotten sick again, no one would have taken the time to do this, and certainly Claudia wouldn't have been able to.

Dez dug out her cell phone and called Derrick. She didn't realize that she was crying until she heard her own broken voice.

"Mama. Where is she?"

There was a pause, a moment of recognition, before her twin spoke. "Mexico. She took off with the McAllisters on their boat about three days ago."

She cried silently with the phone pushed hard against her

ear. The back of her head slapped an unconscious rhythm against the wall. "When will she be back?"

"On the fifteenth, in time for her birthday party. Are you all right?"

"I've been better." Her voice cracked but a quick cough cleared the emotion from her throat. "I'll call you back later, okay?" Eleven days. Her mother would be back in eleven days.

"She's all right, Dez. That whole mess is almost over. She already had the surgery and came through the chemo all right. In a few weeks she'll have a last checkup and we're expecting an all-clear."

"Okay. Thanks. I'll talk to you later," Dez repeated. "Okay." She never knew. All the time this was going on, she never knew.

Her mother was gone and no one told her. What the fuck was Claudia doing in Mexico on a boat if she'd just had chemotherapy? She carefully put the phone away before leaving the house the way she had come.

In the driveway, Dez took a deep lungful of crisp spring air and blinked the grit and wet from her eyes. The crickets played their particular empty music as the last bits of blue bled away from the sky under the silvery blade of the moon. She shoved her helmet on and straddled the bike. The black cherry Ducati 749 roared to life and she sped down the drive and away from her mother's silent house. Barely a mile away, she cruised up to her own gate. The house used to be a church, one she used to pass on her way to school every weekday for years but never entered. Now the sprawling two-story stone-and-glass building was hers, bought and paid for with her dead aunt's money. She'd bought the house a year ago just because she could, figuring that it was the closest she'd ever come to actually going into a church. Dez keyed in the security code at the gate and rode up the long drive and straight into the garage. As she turned off the bike, Dez thought briefly about calling her friends, especially Rémi, to let them know that she was back in town. But her mind shied away from it. She was too raw to face them right now. Even over the phone. Later, sheltered in her new queen-sized bed under cool Egyptian cotton sheets fresh out of the package, Dez slept. She didn't dream.

Dez woke up disoriented. Sunlight tumbled over her naked body, burning through the stained-glass skylight. Shards of red and blue light fragmented her skin and patterned the white sheets that she'd kicked off during the night. Dez felt heavy, weighed down, like she wouldn't be able to leave the bed if she tried. Her flesh steamed. After the cool November of Albuquerque, this warmth felt good, like it was beginning to thaw the ice that had surrounded her body since she got the phone call from her mother's doctor.

Her mind shied away from that call, but the abyss of memory swallowed her anyway, replaying the conversation over and over again until every word was just noise in her brain, thunder that made her head vibrate and hurt. Gradually, the pain floated away and she was able to open her eyes again. Fuck.

But even with her eyes open, she couldn't see. Dez couldn't imagine her mother here in this house, could not see her laughing face at the kitchen table. She could not see her in the library perched on the wheeled ladder, reaching for a book on the top shelf. She could not see her holding Dez's hand in the low evening light, telling her that everything was going to be okay, that one more loss wouldn't break her. Dez couldn't see her mother anywhere but in Mexico somewhere, dying slowly on a beach with cabana boys in tight white Speedos offering an hour's worth of living for sale. She scraped her blunt fingertips across her scalp with its short prickling of hair and stood up to get dressed. She left the house so she could see better.

Chapter 3

The breeze lapped at her cheeks, pressing its comforting salty tang around the edges of her sunglasses as she rode bareheaded at a lazy thirty miles an hour through Coconut Grove. Claudia and death. It didn't seem real. Not when Dez hadn't even heard any of it from her mother's own lips. She shook her head and deliberately turned her thoughts to the smooth stretch of road in front of her bike, the growl of the Ducati between her legs, and the dense border of Spanish moss–laden trees swaying in the light wind. There was beauty before her to enjoy. The other things could wait.

After riding around Miami the better part of the day, she parked the bike at a downtown bar. Dez settled onto a stool and ordered two fingers of her favorite scotch. The place radiated tasteful-boring with its gleaming wooden bar, deep blue teardrop-shaped light fixtures hanging just so above their heads. The only music was the quiet murmurs of the early-evening drinkers, mostly suits with the occasional frilly dress to lighten up the atmosphere. The later the hour became, the more dresses appeared.

Over the rim of her glass, she watched the hem of a pretty skirt flounce by. It belonged to an equally pretty girl. She walked by Dez's stool with three of her girlfriends, each sipping a colored drink with fruit in it. Spelman College type.

Long, straightened hair. A cute little ass swishing under the Gucci skirt. Shy smile. More Derrick's type than hers.

So far Dez hadn't seen anyone that she knew, but that wasn't really a surprise. Aside from Rémi, none of her friends would be caught alive or dead in this particular straight bar. Too many men, too many needy women, not nearly enough dykes.

The way that some of these straight women were draping themselves over one another, some girl-on-girl action may not be too far off in the future. Dez had taken enough straight girls home back in the day to know how easy it would be to get laid in a place like this. Everyone else in the bar seemed content enough, bouncing happily from one potential one-night stand to another, doing a good job of circulating while she sat at the dark end of the bar nursing her drink.

"Excuse me." The pretty girl stood near Dez's elbow looking sweet enough to make her teeth ache. She lost some of that shyness up close. Inside the peach neckline of her dress, her breasts rose and fell with each breath. The girl licked her lips and continued. "I was wondering if—"

"Can I tie you up and fuck you in the ass with my fist?" The girl's eyes widened at Dez's growl. "Because if I can't, you're wasting your time and mine."

The scotch burned a trail across her tongue and down her throat. She nodded as the girl backed away and went back to her small huddle of friends. Dez wasn't in the mood to be nice.

"I guess you're not trying to get laid tonight."

Dez didn't even look up this time. "Not really. Even if you're offering."

"Now is that any way to talk to an old friend?"

Friend? With her eyebrow at a killing arch, she turned to face the source of the voice. And got a little surprise.

"Phil?" She laughed. "What the fuck are you doing here?" She got several looks for that one even as she stood up to hug the tall, leggy woman. In her strappy high heels, thigh-baring skirt, and the scent of a salon clinging to her permed hair, Phillida Howard easily caught the eye of every straight man in the room.

"The same thing you are, I imagine. Getting a drink and maybe a little company for the rest of the night."

"Straight company."

"Like I said, for the rest of the night—not for life." She sat down on the empty stool beside Dez, bringing her cigarette and ashtray with her.

"So where have you been? It's been boring around here without you."

"I'm sure you managed to cope somehow. Rémi knew where I was."

"And she didn't pass on any of that information." Phil took a deep drag of her cigarette. "But the rumor mill did say that you took off with that little gay boy you had a crush on in college."

"Oh, Christ." Dez rolled her eyes. "I did not have a crush on him."

"Whatever." Phil leaned in closer and lowered her voice. "For a while there we all thought you were turning straight on us or something."

"Something else, but never straight," she said with a shrug. "He and I fooled around a little bit, got off together in some spectacular ways, but it was nothing major. He found a straight girlfriend and now he's back here in town."

Phil ashed her cigarette in the heavy crystal tray on the bar. "Are you going to look him up?"

Yeah, and after that I'll search for King Kong and let him fuck me up the ass with no lube. "Maybe."

"Hm-hm." She laughed. "To each her own, baby, that's what I say. Fuck whoever you want. I'm not one to throw any stones."

Ain't that the truth? Even before Dez left Miami, Phil's exploits made Dez seem like a virgin. Group orgies, mother-

and-daughter tag-team sex. There was even talk about some exotic whorehouse for women in Canada where Phil was a regular customer.

"By the way, there's a party going on tomorrow night in Fort Lauderdale. You should come." Without waiting for Dez's response, she scribbled down the address and phone number. "The whole gang should be there."

Phil stayed at the bar long enough to pick up two of the pretty girl's friends. The two who didn't seem quite as innocent. Dez eventually finished her scotch and left. All these straight people in one room were starting to give her hives.

At home she was still restless. Restless and worried. Seeing Phil again had made her forget. Forget Ruben. Her mother's illness. Everything. All the pain had shifted to the background for once and she was able to laugh. She'd missed that. During the two years she'd traveled with Ruben, she kept in touch with her friends, sending them postcards, amusing little letters about whatever town they were in at the time, how easy—or hard—the girls were, and how much she missed Rémi, Sage, Nuria, and even Phil, who she'd only met during her last year of college. These were the girls she'd had to leave behind to follow this boy-dream fever that suddenly took hold of her one night and didn't let go. Not until he jolted her awake by leaving.

After Dez left high school, her Aunt Paulette—the woman she'd sometimes wished was her real mother—had died in a motorcycle accident, leaving Dez shaken to her very foundations. The accident wasn't Paulette's fault, she'd been sober and safe, obeying all the rules she'd taught Dez about riding—and riding around Miami in particular, when some blind little fuck in a souped-up Honda took her out from behind. She never stood a chance. After that, Dez couldn't find an even footing. Her friends hadn't been able to comfort her, neither had her mother. Three years later, still not quite back on solid ground, Ruben Salinas had been escape and alien and fun. The sex wasn't bad either. Dez supposed she should be happy that it lasted as long as it did. But the deepest part of her just wanted him back, wanted to have a taste of that mindless joy just one more time.

Chapter 4

Dez took Phil up on her invitation. On Saturday night she pulled her bike to a stop in front of a grinning valet and handed him her motorcycle keys and helmet. She walked past the well-lit entranceway with its faint scent of jasmine and old money. A steady stream of people, mostly women, flowed toward the house. She slid her hands into her loose-fitting tuxedo pants and went to join them. The wide, marble-paved walkway led to a high, curving balcony overlooking a dimmed dance floor where human constellations mingled and shone together. It would be easy to distance herself from the party, to lean over the balcony and watch the action happen down below. But, as usual, the women and the lights called to her, promising more opportunities for fun than just brooding up here by herself.

The party was well underway with high-energy music and the sound of alcohol-laced laughter, when her feet touched the final step into the opulent ballroom. Dez heard someone call her name. She looked around—glancing past tantalizingly bared flesh, the swell of breasts, wet mouths, and curved backs, past the pleasant distractions—to find the source of that voice.

Phillida stood up from a couch at the far end of the room and waved. She looked gorgeous in a pale, body-skimming blue dress with dyed-to-match flowers sprinkled in her black hair.

"Dez! I'm glad you could make it."

"Of course. You asked so nicely. How could I refuse?" She greeted the other woman with a light kiss on the cheek, eyeing her caramel skin and its artfully displayed cleavage.

"Please. As if I had that much influence over you." She looped her arm through Dez's and pulled her toward the couch. "You remember everybody, right?"

How could she forget these women who she had ran with in high school and then later on in college? They looked much the same now as they did two years ago when Dez left, perhaps only a bit more polished, and a lot more jaded.

"Dez." Rémi Bouchard extended a hand to Dez. When she moved to take it, Rémi grabbed her in a crushing bear hug that drove the air from Dez's lungs. "Bitch, where the fuck have you been?" she demanded with a growl.

The first time Dez saw Rémi, she had to look twice. Before that she'd never known anyone whose looks literally took her breath away. And she didn't even want to fuck her. At least not at first. It was more than the dimpled chin or the devilishly curved lips. It wasn't even the powerful body that she'd seen naked more times than she could count. Feature by feature, Rémi Bouchard was simply the most gorgeous woman that Dez had ever seen. At first sight, all you noticed were the lazy-lidded brown eyes and the mouth that seemed made for pleasure. Later, after the shock of her looks wore off, you saw the deep olive skin with its hints of red, the low-cut wavy hair, and the long elegant hands. At six feet, she was the same height as Dez, only twenty pounds heavier and all of it muscle.

They had been best friends once. In their teens, they'd formed a mutual admiration society, even flirted with each other briefly, with the thought of getting involved. But in time they'd realized the value they both placed on a friendship, being the only two out black dykes in middle school and then later on in high school. After that they'd taken off and traveled for three years together around Africa and the

West Indies, half learning and discarding languages, agonizing over straight women, laughing and crying on each other's shoulders. All that had stopped when Dez's aunt died. Dez had to go back to Florida and Rémi didn't want to stay in Bonaire by herself, so their adventure was over.

"I've been here and there," she said, answering Rémi's question. "I told you in the letters. I just hit Miami last week though."

"What brought you back? I know it wasn't my fine self."

"Some family stuff."

Rémi nodded. Dez would tell her more. Later.

"If the beautiful butch reunion is over, can the rest of us get a turn?" Nuria Diaz leaned her cleavage toward Dez from her seat on the arm of the couch. She pouted prettily then smiled, looking every inch the Dominican princess with her cocoa dream skin and shoulder-length dreadlocks twisted into fat curls. The platinum stud of her labret piercing winked in the light.

"You can always get a turn, baby," Dez said, moving toward her. She scooped the delectable Dior-dressed bundle into her arms and buried her nose in her throat. Nuria smelled like maraschino cherries and peach schnapps. She wiggled in Dez's embrace, setting off a chorus of appreciative laughter and catcalls. The crowd eddied around them, watching their raucous reunion with mildly curious eyes.

"She never hugs *me* like that," Rémi laughed.

"Because you never come out looking like this." Nuria's tongue peeked from between her lips as she gestured to Dez's handsome tuxedo jacket with the loose matching pants that hung off her prominent hip bones and left an inch of skin between it and the tight, lace blouse bare.

"You got that right," Rémi said, touching the brim of her hat. Ever since her family took her to Montana to play with horses, an eleven-year-old Rémi had decided then and there that she was a cowboy. After that, she never left the house without a cowboy hat, spurs, boots, boot-cut jeans, and chaps, or some other cowboy paraphernalia. Never mind that she was deathly afraid of horses and would rather go surfing than riding on the range.

Nuria ignored Rémi's comment. Her fingers traced the strip of skin between Dez's blouse and slacks, before settling on the fold of cotton that hid the zipper. Dez chuckled, helpless to the twitch of stomach muscles and the clenching a few more inches down.

"Careful, baby. I'm only human."

"Why do I have to be careful?" Nuria pouted again. "You just got back into town after, what, eight years of playing hard to get?"

"I never play those games. You know that by now. I always deliver."

"For damn's sake," said Sage, the smallest of the group. "Here we go again. Cool it you two. It's been less than five minutes and you're already starting the same old shit."

"I'm just getting my lovin' in while I can. As soon as all the easy girls in Miami know that The Good Time Twins are back together again"—she gave Rémi and Dez a sly look—"I'll have to fight the crowd just to be able to kiss her . . . ring."

Dez laughed out loud as she untangled herself from Nuria. "Don't be jealous, Sage. I was coming to you next."

"What's up, man? Long time." Sage drew back from their hug, her penetrating stare belying the casual words.

"It has been a long time. Sorry to say. What've you been up to?" Dez squeezed her shoulder.

"This and that. A few new inks, a new girl, nothing too dangerous." Her Jamaican accent, softened by her ten years in America, made the words sound almost like a song. She smiled wide, showing off her gorgeous enamel and the small gap between her two front teeth. "It's really good to see you."

A flash of black ink at her wrist from just beyond the cuff of her striped long-sleeved shirt caught Dez's eye. The tail end of one of her many tribal tattoos. Another swirl of ink only a few shades removed from her deep brown skin peeked from within the shirt's collar. Sage's tatt artist certainly had been busy since Dez last saw her friend.

"We hoped that you would come around to see us. Those postcards and two-minute phone calls didn't count for shit." Rémi's mouth twitched—not quite a smile, but not a snarl either. "So you were fucking the boy. Then he left you for some red-haired bitch. Then what? Why didn't you come straight to us? We would have made you feel better."

"Yeah, much, much better." Nuria gave her most innocent smile. Which wasn't.

"If I'd only known." But it wasn't as simple as that. She met Rémi's eyes and was surprised by her friend's slight smile of understanding.

"Come dance with me, baby." Phil took Sage's hand. "I think the boys need to catch up."

Nuria waited only a moment before following her friends in the general direction of the dance floor.

"Those two seem cozy," Dez said, watching her two friends move easily together on the dance floor. Phil stood almost a foot taller than Sage in her stilettos, but their looks complemented each other: bright and dark, slim and curvaceous. Sage's hand settled on Phil's snaking behind.

"They ought to be." Rémi sat down, making room on the low couch for Dez. "They've been a couple now for almost as long as you've been gone."

"Seriously?" That was the last thing she expected to hear. Then again she was sure that the news about her and Ruben hadn't been the usual fare either. "Are they supposed to be monogamous?"

Rémi gave her a look. "You know better than that."

"Just thought I'd ask. Things change. People change."

"True." Rémi nodded. She leaned forward with her elbows on her knees, her hands clasped loosely together before her. "So, how have things changed for you? You seem different. Is something going on?"

"Can I tell you later?" Dez hated the pleading tone in her voice, but with her friend, the one she'd told so many secrets to in the past, she couldn't help herself. Not even her mother had been there for her the way that Rémi had.

"All right, but you have to call me, or I'll track you down. I'll give you three days or I'm coming for you."

"You are so full of shit. You can't even wait three days for pussy."

"Exactly, so you better call me soon."

"Are you two done yet?" Nuria sashayed over, a pink drink in hand, a pout sitting prettily on her mouth. "I'm already bored looking at the same old tired faces at this damn party."

"We're finished," Rémi said.

"And even if we weren't, Rémi and I could always think of something to do with a girl like you." Dez playfully tugged the flirtatious woman closer.

"Flattery will get you absolutely anywhere," Nuria leaned in with a purr. Her breath was awash in a cocktail of peaches, vodka, and oranges. Dez wrinkled her nose and turned her head to kiss Nuria on the cheek just as Phil and Sage tumbled back from the dance floor, laughing and holding each other tightly.

"Are you all going to stand around feeling each other up?" Phil asked. "As far as I know, it's not that kind of party."

"You never know, baby. The night is young." Dez chuckled and squeezed Nuria's waist.

"Are you taken for the night, honey?"

They all turned around.

"Damn . . ." Sage whistled, not quite under her breath.

Phil glanced at the woman, an eyebrow arched in mute appreciation.

But the object of their collective lust only had eyes for Dez. She was eye-catching in a peach-colored dress that covered her walnut skin from throat to ankle. It was a late nineteenth-century gown with pearl buttons at the wrist and throat, one that barely hinted at her curves, focusing instead on the elegant lines of the body beneath it. As the woman stepped closer, Dez caught the scent of champagne on her lips. Her arm slid from Nuria's waist.

"I could be," Dez murmured, immediately intrigued by the woman's boldness. The topic of the previous discussion fell away from her brain.

The woman's smile was sweet and teasing. It warmed her pretty, doll-like face even more, stretching the small rosebud lips into a wet promise. "I'm Lylah."

Dez's body was paying attention. She wanted to slide her hand in Lylah's headful of curls and pull her closer, feel those lips under hers to see if they were as soft as they looked.

"Dez. *Very* pleased to meet you." She heard her friends' laughter, the vague noises of their conversation as they moved away and deliberately lost themselves in the crowd. "So what do you have in mind?"

"I have the key to a room upstairs. Interested?"

Oh, yes. This was just the thing she needed to get her body distracted from its memories of Ruben. Dez allowed her to lead the way, content to hang behind Lylah and watch the sway of her graceful shape under the dress as she slid through the crowd, then up the stairs and into a large bedroom.

"I haven't seen you around here before," Lylah said, locking the door behind them. "Are you new to the scene?"

"Something like that." Dez shrugged off her jacket and dropped it on a chair near the door. The room reminded her of a suite at the Hyatt—simple, nondescript, yet functional with its wide bed and bathroom just beyond. There was a TV and a DVD player too. *For extended hours of fun*, Dez thought with a wry smile. She reached for Lylah. "So how do I get you out of this thing?"

"You let me worry about that."

Their lips met with a firm, wet sound. No preliminaries. Lylah knew exactly what she wanted. Dez's hands slid into the tempting curls and stroked their softness that reminded her of rougher curls down below that would also feel good on her fingers. The woman moaned deep in her throat and reached for the button at Dez's slacks.

Dez had done this countless times before, gone with the instinct of her body and shared it with anyone that it felt the inclination to. Unthinkably, she'd been faithful to Ruben. Two years without the smell of another woman's cunt on her hands. Two years without the quick, anonymous sex that she and Rémi had perfected in tandem all over Miami and a good part of the world. She'd missed it.

There was a rhythm to this sort of thing that she fell into now, the not thinking, the indulgence in pure sensation that made nothing else matter. Only the blind rush of her own body to possess and share pleasure. The rush that made the woman incidental, accidental. Did it matter that her name was Lylah or Diane or Keisha or Vivian? Or that she crocheted when she was bored or read aloud to herself or had a husband waiting for her in the Keys? No. All that mattered was the soft thighs in their pale gold garters and the stockings that framed the shaved pouting pussy. The scrape of short nails against her naked ass as she pumped against her, riding the wetness like she was running a race to see who could come the fastest. Lylah's nipples were wide and hard under her mouth. Her pussy was wet and welcoming. The gasping words of delight—*Faster. Fuck me. Yes. Harder. Make me come*—weren't unique, but they were enough. Here, that was all that mattered. Dez didn't try to make any more or less of it. She simply buried her senses in it until it was over.

"Thanks." Dez's breath was harsh in her throat. She collapsed back against the bed, thighs trembling still.

Lylah stood up and smiled, licking her fingers. "Any time." She brushed those same fingers over her face and through her pressed dark curls like she was anointing herself with perfume. A quick motion of her body smoothed the wrinkles in her dress. "And thank you for saving me from boredom tonight."

Dez quickly pulled on her pants and jacket before straightening the rest of her clothes. "You're more than welcome."

Lylah smiled then winked at her before she opened the doors to let in the sounds of the party that was still going strong. "See you around." She didn't look back. It was time to go. Dez straightened her jacket again and headed out to find her friends.

She found them one by one, each trying to pick up a little something to take home for the night. She caught each woman's eye, letting her know that she was done and still in the mood for any more interesting options the night might provide.

Chapter 5

"Give me the usual, Gina. To go." Dez passed a twenty-dollar bill to the waitress and claimed an empty stool at the restaurant counter.

Her friends had invited her to go along with them to Novlette's Café in the morning for a late breakfast, just like old times, but exhaustion set in at the thought of it. Too much closeness too soon. She woke up feeling the same way.

After a slow ride around South Beach and her first cigarette of the day, she felt like being around other people. With the wind pressing at her face and chest, she'd headed for what had quickly become her new favorite restaurant by the pier.

The waitress palmed the money and counted out her change, all without looking up at Dez. Her head, bald except for an abstract black tattoo of a winged woman, winked under the light as she finally met Dez's eyes and smiled. The two of them had been carrying on an intense flirtation for the past week, but after Dez got drunk and uncharacteristically spilled half her life story in Gina's lap, they'd both backed off. Some mistakes were easy to see beforehand.

"Your gorgeous brother is here."

"Is he?" She smiled at the puckish waitress, not particularly concerned with her brother at the moment.

Gina nodded at a point beyond Dez's shoulder. "He looks

pissed off right now. Before you came in he was actually happy."

Since the waitress seemed intent on setting up a reunion, Dez turned around. Sure enough, there he was. Derrick sat on the restaurant patio looking vaguely annoyed, with his eyes shaded from the afternoon sun by dark glasses. Dez turned from her brother's frown with a noncommittal noise.

"Did he say anything to you?"

Gina arched a pierced eyebrow. "And why would he do that?"

"Sorry," she grinned. "Had a brain fart." Dez looked over her shoulder again. "Wrap it up and bring it outside for me, would you?"

"For you, anything." She winked and turned back to the cash register, dismissing her. Dez took it all in stride, giving Gina's body the obligatory leer and smile before making her way out to the patio.

"Slumming, Derrick?" she asked, straddling the empty chair at her brother's elbow.

Her more masculine incarnation spared her a brief glance from behind his custom Ray-Bans. Derrick Nichols topped off at six feet six and was gorgeous enough to make even Dez feel a twinge of envy. She liked to think that if she had been born a boy she would have been blessed with identically good looks. As it was, she did the best that she could.

"Nice to see you, too, Desiree," he said.

"You shouldn't lie and chew at the same time, Derrick. Bad for you."

A long time ago she and Derrick had been very close. They shared a lot of the same habits, the same style of dress, even an interest in the same girls. They had even gone out on a triad date with a hot little girl who couldn't decide if she liked girls or boys. That was in the seventh grade. They didn't hang out too much these days.

Dez turned to her brother's lunch companion. Now *this* was far more interesting. His date was soft femininity itself with her striking features and thick hair pulled back from her round face into a flyaway halo of coils and curls. Her hair burned like the color of the desert at sunrise, bright and dark and pale at once. Dez liked what she saw of this woman's lush, ripe body. She liked it very much. The woman stared at Dez with naked curiosity, her fork resting against a lower lip bare of lipstick.

"I don't think we've met." Dez offered her hand and a smile. "Dez Nichols."

This woman, all whiskey gold skin and wide eyes, put aside her fork before taking Dez's hand. "Victoria Jackson. Tori."

Victoria. Dez liked the name. So proper, yet it conjured thoughts of old books and sex, reaching under a long skirt, pussy-slick fingers gripping shelves heaving from the pressure of two joined bodies.

Dez warmed up her smile, resisting the urge to drop her gaze to the swell of cleavage in the neckline of Victoria's cream-colored blouse. Her brother had been hiding this jewel of his since college. She remembered him saying how brilliant she was, and how unavailable.

"So you're the one." Dez released the other woman's hand and glanced at her brother before bringing her eyes back to rest on Victoria's . . . face. "Derrick never said how beautiful you were."

Her brother looked at her as if she just put a dirty tampon on the table. Victoria blinked, caught between flattery and outrage, or so Dez thought.

"By the way," Dez smiled at her brother. "Since Mama is getting in around lunchtime on Thursday, why don't we just go pick her up together? I know that she'd be glad to—"

"Here you go, darlin.' Hot and fresh just like you like it." Gina winked as she slid the nicely boxed lunch under Dez's nose and bent her decorated cleavage for the whole table's inspection.

"Thanks, Gina." And just for the hell of it, Dez tucked a

five-dollar bill between the ivy-tattooed breasts. "See you later in the week."

The waitress grinned and disappeared.

"That was tacky of you, Dez." Her brother leveled a disapproving frown on her.

"What? Jealous?"

"Don't be stupid."

She turned to Derrick's friend. "Do you think that was tacky of me, Victoria?"

The woman blinked again, but followed it with a smile.

"Gina—was that her name?"—she continued at Dez's amused nod—"seemed to enjoy it, so . . ." She shrugged and smiled. "Besides, I've never been one to school anyone else on tacky behavior. You should've seen me in high school."

"What, two years ago?" Dez grinned and leaned in closer.

Victoria laughed. "You are a big flirt, aren't you?"

"The biggest. I'm glad you're not taking offense. You're very attractive, and I don't think a woman can be told that enough."

"Only women?"

"Well, of course, men too. But not by me."

Victoria laughed again, stirring the mouthwatering flesh just above her neckline. She knew Dez was looking.

Derrick had had enough. "Did you want anything in particular, Dez?"

"Hm, nothing much, brother dearest. Just stopped by to say hello and bask in the glow of your gracious company before I go back home." She slid Victoria a look and a smile. "And I guess that was my cue to leave you to your lunch." She stood. "By the way, if you ever want someone to treat you to lunch or . . . whatever, please give me a call." Dez took a card from her wallet and put it in the hand that was already rising to meet hers. "See you both soon."

She picked up her lunch and left them to theirs.

On the way home, her cell phone rang but she let it keep until she pulled into the garage and parked the bike. It was Sage.

"What's up? Didn't get enough of me last night?"

"You mixing me up with your whores again?"

"No mix-up here, baby." She pressed the phone between her ear and shoulder as she stripped off her gloves and, balancing her lunch in the crook of her elbow, walked through the double doors leading from the garage to the house. "What's going on?"

"There's a little happening at our house tonight. Phil and I want you to come."

"Don't you people ever work?" Dez dropped her lunch and gloves on the kitchen counter then opened the fridge. The breath of cool air from inside misted against her face, bringing with it the scent of the guavas she'd bought the day before.

"Not if I can help it and I know you aren't talking, you big lazy ass."

Another thing that had united the four girls in school besides the whole pussy-eating predilection was that none of them were poor.

Dez's mouth twitched with reluctant amusement as she poured herself a glass of rice milk. "What time?"

"Ten. Or whenever you can make it."

"I'll be there." Dez hung up and lifted the glass to her mouth.

The night of the party, Dez pressed past the surging bodies at Sage and Phil's door, biting back her annoyance. It was well after midnight and the party was in full swing. There were women everywhere, most were well past the point of modesty. A foursome pressed itself into a corner, leaving a trail of clothes scattered on the floor. Breasts and buttocks heaved in the flickering light. Flashes of their open mouths, wet thighs, and hands lured her deeper into the house. But the sounds of sex on a nearby couch—rough, flesh-pounding, wet sex—brought her up short. This wasn't exactly the kind of party she was expecting.

Lines of coke ribboned the glass surface of the coffee table. Heads bobbed over the white streaks, sucking up the powdered pleasure, ignoring the naked and sweating bodies around them.

"What the fuck is this?" she asked Sage when she saw her.

"A party. What else?" Except for a pair of shiny boy's-cut briefs, she was naked; her dark, tattooed flesh glowed with flecks of white powder.

"Shit! I didn't know it was going to be this kind of party." She waved her hand at the bodies around her.

"What, you don't like pussy? Come on, have some blow. Shit, have a blow job. It's all free tonight. Welcome back to town, baby!" Sage slapped her on the back and passed her a tumbler with the remnants of what smelled like scotch, before stumbling back the way she had come.

Portishead played heavy and loud from the speakers, the perfect accompaniment to the distinct sounds of sex, of demand and release, of "come here" and "fuck me harder" drifting from different corners of the house. The music and the voices, the intoxicating smell of sex seeped into her as she stood watching it all. Her skin warmed with the beginnings of arousal. Why not? Dez's eyes flickered around the room again. She shrugged out of her jacket and went to find some pleasure of her own.

She found Rémi in the old basement playroom, knocking balls around a pool table. A few slumped bodies perked up as Dez walked down the stairs. She heard whispers, some she could make out, some she couldn't.

"Are you high, too?" Dez asked. Sage's leftover scotch and the nonstop visual stimuli were starting to work their magic on her. She definitely felt more relaxed than when she first walked into the house.

Rémi grinned, leaning over for a shot. "Not yet." She nodded at the beer bottle dripping condensation on the edge of the table. "I'm working on that right now." As she straightened up, Dez noticed the tight black T-shirt that stretched across her breasts and abs. It read, SAVE A HORSE, RIDE A COW-BOY.

"Are you back in town for good, Dez?" A woman in ghost white slipped out of the darkness. The newcomer's dress was short and draped over high, lush breasts in two separate strips of nearly sheer cloth, leaving a wide canyon of brown sugar flesh visible down to her pierced belly button. At the hips the dress hugged tight, cleaving to a thick round ass and muscled thighs. With all that she didn't have to bother with "fuck me" red stilettos or black stockings that snared around her legs like silk invitations, but she did. Dez acknowledged her appearance with the requisite leer. Unlike most of the people she had already seen at the party, this woman seemed perfectly lucid. And watchful. Should Dez even know who she was?

"I'll be here for a while," she said, answering her question.

"Good." Whether or not Dez knew this woman from before, she seemed down for a good time. Isn't that why they were all here?

Dez looked at Rémi across the pool table. The eyes under the black cowboy hat sparkled with anticipation. The woman in white positioned herself in the light, watching them both with a slight smile. Her body swayed slowly from side to side. Rémi went back to her game with the smirking stud who looked about ready to lose. They continued the round in silence until Rémi sunk the eight ball. The two shook hands and the woman backed up to prop herself against a nearby wall and watch the action.

Rémi looked at Dez. "You next?"

The woman stirred in the light. "I want to be next." She slid over to the pool table, taking her time so that everyone could see the way the white silk draped over her body. "I want to play both of you." Her fingers landed on Dez's forearm. "You game?"

Several throats cleared in the room. They *all* knew what she meant. The Good Time Twins looked at each other again.

"Why not?"

Now, when it came to their tandem sports, Dez and Rémi had rules, especially when they were playing with someone they didn't know. Rubber gloves, lube, and lots and lots of condoms. Sage kept a healthy supply in all her guest bathrooms. Dez swallowed the woman whole with her eyes then gestured toward the stairs. "After you." She just wanted to see that ass wiggle up the stairs before she got good and deep in it.

Behind them Rémi didn't bother to hide her laughter. "All the way upstairs, honey. Second door on the left."

Once in the room, the woman—Ashley, Ananda, or something—stripped off her clothes and lay back on the bed. She spread her legs and, watching Dez and Rémi with eyes that glowed, bared her already wet pussy to their gaze. When she was absolutely sure that she had their undivided attention, Ananda took a vial of coke and shook some of the white powder over her bared clit before rubbing it into the swollen pink flesh. She hissed and arched her neck in reaction. Her steady fingers worked it deeper into her pussy, then she spread two thin lines on her belly, two arrows of white leading to her cunt.

"I like to fuck on coke. You're okay with that, right?"

Okay wasn't quite the word, but Dez would go with that for now. She kicked off her shoes and knelt on the bed near Ananda's belly. The smell of her pussy was natural and fresh, much better than the cloying perfume she wore. Dez resisted the urge to dive into it with her tongue and hands. That was for another fuck. Another time. Ananda's skin was buttersoft in the light from the chandelier swaying slightly above them. Shards of light from its crystals danced around the room. The coke hit the back of her throat like ice and fire, numbing and cool at the same time, and she swayed for a moment. Exhilaration and its companion tremors rocketed

through her. She sat up. Rémi came back from the bathroom
with a basket full of goodies, including two hefty dildos and
straps. Ananda's eyes widened and she licked her lips.

"Your turn." She pointed at Rémi then at the line still left
on her stomach.

Rémi, naked now except for her thick swaying dick, grinned
and leaned over Ananda while Dez strapped herself and covered the silicone toy with a condom. Her clit felt hot and ready
against the dick. Rémi's ass in the air, with its black cherry
pucker of a sphincter and wet velvet pussy, drew Dez closer.
The two women had never touched each other as lovers, not
even in the most heated moments, but that didn't stop either
of them from looking.

Dez knew that Rémi usually liked to start things by watching. She loved it when Dez warmed her up, teasing the lay of
the night with her hands and tongue, let the fire build inside
until she was begging for something hard and deep and fast.
But that wasn't how it was going to go tonight. Lightning
and fire thrummed through Dez's limbs. She went quickly to
the bed, her fat dick already well lubed, and drew the woman
up, slammed her breasts against her back and slid inside her.
The woman—Ananda, she had to keep reminding herself—
gasped, laughed out loud, and reached for Rémi, begging to
have all her holes filled.

They arranged her incredibly limber body, twisted and
contorted it until, with Dez at her back and Rémi at her
front, they twined into a sweating three-headed beast, thrusting and gasping against one another in the bed. A hot palm
hooked at the back of Dez's neck and she groaned, heart
hammering in her chest, sweat coating her breasts and back.
Ananda twisted her fingers in Rémi's hair, opening her mouth
wide to receive her deep kiss. Her fingers slid back to squeeze
Dez's ass, the rhythm of her fingers begging for a faster pace.
Ananda's hips bucked and jumped as Rémi slid a gloved finger between them and over her coke-hardened clit, strumming it like a guitar.

That was her friend's cue to quicken the pace, and she did, until the two of them were slamming into the woman from both sides, grunting and twisting as the bed bounced, and they were going faster and yelling and fucking until the woman called out somebody's name and collapsed between them. But they didn't stop. They held her limp body between them, pushing and thrusting and grinding their pussies against her, against their borrowed dicks. Ananda laughed, gasping a yes as her body sparked again. Rémi's fingers sank into her friend's shoulder. Through her clenched eyes, Dez saw a light and chased it, pushing her hips in a savage tempo until she was up on it, then inside it, burning, glowing, then exploding. Her heart galloped in her chest and her body felt hot. She couldn't tell if it was the coke or the fuck.

She pulled out first and rolled off the bed to strip off the condom and gloves and throw them in the bathroom trash. When she walked back into the bedroom, Rémi had the girl's ass in the air and was working it out with her tongue, a long piece of plastic wrap between the girl's hole and her mouth. Ananda wiggled her ass, making encouraging noises with her mouth, as if Rémi didn't know what she was doing. She needed something better to do with her mouth. Dez stripped off her dick and tossed it in a nearby chair, then grabbed some plastic.

Even through the barrier the woman gave fantastic head, she lay between Dez's splayed legs, eating her pussy with the concentration of a surgeon, holding her open, licking her clit and asshole, and tongue fucking her until Dez's hips rose off the bed to meet each movement of her tongue. She held the woman's hair in her fist, slamming her aching wet cunt against her mouth. Ananda didn't stop when her own orgasm rolled through her. She shouted hoarsely and panted into Dez's pussy but didn't slow her movements. If anything, she sped up.

"Fuck!" She met Rémi's eyes over the slope and rise of ass. "She's—ah!—good." Then her world went supernova again.

She slid bonelessly to the bed, having enough presence of mind to crawl away from the girl's mouth so that Rémi could experience it for herself.

She watched the girl eat her friend out, lapping at the pussy in front of her with frantic greed. This one, she thought with lazy appreciation, was worth keeping. At least for the rest of the night. To prove her point, Rémi reached back for the headboard, arching up off the bed as she watched the girl devour her, her teeth skinned back in a feral smile. She came furiously, roaring and rising up, her face a rictus of pleasure. Dez's body clenched in sympathetic orgasm, jerking against the sheets.

"Damn!"

"I second that." Dez sighed at the ceiling, feeling the beginning descent of her high. The hectic breath of the two women mingled with her own. She shivered at the cooling sweat on her skin.

Ananda rolled up to her elbows and held up a little glass bottle that was still three-quarters full of white powder. "You want to go again?"

Hours later she stumbled around the house looking for her clothes. Pleasure had ridden her hard and fast and now her muscles were quivering from the rough use. Her body ached and every orifice felt sore and tender, even her mouth couldn't bear having anything in it any time soon. The sun was already starting to come up but she was nowhere near tired. Her eyes felt like they had been Krazy-glued open, nerves still vibrating from her ride on the bucking white horse.

"Hey, good-looking." Nuria lay by the pool in her bra and panties, smoke from a cigarette curling up to the lightening sky. "What happened to your clothes? Not that your little robe isn't cute. . . ." She laughed softly, eyeing the half a robe that left everything below the top of Dez's thighs bare.

"I think a naked girl stole them off me." The water seemed suddenly very inviting, sparkling and clean in a way that she longed to be. Dez slipped out of the robe and walked to the edge of the pool. She heard Nuria's quiet intake of breath, and she wasn't sure if it was the muscle she'd put on since the last time her friend saw her naked, or the scratches that decorated her arms and back.

"Someone's been busy tonight, I see."

She made a noncommittal noise and dove into the water. Heaven. The warm wetness slid over her skin like a balm. For the moment, her groaning muscles quieted and the gentle noise of her journey through the water, combined with the distant sounds of the party, lulled her into a lovely half dream. Dez slid beneath the pool's surface and floated on her back, arms and legs spread out like a starfish as she watched the crescent moon through the water's wavering lens. She forced herself to just lay there and not heed the call of the frantic energy humming in her blood. Movement near her and the beginning burn in her lungs made her stand up and break the surface.

"I hope you're not trying to off yourself so soon. Half the girls in the place still have plans for you." Sage swam close to, then past her to heave herself backward onto the edge of the pool. Water ran off her tattooed body in thin rivulets.

"That's the last thing you'd ever have to worry about from me, my friend." Although now she wasn't exactly feeling on top of the world. This time she *knew* it was the coke. And she wasn't going to take another hit to make herself feel better. It was going to be a long day. All she had to do was ride it out until she felt sleep closing in on her, then that would be that. She swam backward toward Sage.

"So what else you got to do at this party besides snort, drink, and fuck?"

Someone was banging a drum inside her skull. There was no other explanation for the megawatt pain that made her entire body throb with hurt. Dez rolled over, relieved to see that the curtains were drawn. Beyond the thick burgundy cloth she could tell that it was daylight. And this wasn't her house.

She stumbled to the bathroom where she found and choked down four aspirin with tap water. With a less-than-graceful motion, she moved to turn on the shower only to stumble when a wave of nausea attacked, making her spin to the toilet and clutch its porcelain edges as she retched, bringing up her aspirin, the water, and some other liquid nastiness that had been resting in her stomach from the night before. Her head pounded even more when she was done. *Christ!*

Dez sat down a little unsteadily on the toilet and waited a full ten minutes before trying for the shower again. When she was clean and dry in one of Sage's terry-cloth robes, she took more aspirin. This time she swallowed them dry, willing herself not to gag. Downstairs, she found Sage stretched out in front of the TV with a glass of grapefruit juice balanced on her lap. The house looked freshly scrubbed and cleaned with no hint of the previous night's party. A clock hovering above a doorway told her that it was well past five in the evening.

"Now I remember why I don't do that shit anymore," Dez said, sinking into the couch beside her friend. "Next time a girl says that she can only fuck on coke, I'll tell her to go fuck herself."

"Don't front. You had a damn good time last night." Sage turned down the sound on the National Geographic show, something about pyramids, and slid Dez's pouting pained face a look. "Besides, it wasn't just the coke. It was the scotch and the scotch and more coke. You gettin' old, baby."

"Something. Shit." Dez leaned back into the cool leather. "I feel like something a leper squeezed out of his asshole."

"There's ginger ale and saltines in the kitchen."

"How much coke did you do last night, anyway?" she asked when Dez returned from the kitchen with the box of saltines and a can of Schweppes.

"Obviously too much." Now that her head was a bit more settled, she noticed other things, the weakening light of the sun through the open terrace doors, the sound of voices from downstairs, splashing from the pool, and the occasional sound of laughter.

"You know that I can't dredge up any sympathy for you, right?" Sage turned on her trademark lopsided grin. "Even wrecked you look gorgeous."

"Good genes." She lifted her head weakly to see what was happening beyond the terrace doors. "What's going on outside?"

"Nuria and Phil are out baking by the pool. There's someone else, too, a friend of Phil's, but I can't remember her name." Then she answered the unasked question. "Rémi had to go by the club for a while. I guess she'll be back."

Rémi was the only one of them who had to work these days, although she used the term lightly with her best friend. She was the owner of one of the trendiest jazz clubs in Miami. Since she hired only the best people to manage and run the place, she didn't have to do much more than show up around town looking prosperous and promote the bar.

Another burst of laughter floated up from the pool. With her attentions no longer focused on keeping upright or from upchucking last night's liquid meal, Dez realized that Sage, although she wanted to be out by the pool, had stayed in the house to keep an eye on her. A distant eye, but an eye nonetheless. She even had her little swimming shorts on. For a moment she'd forgotten their system of keeping one another from dying of excess. Suddenly she didn't feel so bad.

"You should go out there and get a tan; you're looking a little pale these days." She smiled at her friend's look. "Go ahead, I'm fine. Just pass me the remote before you go."

Dez sank back into the leather as Sage walked out the door, telling Dez to yell if she needed anything. Yelling was the last thing she intended to do anytime soon. But she nodded and lifted the remote.

Chapter 6

Heavy darkness pressed against Dez's bedroom window. It wasn't even dawn yet. She turned over and picked up her watch: 4:47 A.M. With sleep misted eyes she blinked up at the skylight. Claudia would be coming back today. After almost two weeks of waiting, her mother was coming back. She swallowed past the lump in her throat and closed her eyes. *Go back to sleep.*

The phone rang. "Are you coming or what?" Her brother's irritated voice yanked her from sleep. The sun was full in the sky, scattering bits of red and green and orange through the stained glass. The more sedate gold from behind her sheer curtains told her it was well past noon.

"What time is it?" she croaked.

"Almost one. You know that the yacht is supposed to come in at one-thirty. Why aren't you here? Where the fuck are you?"

"Where did you call, stupid?" She sat up and rubbed at her eyes. "I'll be there in ten minutes, keep your pants on."

In four minutes she was ready, teeth brushed, face washed, and tired body dressed in jeans and a slim fitting T-shirt. Under the sunglasses, her eyes were still at half-mast, sleepy but open. Driving to her brother's office, she scanned the streets, half expecting, even after almost two weeks in Miami, to see Ruben and Caitlyn. She dreaded that day, but also wished it would come so she could stop worrying about it. Dez called Derrick as her truck coasted to a stop outside his office building.

"I'm here." She leaned back in the pale gray leather seats and tried to wake up some more. The Prodigy pounding from the SUV's stereo would at least help with that.

She'd bought the Lexus 400h two days before at her mother's insistence. Over the yacht's sophisticated satellite telephone system, Claudia had managed to call her daughter, skirting the reason Dez was in Miami in the first place, to address her poor choice of vehicles. "You need a car, Desiree," she had said on the phone. "Groceries don't fit well on the back of a motorcycle." Dez couldn't argue with her on that one.

As a silver Firebird slid up, obviously wanting to get by her double-parked truck, Dez glanced at her watch. She was about to move when she saw Derrick walk quickly from the glass doors of Silverman, Johnson, and Meyer. With a quick flick of her wrist, she turned down the stereo and changed the CD to Sade. Her brother jogged the last few feet and jumped into the truck.

"What happened to your AC?" Derrick asked with an annoyed glance at Dez, unbuttoning the jacket of his charcoal gray suit and throwing it in the backseat. He buckled his seat belt.

"It's not on." Dez guided the truck into the light Saturday-afternoon traffic.

"I see."

Dez watched from the corner of her eye as Derrick tried in vain to look comfortable in the late October heat. She turned on the air conditioner and put up three of the truck's windows.

"Thanks." Derrick smoothed his tie and settled back to watch the neon Miami scenery slip by his window. After a moment he took out a folder from his briefcase and started looking through it.

"What's up? You look a little uptight today."

"Uptight?" He looked up from his paperwork with irritation. "I guess next to you anybody can seem uptight. You don't work, you have all of Aunt Paulette's money to wallow in, and all those girls to entertain you in case you get bored."

"Uh huh. Is this about your friend?"

"My friend?"

"You know, what's her name . . . Victoria."

"Leave her alone. She's a good woman who doesn't need to fuck around with somebody like you."

"Calm down, killer. All I did was invite her to hang out with me sometime. It's not like I'm going to fuck her hello then drop her off at the curb."

He made a strange noise, and then flicked his eyes contemptuously over her. "That's not going to happen, even if that *was* your plan. I'd just like her to run with a higher class of friends."

Ouch. "All right then." She downshifted the truck, pulling up behind a red convertible Mustang as they approached a yellow light. The driver, a sexy light-skinned woman in a dress she could have had on from the night before, looked at them through her rearview mirror. Dez doubted that she could see through the tinted windshield, but the woman adjusted her legs anyway and let the shimmering green silk fall away from her thighs. Dez revved the engine and chuckled at the seductive display. She was still smiling when the Mustang pulled away, leaving them in the proverbial cloud of dust. Dez turned her attentions back to her brother.

"What did I ever do to you, Derrick? I don't think I deserve any of this shit that I'm getting from you."

"Cut the innocent bullshit, Dez. You deserve this, and more. You run off and leave Mom like you didn't give a shit about her, then just because you find out she's sick you come running back like some fucking prodigal daughter." Derrick turned to face her. "You knew that you were her favorite. You knew that she needed you, and you abandoned her."

"Now *that* is bullshit. She sure as hell didn't need me any more than she needed you. I never abandoned Mama, and you're delusional."

"Right. At least I care for Mama and let her know it by my actions as well as my words." He made a noise of disgust. "You are a selfish bitch, Dez. You always were and apparently that'll never change."

"Tell me how you really feel, big brother."

The truck pulled up to a high metalwork gate and she leaned out the window to give her name to the voice that crackled with distant authority from the speaker. With a well-oiled sigh, the gate slid open to let them in. Bracketed by miles of well-tended lawn and cameras masquerading as statuary, the driveway was the long and boring kind, designed to build anticipation until it propped you up on the hill where the mansion suddenly loomed in its salsa picante colors— brilliant reds, yellows, and greens—and strangely inviting ostentation. Dez bypassed the main house and navigated the truck down the small road leading to the dock at the rear of the mansion. Derrick was silent.

Before this, they'd fought over who would pick up their mother, not with shouting matches like in the old days but with deliberate attacks of silence and looks meant to make the other feel small or guilty or generally incapable. In the grudgingly declared truce, they both won the prize of driving to the McAllister mansion to retrieve Claudia and take her back to her relatively modest four-bedroom bungalow in Coconut Grove. Dez slid her brother another look. He sat back in his seat, apparently still absorbed in his paperwork. Hard to believe that they were even related sometimes. But, unfortunately, she had the scars to prove the relation.

It wasn't that long ago that the four of them—Dez, Derrick, Claudia, and Warrick—used to come out to this very mansion and play with Claudia's friends. On countless sunny days, Warrick had held Dez's slight body as she splashed around in the water, telling her she could make it all the way down the length of the Olympic-sized pool, while her twin, their mother, and the McAllisters cheered her on. Their family of four was perfect. A successful and handsome papa, a fragile yet iron-willed beauty of a mother, and a smart twin brother who she could always borrow shorts, ties, and homework from. Then, thirteen years ago she did a double backflip and somersault out of the closet, and that was the end of that. Warrick pulled his love away from her, her mother's frailty became more apparent, and, of course, the divorce happened.

They pulled up to the drive of a tiny house—a cottage, really—at the rear of the mansion. It was a cozy little place, straight out of someone's gingerbread fairy tale. Two women sat on its porch drinking what looked like lemonades. Their heads lifted to watch Dez and Derrick get out of the truck and walk toward them.

The last of the day's coolness had burnt away under the rays of the high noon sun. Even though it was hidden behind the much larger mansion, this little yard was lush and beautifully manicured with its abundance of multicolored bougainvillea and hibiscus exploding from every hedge. Creeping star jasmine clambered up and over the railing of the buttercup and white house. Beyond the tropical green yard and its profusion of flowers, the McAllister yacht floated, shimmering white and blue in the water, placid in her majesty and extravagant show of wealth.

The daughter of the house—a tall elfin creature with her slenderness, slightly pointed ears, and dark curls cut close to her head—pursed her lips, then winked as Dez drew closer. Money had always bought Paj McAllister everything she'd ever wanted—a good education, beautiful toys, a life of idleness and ease. For a moment, it had even bought her Dez, trapped her happily on Paj's long leash in awe of her freedom, her extravagant parties, and good looks. Even Aunt Paul's overindulgence and her professional parents' solid upper-middle-class money could never buy her an entire island to vacation on—with the accompanying servants—or a sixteenth-birthday Porsche, or Lenny Kravitz's company on her twenty-first birthday. Dez had eventually pulled herself out of that thrall, but she still thought of Paj as beautiful and worth a long evening's attention. Despite (or perhaps because of) a belief in her own superiority, the McAllister girl was still kind. As Dez approached, she tilted her head back, baring her slender throat and the platinum Tiffany-heart charm necklace that sat below it. Her smile was dazzling.

"Professor Nichols said you were back, but I didn't believe it." Long slim legs and a curved bottom in khaki shorts flashed as she stood up to pull Dez into a quick hug. Her smell was pure sea air and the faintest hint of almond soap.

Beyond her sat Claudia, not at all put out that her young companion and former student just called her a liar. With her legs tucked under her and her jaw resting in the bed of her cupped palm, she looked just as relaxed and youthful as her twenty-four-year-old friend. She was thin, yes, and her once-beautifully-thick hair wasn't quite so much now. It lay in fine curls against her skull, making her look vulnerable and small.

"Hello, loves." She greeted her children with a slow smile.

Paj pulled herself from Dez's embrace. "I'll go tell Delores and Gael that you're here."

She didn't need to tell her parents anything, but she met Dez's eyes and saw her old friend's need for privacy. Dez turned to watch her graceful shape flounce down the stone path toward the yacht.

"You look thin, Desiree." Dez stirred as Claudia reached for her. "But you're still my beautiful baby girl." Heat bloomed in Dez's cheeks as her mother tugged her down to the chair beside her and touched her face, flicking the sunglasses aside to look into the bruised brown gaze. "I'm sorry I didn't tell you, but I couldn't." She already seemed to know what her daughter was thinking. Dez shook her head, an automatic refusal to talk about this in front of anyone, especially her brother.

"I'm glad you're back," Claudia said. "Paj tells me that Jackie's has a special on mother-daughter manicures and pedicures this week. Come with me. My treat."

Dez shook her head again and choked on her forced laughter. On the wind, she heard Paj's high, carrying voice, a warning that their private time was up.

"Sure, Mama. Whatever you want."

After greeting and saying good-bye to the elder McAllisters, Dez and Derrick drove off with a drowsy Claudia in the backseat. She yawned and stretched herself full out on the gray leather, gratifyingly confident in her daughter's driving abilities. At her house, she begged to be left alone to nap in peace. Dez took her brother home with his briefcase full of paperwork, then drove back to her mother's house where she sat on the couch near Claudia's bed and watched her sleep.

Chapter 7

Claudia was forty-nine today, beautifully middle-aged, although she didn't seem to know it.

"Fifty is middle age. I am *not* middle aged!" Her voice rose above Derrick's laughter.

At eight-thirty in the morning, the house already buzzed with activity, radio playing, Claudia's ambitious soprano accompanying the studio-recorded voice, the cheerful clanging of pots and pans in the kitchen, even Derrick's loud and frequent laughter. Dez hugged her cup of morning coffee and took herself out of the way until she was all the way awake. That might be a few hours yet.

Was this how it had been when she was gone? Derrick and her mother cooking, sloughing off her absence like old skin on a healing wound? It cheered and depressed her at once, that her mother could still be happy, especially after all she'd been through. All she'd been through and told Dez nothing about. Nothing. Dez leaned on the railing, sipping her coffee and staring down at the shimmering blue of her mother's pool. The caffeine woke her, but a small part of her preferred her mind insensate and numb, taking nothing in. Yesterday, Derrick's words had meant to make her feel like shit. Today she actually did.

"Are you coming in to help us cook, love? Leisure suits

you, but you're not on vacation anymore." A damp towel smacked her on the rump through her pajamas.

"I didn't think you needed my help." Dez balanced her nearly empty cup on the railing of the deck and tilted her head to look up at her mother.

"Not your help so much, darling, as your company." Claudia draped her arm over her daughter's back and pressed close. Her talc-and-lavender-blossom scent reminded Dez sharply of before, of her childhood, when questions were easily answered and her Aunt Paul was only a room away.

"I can handle that," Dez said, swallowing past the lump in her throat.

"Good." Claudia stepped away. "And be nice to your brother while you're at it. He's not that bad once you get to know him."

"I'll take your word for it."

The three of them made breakfast together, slipping easily into the rhythm of old times with their laughter and soft-edged criticisms of technique and execution. Dez only elbowed her brother once and it was almost an accident. After finishing up the obscenely large meal, they staggered away from the dining table, undoing too-tight buttons as they went. Claudia escaped to her bedroom for a nap while her children stayed to clean up the kitchen and begin the birthday dinner.

There, they didn't have to talk. There was nothing to disagree about. They both knew what Claudia liked to eat and they both cooked very well. Spices and utensils changed hands, grunts and nods took the place of conversation, and soon the smells of harmony, of a well-made meal for a woman they both loved, filled the space.

People started coming in at around two in the afternoon. It wasn't especially planned that way, but Dez could bet that her friends just woke up hungry, showered, shaved, and then

showed up. Rémi still looked bleary-eyed from the night before.

"Hey, Dez." She gave her friend a cursory pat on the shoulder before walking into the house. "Smells good in here."
When she saw Dez's mother, her whole demeanor changed.
"Ms. Nichols. You look lovely, as usual." She swept off her
hat before producing a bouquet of silver and scarlet roses
from behind her back. "These are for you."

"Thank you, Rémi. They're lovely." Claudia took the
flowers, smiling.

"You bring out the kitty in me, Ms. N."

Dez rolled her eyes. "You want to come help out in the
kitchen or just sweet-talk my mother all afternoon?"

"Well, if you really want—"

Dez dragged her to the kitchen before she could say anything else. The Cornish hens were almost done. Their rich
scent mingled with the gravy simmering on the stove and
with the bread pudding warming on the sideboard.

"Did your mom do all this?"

"Hardly. She helped with breakfast. Dummy and I took
care of dinner. If anybody falls over dead it's his fault."

"Good to know." Rémi opened the fridge. "Any breakfast
left?"

"No."

But Rémi quickly homed in on the freshly made bread that
was still warm and exhaling its textured rosemary scent from
where it sat on the counter. When Dez looked at her friend
next she had the honey butter out of the fridge and was making herself a heart-attack sandwich with the bread and the
bacon, egg, and grits she found on the backup stove near the
rear kitchen door.

"When you're done mooching you can mash these potatoes. People should start coming in about an hour."

But the doorbell rang barely fifteen minutes later. It was
one of Derrick's friends—but not Victoria. That was one pair

of C-cups that Dez wouldn't mind seeing again. Claudia poked her head in the kitchen.

"I think your brother has a new girlfriend."

Dez rolled her eyes. "It's probably just some hooker he paid to come here and make nice."

"Darling, don't be mean," her mother said, although she couldn't quite hide her smile. Her head disappeared back into the living room.

"I wonder what skank he brought home this time?"

"Don't be a bitch," Rémi murmured around a mouthful of food from her seat on the counter. "You know he only runs with classy broads, unlike some other people in the family I won't name."

"What the hell do you mean by that? All my women are classy." Then she decided to change her statement. "At least the ones I decide to bring home to my mama."

"You think so?" Rémi snickered.

"Are you girls playing nice in here?" Nuria walked in looking perky and awake in her designer parent-meeting gear of a high-necked (but sheer) white blouse and a black mermaid-cut skirt that flirted around her knees as she walked.

"We always play well together, baby." Rémi smirked and took another bite of her sandwich.

Nuria received her kiss from each woman before taking her turn at the fridge. "By the way, Sage and Phil won't be coming. I think they're in the middle of one of their marathon fuck sessions or something."

"That's cool. I'll catch up with them some other time," Dez said.

Nuria poured herself a glass of orange juice and leaned on the counter beside Rémi. "Your brother is a cutie, Dez. I keep forgetting about that until I see him again. Delicious."

"Yeah, it doesn't seem fair that an asshole should have such a cute face, does it?" She opened the fridge door and took out the package of unsalted butter. "Family curse."

Derrick chose that moment to slip into the kitchen. "I'm

going to start setting the table since people are already start-ing to come." He gave each woman a pointed look.

"Just play host and start passing out the liquor," Dez said. "By the time all the food is done they'll all be so drunk that they won't care anyway."

"Why do all that? People know that you don't come to a birthday dinner at two in the afternoon."

"So what's your girlfriend's excuse?"

"Shut it, Dez." He backed out of the kitchen with an arm-load of china.

"You two don't like each other, do you?"

"How can you tell?"

Rémi finished up her food. "Compliments to the chef once again. Your mama can really throw down in the kitchen, Dez. I'm telling you, one day I'm going to have to marry that woman."

"How many times do I have to tell you, Rémi? Stay away from my mother."

Her friend made a dismissive noise as she hopped off the counter. "Nuria, Dez wants you to mash those potatoes for her." She walked out of the kitchen.

Moments later they could hear her paying effusive compli-ments to Claudia. Nothing that would make Dez rush out there and lay her out on the floor, but just enough to make her grind her teeth in annoyance.

Nuria laughed. "She's just doing that to get under your skin, baby. I hope you haven't been gone so long that you forgot how much she loves to do that."

"Just like the annoying sister I didn't want."

Nuria sucked her teeth. "Where are those potatoes that she was talking about?"

Dez hid in the kitchen for as long as she dared. A party was definitely going on in her mother's living room. She could hear the low contralto of Derrick's girlfriend mixing with her brother's low baritone. Eden, her mother's best friend and colleague from the university, came an hour ago and was circulating easily among the mostly younger crowd. She and Claudia laughed often, usually in response to something Rémi or Nuria said. She didn't envy her mother that laughter, just the source of it. Dez basted the hens one last time and turned down the fire under the gravy. As she was straightening up from the oven, she felt another presence in the kitchen. She turned around.

"Hello." A woman stood just inside the kitchen door. "Your friend Rémi sent me in here to tell you to come out and play." She held up a glass of Irish cream in a frosted glass. "This is for you."

Tall, teak, and lovely. A smile tickled the corner of Dez's mouth. *Rémi, you troublemaker.* She slid off the oven mitts and dropped them on the cluttered counter.

"And you are?"

"Trish. Derrick invited me."

Of course. Despite her teasing, Derrick always did have great taste in women. The absent Miss Jackson was ample proof of that. And Trish wasn't bad either. Dez accepted the glass of liqueur and took a sip. "Thanks. I'd hate for you to come sweat in this hot kitchen for nothing." She gestured ahead of her. "Shall we?" She didn't bother to look away from the enticing glide of ass and hips under Trish's copper and cream dress as she walked ahead of her.

When they came out of the kitchen, Rémi winked at Dez from across the room. Nuria shook her head, discreetly wagging her finger at them both.

"The other chef has emerged from the kitchen," her mother announced. "Does that mean everything is ready?"

"Almost. Give it about another hour or two."

Rémi, the bottomless pit, groaned the loudest about the delay. "Are you trying to starve us?"

"I'm sure you can find something to occupy your time until the food is ready." Dez glanced at her brother. She bet that he could think of a couple of things to do with that hot little number he brought home. Too bad he didn't believe in sharing.

"If anyone brought suits, there's always laying out by the pool," their freshly tanned mother suggested.

"I didn't bring a suit, but I'm definitely for laying out." Everyone looked at Nuria. "What? God didn't give me anything that I'm ashamed of."

"I have some bathing suits in the guest bathroom down the hall. There is enough of an assortment in size that everyone should be well provided for."

"We'll keep that in mind, Mother," Derrick said. He didn't seem wedded to the swimming idea at all.

"Ah, well. There are worse things to do besides what we're doing now." Nuria sipped her vodka on the rocks from the arm of the brown leather sofa and dimpled prettily at Derrick and Trish.

Eden intercepted Nuria's suggestive glance and the younger woman blushed. Against her will, Dez felt herself starting to relax. The Irish cream mellowed her enough to be nice to her brother and his date, but not enough to invite the petite woman in the kitchen for a quickie. She could see Nuria already considering that route, only with Derrick invited along for the ride, too.

"How are you doing, love?" Claudia asked, sitting beside Dez on the overstuffed love seat. "You seem pensive."

"More like maudlin, really." She smiled at her mother to let her know that she was at least partly joking. "But I'm fine. Just thinking too much right now."

"Thinking or drinking?" Her mother looked meaningfully at the glass of liqueur, her second that afternoon.

Dez chuckled. "Maybe a bit of both."

"In that case, you and Derrick go in and finish up the food so people can eat. Breakfast wore off a long time ago and I'm starving."

Within two hours, everything was ready. Derrick herded everyone into the dining room while Dez put a round of Jazz

CDs in the stereo and pressed PLAY. A mellow saxophone settled in the background. Rémi rubbed her hands together as she sat down at the table. "This is the best-looking spread I've seen in a long time. Did you two do all this?"

"Of course." Derrick pulled out the chair for his mother. "This day and this meal are for a very special lady, so we did our best."

"Your brother is good, Dez. You could learn a thing or two from him. At least in the charm department."

Dez didn't even spare Nuria a glance. She handed the tongs to Claudia before taking her own seat. "Start whenever you're ready, Mama."

But the older woman seemed too in awe of the lavish meal in front of her to even touch it. The Cornish hens were a deep golden brown and still steaming. Ten of them sat in deep serving platters surrounded by bowls brimming with steamed broccoli, garlic mashed potatoes, herbed corn-bread stuffing with pine nuts and golden raisins, and cranberry sauce. Dez and Derrick had taken out the good china, and the translucent amber plates and goblets glowed in the softened light.

Claudia cleared her throat. "Before I desecrate this gorgeous arrangement of food at my daughter's request, I just wanted to say a few words." She glanced at everyone around the table. "It's good to have both my children back with me. It's been too long. And I'm thankful that they could put aside their"—she looked from Derrick to Dez—"endless quarrelling to make this meal together and share this day with me and with all of us. Thank you, darlings."

Everyone raised their glasses of water in agreement. Dez quickly sipped hers so she could swallow past a suddenly dry throat. "Hear, hear." She met her brother's eyes across the table and nodded briefly at him.

He opened his mouth to say something but the sound of the doorbell cut him off. Dez waited a second, then two, to see what he would say. When nothing came out, she stood up.

"I'll get the door," she said.

"Am I too early?" Victoria Jackson asked, holding a brightly gift-wrapped present as she stood in the doorway.

"Who is it?" Derrick called out from the dining room.

"Your friend," she yelled back, looking at Victoria.

"Tori," the woman said with a slight smile.

"I haven't forgotten," Dez murmured.

"Quit stalling and bring her in." Derrick's voice rose, light and teasing from the dining room. "We're all about to pass out from hunger in here."

Dez gestured for her to come in. Was it her imagination or did the woman look even better than the last time, like a dressed-up version of last night's wet dream come to life in her mother's foyer? She walked ahead into the house and Dez could only blink in the after-image of her. Hair twisted up and back away from her face. Burgundy-painted lips. The slope and rise of her breasts under the white blouse. Reaction settled deep in Dez's belly. She took a deep breath and followed after Victoria.

"You ass," Victoria said to Derrick as everyone made room for her at the table. "You told me dinner was at five." It was barely four-fifteen.

"I'm glad you made it, honey." Claudia kissed her son's best friend on the cheek and tugged her gently into the chair next to hers. "You're right on time."

Dez watched their exchange with interest. Was she the only one who hadn't met Victoria? Even Eden chatted her up with some familiarity, teasing her about trusting Derrick, who ate when the food (and he) was ready, no matter what time of day it was.

"And now, let's really get started." Claudia brandished the tongs. "Who wants a Cornish hen?"

Victoria was a meat eater. She tasted some of the tofu with red and yellow roasted bell peppers that Dez had made for Sage and Nuria, but ended up eating a hen and a half, throwing compliments at Dez and Derrick between bites. Her lips glistened from the olive oil and from her tongue's repeated journey over them.

"You never cook like this for me," she chided her best friend around a mouthful of mashed potatoes.

"I think everybody at this table knows that you're lying," Derrick pointed his fork at her. "That was one of the first ways I tried to get you to fall for me when we first met."

Victoria blushed and laughed, the subtle color moving like a wave under her butterscotch skin.

Dez caught her eye over the centerpiece of floating candles and flower petals. "You should taste what I can cook up in the kitchen."

"I think she is, darling." Eden shot her an amused glance. Dez smiled back. As soon as Eden looked away her smile faded. She suddenly felt very tired.

The dinner was wonderful, almost like old times, even before their father left, with Claudia being the brilliant diamond in their midst, laughing and showering her light on everyone at the table. Dez took part in the festivities, may have even seemed like her old self, flirting shamelessly with all the women, talking the usual round of shit, and eating much more than she should. But inside she felt herself slowly shutting down. Sensations came and went, lightning fast, before she could access them. Even Victoria's presence couldn't engage her. After the first course, Trish asked if she was all right. Dez nodded a yes and found somewhere else to look. What else was she supposed to say?

Derrick went into the kitchen to get his dessert masterpiece, an exquisite guava-and-cream-cheese flan with slices of the pink fruit fanned out on top. That was what Claudia said she wanted for her birthday, not cake. So her children obliged her. The women oohed and aahed over the gorgeous dessert, some eyeing Derrick like he was part of the meal. Dez excused herself to smoke on the deck. In that moment, she felt too heavy to be among all those bright and laughing people.

Dez lit her cigarette and took a long drag. Smoke hit her lungs in a deep, burning stroke. Yesterday she was fine. Even this morning. She had managed to all but forget that her mother could be dying and that Claudia had told Derrick about it and not her. But now the memory of the call from the doctor's office rose up to suffocate her. Dying. Death. Dead.

"Dinner was marvelous."

Dez put away her emotions before turning to face Victoria.

"I thank you and Derrick thanks you." She looked beyond her to the party still going on inside. "Is it time to open presents?"

"Almost, but not yet."

Dez ashed her cigarette over the railing and turned so the smoke wouldn't blow toward Victoria. She took a deep breath. "So what brings you out here?"

"You."

She attempted a smile. "Really?"

It had rained while they ate so the air was cooler now. Victoria shivered in her thin white blouse and crossed her arms to warm herself. Dez deliberately kept her eyes on the other woman's face.

"Your mother highly encouraged"—Victoria said the word with a wry grin—"me to tell you to get your ass back inside."

"Ah, I see. No other motives, then?"

She smiled. "None whatsoever." Her eyes caught a flash of something from Dez. "Are you all right?"

"Not really. But I'll live."

Victoria's mouth began to shape a question, but Dez never found out what that question was.

"Desiree, stop brooding and come join the party."

With a low sigh, she crushed out her cigarette and tossed it into the darkness behind her. "Coming, Mama." She waved a hand before her. "After you, Ms. Jackson."

That night, sleep came easily. So did the dreams of decay and death and the rapid drumming of her heart, heavy and full in her chest. Dez woke to stare wide-eyed at the ceiling. The clock winked a soothing electronic blue. It was barely midnight. The party ended hours ago but the feelings that had trailed her in its last hours remained. She pushed the light covers away and sat up. A thought carried itself from her dreams, made her call Claudia's number and croak out a plea. She left her house a half an hour later to meet her mother.

Chapter 8

She rode into the front entrance of the Coconut Grove Cemetery in first gear, coasting over the smooth pavement that wove like gray thread through acres of manicured grass and marble tombstones. The night was already damp and sweet from the drooping jasmine and honeysuckle. Dez looked over the wide expanse of green and found her mother. Claudia was right where she said she would be, on the steps of Aunt Paul's tomb with its twin columns and blue marble vases still bright with fresh flowers. She looked tired. Her jaw split in a yawn even as Dez brought the bike to a stop and turned off its engine.

"You going to make it, Mama?"

"I assume that you have a good reason for getting me out of bed at this ungodly hour." She yawned again.

"Yes." Dez held up a paper bag. "Snacks."

Claudia rolled her eyes in a most unmotherly way and huddled deeper in the blankets tucked around her. Dez twitched with guilt.

"It's not that cold, is it?"

"For me it is, love. So could you please get to the point."

Dez sat down next to her mother and unfolded the contents of her paper sack—a thermos with fresh mint tea, small corned-beef sandwiches that she knew Claudia loved, and oatmeal raisin cookies. "Here." She poured a cup of tea, then leaned back against a column as Claudia smiled her thanks before bringing the steaming brew to her lips.

"Thank you."

"No, I'm . . . thank you for coming."

Claudia watched her daughter with alert eyes. "I guess you're not okay, then?"

Dez forced a smile. "No, I'm not." She shook her head. "I'm sorry."

"Don't be sorry. Just tell me what's wrong." Claudia cradled the tea in her lap.

"I'm worried about you and I'm angry." She bit into a cookie and chewed slowly, forcing herself to swallow although it felt like dust in her mouth.

"That doesn't surprise me."

Dez looked up at that noncommittal response. She didn't know what else to say. Her family was never big on sensitive chats. Things just *were*. She came out as a lesbian by bringing a girl home when she was thirteen. There was no discussion, just acceptance—a grudging one on her father's part—of the way things would be from that point on. Her aunt was the only person she'd been able to really talk to.

"Don't go home with a woman you just met," Aunt Paul had told her over ice cream and cake, her face perfectly serious. "Unless you're with someone else who can take care of themselves and you."

Paul was never fond of giving advice, but she did so then because Claudia, unsettled by her daughter's lesbian revelation, had asked her to. Dez could never forget that day. It was the first day that her aunt took her out on the back of the motorcycle for more than a cruise around their small Coconut Grove neighborhood. They rode around for over an hour before finally stopping at a little dessert shop in Fort Lauderdale. Only now did Dez realize that her aunt had been buying herself time to find something appropriate to say to her sister's child. At the café, Paul was charming and relaxed. She flirted with the cute waitress who promptly hopped over to take their order, making it seem like she was just taking Dez to a casual dykes' day out.

In Dez's eyes, Paul had been the perfect gentlewoman in every aspect of her life, especially that day when she'd gotten the waitress's number, eased her niece's fears about being abandoned by the rest of the family, and treated them both to a towering strawberry shortcake and ice cream concoction.

Dez spread her fingers wide over the stone steps leading up to Aunt Paul's tomb and refocused on the reason she and Claudia was at the cemetery so late at night.

"You told Derrick about the cancer." It wasn't a question.

"Yes." Claudia's eyes flickered away and she briefly looked ashamed. "He was here and I thought he could handle it better."

"Since he's a lawyer and everything?" She didn't bother to hide her sarcasm.

"Darling, don't."

Dez took a breath. "It's hard not to. Not when you kept something so important from me and I had to find out by stupid accident."

"I guess that means that you were destined to find out."

"Otherwise known as 'you shouldn't keep important things like that from your children, no matter how incompetent you think they are.' " Tears burned, but she bent and poured some tea for herself, making the preparation of it slow so that by the time she looked up, the threat of tears was gone. "How could you trust Derrick over me? I'm not reliable enough? What would have happened if you had died when I was on the road?"

"I was preparing myself to tell you."

"And after all this preparation, when would you have finally let me know?"

Again, Claudia looked away.

Dez shook her head. This was so fucking hard. "Every night I dream about you dying."

"I thought I was doing the right thing, letting you be free

without having to worry about me. I thought that you would only come back to Miami if you knew."

"And I did. I'm here for you."

"You've always been, darling. I just don't want you to be here because of some misguided notion of filial loyalty. I don't want you to give up your life for me."

"I'm not, Mama. There's nothing—"

A beam of light cut through their darkness. "What are you two doing here?"

The official-sounding voice made Dez glance up sharply. "Take the light out of our faces and I might tell you." She put up a hand to block the light.

Across from her, Claudia quietly put her teacup down on the marble steps of the tomb and squinted up at the officers. "Is it against the law to visit loved ones in the cemetery?" she asked quietly. The light on her face moved away.

"Do you have ID?"

Dez cursed.

"Keep your hands where I can see them, sir."

"Desiree, please don't antagonize these people." Her mother's voice was low with warning.

"Can I see *your* identification?" Dez said, standing up and keeping her hands in plain sight. Despite her annoyance at whoever these two assholes were, she was no fool. The beam from the flashlight went south, down her body, following the stark lines outlined by her white T-shirt, black leather jacket, and black jeans; then it fell away.

"It's not safe for two women to be out so late, especially in the cemetery."

The smaller officer made a vague gesture with his flashlight. "You ladies might want to do your visiting in the day-time." His gravelly Southern accent threatened to scrape her nerves raw. "Vandals and other undesirables have been known to come through here at night. We're just looking out for your interests."

His partner only nodded, looking grim in her dark uniform. Why would anyone need to wear sunglasses in the pitch black of night?

Everyone exchanged IDs and thanked one another. Then the officers escorted the women to their vehicles. Dez thanked them again with a meaningful look. The officers didn't budge.

"I'll be fine, love. Call me when you get home, okay?"

"Okay." She waited until her mother pulled off in her little convertible before she got on her bike and cruised out of the cemetery, ignoring the twin stares at her back.

She didn't call when she got back home. It was after three and she was exhausted. Tomorrow, she promised herself. But the day came and went. Dez called Derrick to check up on their mother, but he was his usual charming self and told her to call Claudia herself. But her mother beat her to the punch. Dez heard the message as she stepped out of the shower, dripping water all over the hardwoods.

"Hello, love. We didn't get to finish our talk the other night. I'd like to. Call me or come over to the house." The machine beeped as she hung up.

But she didn't feel up to talking with Claudia just then, so she dried off and pressed the PLAY button again and again until it was time for her to leave the house.

Chapter 9

Dez walked through the automatic doors of the neon-lit supermarket. The cool air, unbelievably a few degrees below the chill air outside, washed over her face as she stepped past the threshold. She wanted to be able to invite her mother over to her house for dinner, to sit her down and have a civilized, grown-up conversation. She didn't want to be sniveling and whiny and all the other ten million things that she despised about the way she'd acted in the past. But for that dinner, Dez needed food.

At ten past midnight, the market was nearly empty. The security guard and the bored cashiers glanced up and past her as she walked by. She nodded a greeting to the thickly muscled woman with her rent-a-cop gun strapped high on her waist, then took out her long grocery list. Dez didn't have a clue what she would make when she invited Claudia over for dinner, only that it would be good and plentiful, a meal that would remind her mother of better times. She unhooked a shopping cart from the long string by the door and pushed it down the nearest aisle.

Years ago, when she and her brother were young, their lives seemed to revolve around food. Between grading papers and putting together lesson plans, Claudia always made time for food-gathering field trips. Most times, she took the twins to the farmer's market on the outskirts of Miami. The scent of their childhood was of crisp apples, luscious red tomatoes, water-veined celery, and the sweet ripeness of mangoes, Jamaican June plums, and the thick almost-smell of eggplants. Their days together were measured by the meals they prepared side by side—Claudia in the middle and Derrick and Dez like animated parentheses, laughing and tasting, creating meals that were invariably delicious, flavored as they were by their shared joy.

It was only when at thirteen Dez discovered girls that her interest in food and her mother waned. Then she and her brother started fighting—over girls, space, and anything else they could think of. Dez lingered over the barrel of jasmine rice, inhaling its faint popcornlike scent and the lingering flavor of her childhood memories. As she reached down for more rice, her cell phone rang.

"Yes?" She deftly emptied the metal scoop into the two-pound capacity plastic bag while balancing the phone between her ear and shoulder.

"Hi, there," a low female voice purred in her ear. "Is this a bad time?"

Who is this? "Not at all," Dez flipped through her mental Rolodex for a name to match with the voice but came up empty. "I'm just doing a little shopping."

"Good. You said whenever I felt like doing lunch, or any sort of meal, to give you a call, so . . ."

"Ah, you're asking me out. I like that." Something suddenly clicked in her brain. *And I definitely remember you, Miss Victoria of the tasty cleavage and a mouth I would love to come all over.*

"Are you free next Friday night?"

"I think so." Dez was actually sure of it. "What do you have in mind? Something kinky, I hope."

Victoria laughed, a husky vibration that made Dez want to reach through the phone and start her meal right now.

"Not quite, at least not yet. Just dinner." A pause. "How about my place? Eight o'clock?"

"Sounds good to me."

"Great. Dress casual. Here's the address."

She dug out a pen from her inside jacket pocket and scrawled Victoria's name on her hand. "Go ahead." Dez took the address down, then repeated it twice to be sure. She didn't want to get lost on her way to *this* appointment.

"See you then."

Dez closed the phone and smiled. Now she had two dinner dates to look forward to. As she reached up to put the phone back in her pocket, someone jostled her from behind. Her phone fell, breaking neatly in two pieces.

"Shit!"

"I'm sorry. Fuck, I didn't see . . ."

Dez looked up from retrieving the pieces of her phone as the voice trailed off. It took a moment for the red hair and pierced lip to register. The woman—Caitlyn—cursed again and ran her tongue across the silver ring encircling the center of her full lower lip. Dez stood up.

"Cait, did you find those tomatoes I like?" Ruben appeared from the next aisle, pushing a cart already half-filled with groceries. He looked good. Dez stepped back as if that measly distance would lessen his effect on her. It didn't. His body was as slim and hard as ever, gay boy muscles alive under his tight blue shirt. He had cut his hair, and now it lay in conservative, Anglo-looking waves against his head. The style only made his liquid eyes more noticeable. They became startled and soft when they noticed her and his dimples went back into hiding. He was still beautiful.

Dez endured her stomach's sickening plunge and the way the temperature of her hands suddenly dropped ten degrees. Fantastic. She gripped her shopping cart and swung it around, away from them. Her face felt tight and cold, but she forced herself not to run. Moving in a fog, Dez took her time picking a bag of black beans from its pyramid display, then after she was sure that it was the one she wanted, she put it in her cart and walked away.

*   *   *

He followed her from inside the store. Not with his body, but with everything else. Otherwise, how could she explain the smell of him pressing close, the sound of his voice, the phantom feel of his hair between her fingers? It took her three tries to open the door. Dez loaded her groceries into the truck with shaking fingers, again measuring each movement. No one, not even Ruben, was going to make her rush. Even though she needed to be alone with the sudden memories of him, of them together. She left the shopping cart where she'd unpacked it and backed the truck out of the parking space. A pedestrian yelped behind her and barely jumped out of the way in time to avoid being hit. Damn Ruben.

Long before she'd been to college, Dez had made her choice. It was going to be girls. Or at least that was what she thought. And then she'd seen the hot boy at orientation that first year at the University of Miami. He was all pretty mouth and round, tight ass—two things she normally only liked in girls. She'd been ashamed. And it took her three years to actually approach him, three years of watching him fool around with boys and sneer at the infatuated coeds. Shit, they were even in the queer students alliance together. But she still wanted him. She'd denied herself, sleeping with more women during those three years of confused longing than she had before or since.

Then, it happened. One night at an impromptu, post-study-session boogie-run to one of the hottest new gay clubs in Miami, Dez got her boy. She and seven of her classmates had stumbled into the place, badly needing a distraction from school and the midterms only a few days away. Samantha Morris, one of the more adventurous girls in Dez's lit class, passed out tabs of X to each of her stressed study-buddies; then they were off. Ten minutes into her high, Dez found herself staring at the club full of gyrating bodies, her own skin itching with the need to dance.

"Come on." Ruben rushed at her from behind and pulled her into the fray.

His palm against hers felt electric and slick. They pushed into the crowd and she couldn't help but prolong it, that delicious slide against foreign skin, the pumping push-pull of the crowd dancing to the infectious rhythm of Kylie's "Can't Get You Out of My Head." Never one to hold back on the dance floor when she was sober, Dez threw herself even more into the high energy music, writhing up against the glowing rainbow boy that Ruben had become. Sweat dripped from both their bodies. She and Ruben passed a giant bottle of water back and forth until it was empty, until she wanted something else to put her mouth on.

Dez licked his face, and he licked back, passing a hot wet tongue over her cheek and eyelashes. She quivered and rubbed her breasts and belly against him. Ruben was the angel of sex, slippery and hot, rocketing her temperature through the roof, sending her skin shuddering in tiny orgasms just with his touch. The other dancers disappeared and it was just the two of them, sweetly trembling, together. Somehow they ended up away from everyone else, pressed belly to belly in a narrow hallway that smelled of latex and fresh sex. She drew his shirt off, then hers, too. She undid her pants, then his. Ruben's dick was hard. He fumbled with the condoms he'd brought along to use with someone else and managed to cover himself without coming. Dez grabbed his ass and pulled him into her. Everything was on the surface, her lust, her sweat, her need. One thrust. Two. Dez's body exploded deep inside, clenching him and pulling him into her, into the shimmering, pulsating light overtaking her. His breath huffed against her neck. And his voice, rough and soft at once, wailed around them. She clung to him, laughing.

They spent the rest of the night together, wringing the rest of their X trip for all the fun that it was worth. Neither of them advertised their lust-affair, but they didn't hide it either.

One day they were passing acquaintances and the next day they were fucking each other like nymphos on speed. With Ruben she'd felt renewed. Her period of self-denial was over and she reveled in her obsession and love for him. They made after-graduation plans, then left. Together.

Now, two plus years later, she was alone. Dez blinked away the sting of old memories and forced herself to focus on the road ahead.

Chapter 10

Dez was good at pushing aside her emotions. By the time Claudia knocked at her door a few nights later, the unexpected reunion with Ruben and Caitlyn was barely a ripple in her calm sea. Dez was able to smile her thanks for the bottle of wine and even laugh at her mother's Alaskan wilderness gear of goose-down jacket and gloves in the sixty-degree chill.

"Come in." She waved Claudia inside and closed the door on the cool night air. The house was warm and fragrant with the scent of cinnamon and apples, the steaming hot toddy Dez had prepared for her mother to ward off any lingering cold from her short drive. She took Claudia's outer layers and led her to the kitchen.

"I don't want to mess this up like I've done everything else." Dez stood with her back to the counter, her hands moving restlessly over the cool marble behind her. "I haven't made dinner yet because I wanted us to cook together. Make it like it was before Aunt Paul died."

Claudia sat on the bar stool with her toddy clasped between her palms. "You don't have to reach into the past for me, Dez. I'm right here. Sometimes things are just a little different now, that's all."

"They're not a *little* different, Mama. Even I can tell that. I feel like I've lost you already."

"No. No, you haven't." Claudia put aside her drink and reached for her daughter, grasped the cold hands in hers and squeezed. "Stop being dramatic. I'll be here for you as long as I'm on this earth, no matter how things may seem or how far we are away from each other. I know I made a mistake by not telling you I was sick. I thought I was doing the right thing, but that was obviously wrong. Please don't be angry." When Dez didn't say anything, Claudia stood up and tugged her toward the refrigerator. "Come, let's go make dinner."

They made Claudia's favorite winter food—sage-spiced quiche with Italian sausage and red pepper flakes and a pot of pumpkin soup. Dez insisted on having bread with the meal and rummaged around for the bread maker. While her mother took out and measured the ingredients for the honey wheat bread, she turned on the oven and broke the eggs for the quiche.

"This is a nice bread maker, love. I didn't know you liked to make your own."

"I don't. But I knew that you would come over one day."

It was the best invitation for a closer relationship that Dez could offer. The last two years before she'd left for college, she and her mother had been distant, cooking together only on the requisite holidays, and even then the rapport had been different, off somehow. More dead space had inexplicably sprung up between them while Dez's mind was on her aunt more and more, wondering if she could have done anything to keep Aunt Paul around for just a while longer and hating that her only confidante was gone. She took Claudia for granted, assuming that she would always be there yet would never understand her as well as her dyke aunt had. Their last conversation before Dez left was simple.

"I have to go," she had said. Then left. No promises to write or call, no certainty of when she would return to Miami. Claudia seemed to accept it. Although a single look that spasmed across her face said *something*. Dez did not take the time to find out what. She had a ride to catch, but more importantly there was that history of silence between her and Claudia that was too hard to breach. Over the two years, her mother had written to her, scented letters filled with the minutiae of her days, delicate tendrils of connection that Dez hadn't been able to return, but had cherished nonetheless.

Still, in this new kitchen, over the milk, eggs, and wheat and yeast, they managed to talk. Dez finally found out when her mother knew about the cancer—during a routine exam eight months ago—and how she was going about taking care of herself. Dez's stomach turned over at her mother's matter-of-fact description of her illness and her chances for survival.

"My chances are good. We caught it at stage one," Claudia said as she poured the dough in the bread maker and set the timer. "Dr. Charles scooped out all she could during the last operation. She did some tests at my last visit so I have to go and see her in a few days to get the results."

Scooped out? Dez's insides quivered with the beginnings of nausea. But she wanted to know more. This wasn't something that anyone should go through alone.

"Can I come with you?"

Dez settled the liquid ingredients of the quiche into its store-bought crust and ignored her mother's look of surprise. "I won't get in the way. Promise."

"I know you won't," Claudia said. Her gaze was considering. "Okay, you can come."

"Thank you." Dez looked up. "What should I bring?"

"Just yourself."

"Okay." A blast of heat flashed over her face when she opened the preheated oven and set the quiche inside. "I promise not to cry and act like a complete baby in front of your doctor."

"She's used to that kind of thing. Your father almost broke down when he found out."

Her tentative smile disappeared. "Daddy knows?"

"Warrick was the first person I told." Claudia's smile was

wistful. "He came in with me for the operation, although, obviously, he didn't have to. Everything went fine and he was really great. It was almost like old times."

"Then he went back home to his wife," Dez sneered.

"Don't be unkind, Desiree. He was my friend before we were ever lovers. Just because we didn't work out doesn't mean that our friendship is over."

Words of protest crowded onto Dez's tongue, incidents of Warrick being a complete asshole to everyone in the family, especially his wife. Then there was that whole abandonment thing. "I'm glad he was there for you, Mama." Water gushed in the sink as she turned on the tap to wash her hands. "But what about Eden, or any of those other women you hang out with these days?"

"Your father was my choice, Desiree. He was the right one."

Properly chastened, she backed off. "Sorry."

"Don't be. Just accept the things that I need. And realize that I need you, too." Claudia bumped her daughter's hip with her own. "Although I have been a stupid old woman for not showing you that."

Dez smiled. "Well, you may be stupid, but you're certainly not old. Now Warrick, he's got a face like—"

Claudia poked her in the belly. "I can see where this is going, so let's just stop it right here."

"I'm just kidding. The old lady can't take a joke?"

Claudia came after her with a bony elbow again. Still laughing, Dez easily dodged her and slipped past to the other side of the oversize kitchen. Their evening went by quickly. Dez forced herself to pay attention to every detail of their time together—her mother's laughter, the new lines at the corner of her mouth, the sometimes fragile way she held herself, like a moth waiting to fly off for a new light source. She had not always been so delicate. Perhaps it was because Dez knew of the illness and was seeing things for the first time that had always been there. She could be oblivious at times.

They sat at the dinner table surrounded by soft music and candlelight, like old friends, sharing bits of their lives previously held separate. When Claudia revealed that Warrick had been her first lover, Dez held up her hands in surrender.

"That, my darling mother, might be too much information."

Claudia laughed. "Stop being such a prude."

"I'm sure you don't want to know everything about *me*, Mama."

"Of course I do. It feels like it's been years since you and I had a real conversation. I want to know everything you've done and been and seen and felt since you were fourteen."

"Fourteen!" Dez laughed. "I'll have you know I was sharing plenty with you after that."

"Right. Your feelings about being treated like a child you mean—at high decibels."

Dez quieted. "Did I? Was I that bad? Why didn't you slap my face or something?"

"Your father believes in that kind of punishment. I don't. There are other ways to discipline a child."

Dez remembered her mother refusing to speak with her until she calmed down. Those brown eyes going flat and cold had been more effective than any beating her father ever gave her. "No kidding."

"But really, love. Tell me. I want to know you again. Tell me everything."

"Are you sure about that?"

"I wouldn't have asked if I wasn't."

Dez glanced down at her hands then back at Claudia. Her mother's eyes burned with a warm fire, the long elegant hands—so much thinner now—loosely clasped around her wineglass. Light from the candles winked around them, reflecting in the diamond studs in Claudia's ears as she cocked her head to one side. She smiled.

"I hated you for being weak," Dez said. "Warrick just threw us away, all three of us, and you folded. You let him walk all over us." Her mother shook her head quickly in denial, and her mouth opened, but she said nothing. "Whenever he talked shit about Aunt Paul, you never called him on it. Not once. I thought part of it was because she was only your half sister. When I grew older that wasn't even an excuse anymore. And later that made me feel ashamed about being gay. I felt that you loved me less somehow."

Now Claudia did interrupt, shaking her head more violently. "I never loved you any less. Nor Paulette. She was my little sister. She was the one who forced me to see that there was more to life than just sacrifice and preparing eight course meals. Whenever Warrick said those things about her, I told him to stop. I usually took him aside so you and Derrick wouldn't see us arguing. It never did any good, but I told him that it wasn't okay. He got worse about it when you told us you were gay, too. He felt that it was somehow Paulette's fault that he lost his little girl. Warrick has issues of his own, separate from us that make him the way he is. I'm not making excuses for him or for myself, that's just how it is."

Dez nodded. She could tell her mother was trying her best to react logically to all this instead of with her emotions. The strain showed on her face. "I can understand some of that now, but before, I couldn't. When Aunt Paul died, I felt, suddenly, completely alone. I knew you were there, and I knew Rémi was there, and"—she laughed ruefully—"I guess that was it." She laughed again. "Anyway, I felt like my whole world became different overnight. I went on to college because I promised her I would. I went off with Ruben because he made me feel something else besides pain and loss and loneliness, which is pretty ironic right now, but that's a subject for another time."

"No, sweetheart. Tell me now. Everything, remember?"

Dez sighed and pressed her fist to her mouth. She blinked down at the table. *Emotions are very scary things*, she thought for the millionth time in her life. *I'm never ready for them*. The fire and flood of her relationship with Ruben had left her in ashes. With the news of her mother's illness coming so close to his leaving, she hadn't really made the time to feel what he'd done to her. She poked at the remnants of it, and it still burned.

"On my worst days, I feel like since I was fourteen, my life has been hell. I came out, and my father, the person I'd relied on before to protect and love me no matter what, shut every door in my face. Then your marriage was gone barely a year later. Before I could even think about being a well-adjusted adult, Aunt Paul left me, and I fell in love with a gay man who opened me up and broke me down emotionally only to dump me for another woman." Dez rubbed her hand over her eyes and cursed softly. Her insides hummed with pain, but it felt good to get it all out. "And last, but certainly not the least of it, my mother had or has cancer. The injury on top of injury is that you never told me, but you told my brother and my father and God knows who else."

"Sweetheart . . ." Her mother's voice broke. "My sweetheart."

"I know that my life isn't just misery. I *know* that. But sometimes, I feel it all come down on me at once. And it's too much."

Dez's throat ached from talking and her voice was a bare rasp that Claudia had to lean closer to hear. She finally looked up to see her mother's quiet tears. Her lashes swept down against the suddenly unbearable glare of the candle-light.

"I did ask if you were sure," she said.

Claudia's hands reached across the table and cupped hers. "I'm still sure."

Chapter 11

Claudia was here, but for how long? The question haunted Dez long after their dinner plates had been cleaned and put away. Still, she tried to run away from it. When Dez was younger, people used to ask how it was that she managed to stay so even-tempered—they would never go as far as to say "cheerful"—all the time. When her parents were going through their divorce and she told someone about it, they thought she was joking. After her aunt died, no one could have known how devastated she was. Truth was that she just didn't think about it. She banished it all from her mind like a bad dream. Voluntary amnesia. These days there weren't many people around to see her smiles, or lack of them. Dez threw herself into sex or food or other sensual pleasures the way some did drugs. With thoughts of Claudia and her illness and Ruben creeping back to her, Dez escaped the house after giving Rémi a call. Drinks? At their favorite straight bar? Why not? Rémi was always up for just about anything.

Dez sat on her bike outside the bar, smoking a cigarette and waiting for her best friend to show. The night's entertainment seemed promising. Women walked past her, darting their eyes over her even as they clutched the hand of the men by their side. Dez's tank top stretched taut over her chest, cleaving to the tight body, the small high breasts, and flat stomach. Worn blue jeans, a thick leather belt, and Timberlands completed a package that Dez knew was fuckworthy. She didn't have to see the want in these women's eyes to know that. But it didn't hurt.

"When you're done posing, you want to come with me into the bar?" Rémi rode up on her bike, the laughter rich in her voice even under the dark helmet. She wore all black today. And spurs on her motorcycle boots.

Inside, they turned their helmets over to the bartender and parked themselves at the bar with two shots of tequila, a pitcher of beer, an ashtray, and a pack of cigarettes between them. The crowd was hot tonight—affluent, beautiful, a nice mix of races and cultures. A conversation in Spanish tickled her ear from halfway across the room and from somewhere else a hint of Jamaican patois rubbed up against Haitian-accented French. Rémi knocked back her tequila.

"Nice." Her glance traveled around the bar, taking in the view.

It didn't take long for the festivities to begin. A silver-bangled arm nudged Rémi's, then the accompanying body did the same.

"Excuse me," the stranger said. "I didn't see you sitting there."

Liar. The brown-skinned mami licked her gaze up and down Rémi's body, taking her time at the highlights—breasts, hips, ass. She wasn't bad either, with her curvaceous form poured into a Donna Karan the same luscious tone as her skin. But she had on too much makeup.

"Please, excuse *me*," Rémi said, moving neatly back and out of her way. Turning to ash her cigarette in the heavy silver disc in front of her friend, she turned to Dez. "I wonder what's keeping Ricky. You can't trust boyfriends for shit, huh?"

The girl almost swallowed her tongue in surprise. She ordered a drink she probably didn't even want and fled.

"That wasn't nice."

"What do you want me to do, give her a pity fuck just for

trying?" Rémi snorted and took a sip of her beer, balancing her cigarette between her fuck-fingers and the glass. "I didn't see you offering your pretty little self in my place."

"It was you she wanted, not me."

"These days I'm not settling for just anything."

"When have you ever had to settle?"

"You'd be surprised." Smoke spiraled up from Rémi's cigarette and she squinted against its bite. "Nowadays any pussy that comes to me has to be good pussy, or at least interesting pussy. It can't just be any old shit."

"I still don't know when the hell you've ever had to take just whatever."

"Two years is a long time, isn't it?" Rémi put down her drink and looked at Dez. "There's actually someone—"

"Baby, you must be a model," a voice interrupted. "That body of yours is just *too* fine."

Dez looked past Rémi to the guy with the midnight skin, beautiful teeth, and asshole leer.

"You play ball?" he asked.

Rémi turned to look at the two men. That was an original question. What else would two six-foot-tall black women do for a living or for fun?

"We don't play with balls." Her amused eyes flickered over them, then turned away in dismissal.

"You?"

His friend eyed Dez and tried a leer of his own. Whenever they were out together and straight boys saw Rémi first they always asked if the women were models, trying to lure them into some vanity trap because of Rémi's pretty skin, quiet self-confidence, and devil's mouth. But when they saw Dez first, the lead-in was usually about basketball or some other height-required sport. Never mind that the two women were the same height.

"No, thanks, I already got what I'm drinking," Rémi said.

"What about you, baby?"

"Same thing," Dez said, holding up her beer. "I'm good, thanks."

Admittedly, most men often saw what they wanted to where women were concerned, but wasn't it obvious that she and Rémi were dykes? Or was this about the challenge and a potential foursome? The men looked expectantly at them.

"We're not interested," Rémi finally said.

"You sure?" The first one asked, looking Rémi up and down.

"Very."

The two women found something much more interesting to look at when a dark-skinned honey slid up to the bar, insinuating her body between Rémi's and the interloping men.

"Hey, handsome," she murmured, leaning in even closer to Rémi. "I would *love* to eat your pussy."

The silence in the immediate area was deafening. Dez and Rémi sized her up—striking features with pillowy lips touched by a hint of lip gloss. Low-cut hair and long silver earrings dangling to her shoulders. Short skirt showing off lean legs and a juicy ass. Very nice.

The two women exchanged a look. Very, very nice.

"Want to make it a three?" Rémi looked her over again. "My friend here really loves your ass."

The woman glanced from one to the other. This was probably the best two-for-one deal she'd ever had. "Sure. My place is just up the street."

"Damn! It's like that?" The cocky boy who hit on Rémi first was the first to speak. A domino of speculative murmurs fell around the bar.

Dez and Rémi quickly settled up with the bartender, grabbed their helmets, and followed the woman out of the door. They rode the short five blocks behind the woman's black Infiniti truck. It turned out that her name was Jeanne and she lived in a town house near the beach. No roommate, boyfriend, or girlfriend at home.

The two women parked the bikes in her drive, refusing the

use of the space behind her in the garage. They weren't going to stay that long. Once in the house, Jeanne's cool composure melted.

"You are so fucking hot," she grabbed Rémi, touching her through her clothes and kneading the solid muscles with wonder.

The tall woman let her, chuckling while the slim hands burrowed beneath the leather and cotton. She grinned at Dez over the woman's head. Rémi lived for moments like this, when a woman appreciated how much time she spent making her body look perfect.

Jeanne reached back and tangled her fingers in Dez's shirt, pulling her up hard and rubbing the sleek, denim covered thighs as she angled her head up to sample Rémi's mouth. She pressed herself deep into the soft chest and purred.

The woman felt hot against Dez's breasts. She nuzzled the back of Jeanne's neck and reached around to cup the heavy breasts in her hands. *Oh. What's this?* She fumbled to unbutton Jeanne's blouse, but the woman eluded her, pulling back from her and Rémi both to watch their faces as she tugged off her blouse and the tiny skirt.

Oh, yeah? Jeanne wore nipple clamps. Silver beauties pinched tight to her fat nipples with a chain dangling low on her belly and attached to the matching clamp on her clit. Rémi's eyes became megawatt bright.

Jeanne stood posing in the middle of the spacious living room, the light bouncing off the Y-shaped chain attached to the clamps. "Would you two like a drink?"

"We don't want anything to drink," Rémi said. "We want to fuck. Isn't that what you brought us here for?" She took off her jacket, then pulled a pair of latex gloves from her back pocket and put them on. "Come here."

Jeanne came obediently, but still teased with her head held high and her mouth curved in a secret smile that said she was doing Rémi a favor by walking across the room to her. The chain wriggled against her skin as she moved.

"Nice jewelry." Rémi gripped the chain where it caressed Jeanne's belly, and tugged.

The woman gasped in pain, a thank-you, even as her ass rolled and turned up asking for more.

"I'm going to change your script a little," Rémi said, meeting Dez's eyes over the woman's head. She wanted that ass. Dez nodded and backed up to sit in a nearby armchair, a pretty floral thing that smelled faintly of perfume, and wait. Rémi was running this show.

She kissed Jeanne, sucked her plum purple mouth, and turned the woman's ass for Dez to admire. When Rémi bent Jeanne just a little, Dez licked her lips at the glistening pink slit and the darker pucker of her asshole that Rémi fingered and teased, her gloves wet with lube.

Her friend worked the woman, caressing and kissing her, tugging on the Y-chain until Jeanne gasped and the tips of her breasts became swollen and distended. Her thighs gleamed wet with cunt juice. Rémi turned her again, and showed the woman's tits to Dez as she squeezed them from the back, ran her gloved hands down Jeanne's belly and toward the swollen clit, while Jeanne's eyelashes beat uncontrollably and her mouth fell open to swallow more air.

Dez eased back in the chair and undid the buttons of her jeans. She slid the pants down and over her ass as she watched, her pussy getting juicier, tightening, anticipating the mouth that would surely lick it wet then dry after all this buildup. Her tits throbbed with a sweet pain under the little tank top.

Rémi spread Jeanne's legs, pushed her slightly forward toward Dez, as if asking her for a light or something equally incendiary. Her face changed when Rémi started to fuck her. She seemed to stretch, elongating herself to accommodate Rémi's fingers and her desire, her face becoming taut and hard, needful. Low, long sounds left her mouth. Jeanne leaned forward, bracing herself on Dez's chair. Rémi slowed the pace of her fucking.

"Make my friend come," she said. "At least twice. She's

very particular. No hands, and don't put your tongue in her pussy." She flicked Jeanne's clit and the woman jumped, almost falling to her knees in front of Dez. "No matter what, don't stop. Understand?" When Jeanne nodded, her body quivering and damp with sweat, Rémi reached into her pocket for a pack of dental dams and took one out. "Use this."

Jeanne reached blindly for Dez's naked pussy, opening her mouth wide for it despite the awkward angle of the jeans rucked up at her knees. Even through the barrier of the plastic, her tongue was heaven. Heated mouth, the flat of her tongue against Dez's shaved pussy, hot suction on her clit as Jeanne anchored her hands on her hips, her head bobbing with each yawn and snap of her mouth. Dez loved the hungry noises she made in her throat. They made her pussy feel wanted, made it open up and salivate, eager to be devoured. She pressed Jeanne's head deeper into her pussy. The thick hair tickled her palms as she guided the skilled mouth to exactly where it needed to be.

Jeanne knew what she was doing. Even with Rémi working her pussy hard from the back, fucking her with a lovely liquid sound, she focused on the task at hand. She damn near swallowed Dez's clit. The come snuck up her, lifting up her hips and carrying her away on a swift tide of sensation that left her breathless and shaking, but still wanting more.

Beyond the rising peach curve and cleft of the woman's ass, Rémi fucked her with gloved fingers, plunging in deep with her face a hard mask of concentration and her lips skinned back against her teeth in a feral grin. Her breath whistled with each exhalation. As Dez shuddered in the throes of her first come, Rémi pulled her fingers from the sticky sheath of Jeanne's pussy and slapped her hard. The woman jumped, bumping her mouth hard against Dez's clit.

"Shit!" The woman's muffled cry of surprise sent a jolt of electric heat slamming between Dez's thighs. She moaned and widened her thighs as far as the jeans would let her.

Rémi slapped her again and again, the sounds thick and

hot in the room, mingling with the slurp of Jeanne's mouth on Dez's pussy, her groans, and the steady heavy breath whistling through Rémi's teeth. She slapped her ass cheeks, her thighs, and the tender flesh between them. Jeanne gasped and jerked, eating Dez's pussy in earnest as the pain spread through her body. Dez knew exactly how she felt, could feel the heat in her own thighs, the sweet clench of her pussy at that twin-edged pain. A fiery wave rolled through her. She threw her head back and held on. This one was going to be good.

Rémi started to fuck their little playmate again. Jeanne's tongue flew over Dez's clit, licking the tender bundle of nerves harder and faster. Through the haze of pleasure, Dez looked up at Rémi. Her friend nodded. They pulled off Jeanne's clamps at the same time. The woman screamed and her knees buckled, but Rémi held her up. Jeanne kept at Dez's clit, licking and sucking until her wave crested and Dez bucked against Jeanne's mouth, holding her head steady while her pussy fisted, flooding come against the plastic barrier of the dental dam and on the pretty floral chair.

"Fuck yes!" Dez groaned.

Jeanne's head hung low as she panted between Dez's thighs. "Damn."

They weren't done yet. At a signal from Rémi, Dez stood up despite her wobbly knees so that her friend could take her place in the chair.

"Now, if memory serves, you mentioned something at the beginning of this evening about my pussy and your mouth." Rémi tugged down her zipper, showing off her thick, curling bush. "Come. I'm ready."

Chapter 12

Dez pressed the doorbell of Victoria Jackson's teal and white Spanish-style house. Even as she waited for her date to open the door, her mind still lingered on all that had happened at the dinner with Claudia two nights before, replaying each twitch of her mother's mouth, each shift of eyebrow, trying to decipher what had really happened between them. She sensed that they had come to a resolution of sorts, had acknowledged a mutual desire to reconnect and deal honestly with each other, but that was all. She wanted to sit back with that, content that it was enough. But she couldn't. Not yet. The door before her opened.

"Come in."

Oh. Dez's breath caught and released in silent acknowledgment of the woman's sensual appeal. *That's why I gave her my card.*

"Thank you."

As she slipped past her into the house, the scent of tangerines and honey, nestled in the soft places of Victoria's body, teased her nose.

"These are for you." She produced her gifts from behind her back—lavender tea roses growing in a small terra-cotta pot and a bottle of red wine. Dez had taken the chance that a woman like Victoria preferred living flowers to the dead things tucked inside pretty plastic and paper. At her wide, full-lipped smile she knew that she'd made the right choice.

"These are gorgeous." Victoria delicately sniffed at the still-moist roses. "Thank you."

Aren't we a polite pair?

"Dinner is almost ready. Let me just take your jacket." She put the black leather in a little hallway closet then gestured to Dez. "Come."

Dez followed her past a profusion of vines and blossoming indoor plants. The last rays of the sun slanted through the high windows lining the short hallway and bathing the women in orange and yellow light.

"This is a gorgeous house. Very warm." Dez looked around, intrigued by the clues to this woman that she saw in her whimsically decorated house. The plants with their richly colored blooms arching up toward the sun from their resting places on the shelves, bookcases, and the tiny iron-worked table. Thickly green vines slipping over walls and windowsills and crawling under light that was everywhere at once. Her towering shelves were neatly stacked with books of all sorts, and everywhere pens and pencils stuck out of odd places—a planter there, between two books, on the kitchen counter. The feeling was of ordered chaos, a vined jungle retreat from the outside world. Only the ever-present light prevented it from being a cave.

In the kitchen, she leaned back against the counter to watch Victoria move around the small, light-filled room.

"I don't imagine that you invite many strangers here."

Victoria smiled and looked up from checking the dampness of the soil in her new roses. On the stove, a saucepan simmered on a low gas flame. "I don't. But you're not a stranger. You're Derrick's sister." She put the roses aside and rinsed off her hands. "I feel like I've been hearing about you for as long as he and I have been friends."

"Should I be scared?"

"Only if you want to be. It would be interesting to see if all the things he said were true."

Jesus! Not this shit again. "That boy doesn't know me half as well as he thinks."

"Let's hope that you're right." She turned to Dez. "Do you mind helping me set up for dinner?"

"Not at all."

Victoria opened a cupboard and pointed to a neat row of glassware. "Bring those glasses, will you?"

Dez grabbed two and followed her. They passed through a narrow hallway—also lined with books and flowers—to get to a dining room glowing with light. A very modern chandelier hung from the ceiling, like fat amber teardrops of varying lengths, suspended a few feet above the round dining table set for five.

"Are you expecting more company?" Dez asked as she set the two glasses down neatly to the right of matching dinner plates.

"Yes. A few girlfriends of mine will be joining us." She slid her a guileless look from beneath her lashes. "Do you mind?"

"If I did it would be irrelevant, wouldn't it?" Dez made sure to follow up that comment with a smile.

"True." She smiled again as if Dez had just passed a test. "They'll be here in half an hour."

Dez went to get more glasses. Never one to bullshit around the park, she asked Victoria the burning question as soon as she came back into the dining room. "So why the other women? I thought it would just be you and me."

"No reason, really. I just thought it would be nice to have some women over for a homemade dinner. Since you're Derrick's sister, I hope you and I can be friends."

"I don't want to be friends with you, Victoria. I think you know that."

Victoria's neck colored in the most charming way. Dez wanted to kiss it, to press her against the cabinet and explore under that teasing floral skirt. But she kept her distance. She leaned back against the cupboard and watched her reach up to a high shelf, showing off the gorgeous curve of belly and breast and throat.

"Then what do you want?"

"Look at me." She waited until the other woman faced her. "I don't play games. At least not without the immediate promise of pleasure." She couldn't resist. "I want you. If you don't feel the same I can leave. It's that simple. You don't have to bring bodyguards to shield yourself against me. I've never taken anything that wasn't freely given." She took a breath, watching the soft body next to hers. "So tell me, what is this going to be?"

Victoria laughed nervously. "You are direct, aren't you?"

"I try to be. Given how I lead my life, it's the best route." She noticed Victoria's movements, the loosening motion of her shoulders as if she were trying to force herself to relax. "You are a dyke, aren't you?"

This time she smiled, a genuine thing that took Dez's breath away. "I do partner with women, yes."

"What, you don't like that word?"

"Not especially, but it's not something I'm hung up on either."

"Hm. But back to the matter at hand."

Victoria cleared her throat. "I do find you attractive." Her glance limned briefly over Dez, her splayed legs in loose black jeans and the tight black shirt that stretched across her breasts like bait. "But I'm also being careful. You're my best friend's sister. Things could get messy."

"If you had misgivings, then why did you call?"

That flickering glance again. "The usual reasons."

Dez chuckled. "I see." She pushed herself off the counter. "In that case, to prevent any future complications, why don't we see right now if any of this is worth it?" Four steps took her within a hair's breadth of Victoria's mouth. "What do you say?" Her breath teased the wet and parted lips.

"Why not?" Victoria's voice roughened. "Can't do any harm, right?"

Up close she smelled like honey. Sweet, sun-warmed, melting-over-the-tongue honey. Dez made a noise of appreciation that became a groan when Victoria settled a warm palm on the small of her back, then another on her hip. Succulent, heavy breasts nestled just below her own.

"Right." Her mouth was soft. Soft and pliant and yielding and wet. Dez moved her hands in the loose hairs at Victoria's nape. They tickled her hands, twined around her fingers. Victoria's tongue sought entry, flicking lightly at the corners of Dez's mouth, teasing. Then she was inside. She was all sweet and spice, this one, tongue wicked and slow against Dez's, inciting a riot inside her boxers. She slid a thigh between Victoria's and cupped her ass, bringing her firmly up against the place that needed it the most. Dez's hands burrowed under the skirt, up to find a clenching thigh and luxurious bare skin higher up. *Christ!* She didn't have any panties on. Then the doorbell rang.

Victoria groaned. Dez did, too, still reaching for her goal. But Victoria shook her head and backed away, breathing heavily from her wet and reddened mouth.

"I have to get that."

"Of course." Dez wasn't breathing so evenly herself. "But you might want to fix your skirt first." *And those perky little nipples, too.*

As Victoria walked away straightening her skirt and blouse, Dez wiped her lips with a paper towel, dabbed at the wet stain on the cloth over her thigh before smoothing a hand quickly down her shirt front. Damn Victoria's friends. If only they'd come just a few minutes—maybe even an hour—later. Dez laughed. And that was exactly why they were here. She picked up the glasses and went to finish setting the table for dinner.

*   *   *

The women came into the house whispering. Dez smiled to herself as she carefully placed the wineglasses near each dinner setting, wondering if she would be allowed to sit next to Victoria. Their voices were quiet but excited. She heard Victoria telling them to put up their jackets, hearing the raucous fluting notes that signaled long-standing friendship and camaraderie.

"She's in here," Victoria said just as Dez straightened from putting out the last glass. The three women walked in with unabashed curiosity, obviously having been told a thing or two about the new dinner guest beforehand.

"Hello, ladies." She moved from behind the chair. "Dez Nichols."

Victoria had some very sexy friends. Dez stopped her mind from going where it normally went when presented with a vision like this one. Or at least she tried to stop it.

Victoria brought up the rear. "Dez, this is Kavindra."

"Kavi is fine." The slim, sloe-eyed one with skin like creamed cocoa held out a hand and a smile. She seemed pleased by what she saw. Her heavy, waist-length hair slid forward into her eyes as she nodded to Dez. "Good to finally meet you. I've met your brother a few times."

"My brother and his good fortune strike again. I'd never been jealous of him before now." Behind Kavi, Victoria rolled her eyes and smiled as if she were used to people making fools of themselves over her beautiful friend.

"This is her girlfriend, Michelle—um Mick." Victoria nodded at the seal-sleek woman with a proprietary hand on the small of Kavi's back. Her bald head gleamed under the light, matching the warning look she lasered at Dez.

The two women shook hands and Dez tried not to wince at the crushing grip. "And Abena." The amazon bypassed the hand Dez held out to enfold her in a sandalwood scented embrace. Her wavy dreads, held up and back with a thick band of cowrie shells, swirled briefly around them before she straightened, settling the thick mass against her hips and thighs. "You're just a little piece of gorgeous, aren't you?"

To this woman, anybody six feet and under was "little." Dez had to look up at least three inches to meet her eyes. "A pleasure," she murmured, stepping out of the clinging arms.

"Everybody hungry?" Victoria asked, still smiling.

"Yeah, girl. I know whatever you cook is going to be good." Abena squeezed Dez's shoulder. "One thing about our Tori, she sure can throw down in the kitchen."

"True, true." Kavi aimed her welcoming smile at Dez. "If things go well, that's only one of her pleasures you'll be sampling soon."

"Kavi!"

"What? I'm not the one who came to the door with lipstick sucked off my face and looking like I need a cold shower."

Dez passed a surreptitious hand across her mouth to wipe away any lingering traces of Victoria's color. The other women laughed at their friend even as they offered to help her out in the kitchen. In the end it was Abena and Victoria who set out the meal, walking between the living room and the kitchen and speaking in low, laughing voices while Kavi lit the fireplace.

"Tori tells us that you just got back into town." Mick looked up from pouring wine in each glass. "How long were you gone?"

"Just a couple of years. I was traveling with a friend for a while."

"A woman friend or just a friend?"

"Mick, stop being invasive." Kavi spoke from her crouch in front of the dimly flickering logs.

"Well, we have to know how available she is. If you're still pining over some ex-piece, you might as well leave here now because Tori doesn't need any of that bullshit."

"I guess you'd be the welcoming committee?" Dez arched an eyebrow at Mick, not bothering to hide her smile. "Don't worry about it. Victoria can get into whatever she wants with me. From my position she looks like a grown woman. Those types tend to make their own decisions."

The bald woman made a dismissive noise and walked off with the empty wine bottle toward the kitchen.

"Don't mind her, she's just very protective of Tori," Kavi said. "We all are."

"Isn't that why you're here?"

The fire leapt lively and bright behind the grate after Kavi was done with it. She excused herself to go wash her hands, then came back and took a seat at the table. Dez sat in the chair next to hers. She'd rather look at this lovely specimen than Mick's hostile puss any day. The bald woman walked from the kitchen and stopped short, shooting Dez a poisonous look when she saw where she was sitting. But Mick didn't say anything.

"You know I never did see the point of fireplaces this far south," Dez said, turning to Kavi.

"For the romance, of course. To make your lover feel special," Mick supplied helpfully. "Or do you just always fuck and run?"

Victoria and Abena came with the rest of the food, then stopped when they saw the looks on the other women's faces.

"What happened? Did we miss something?" Abena carefully placed her covered platter on the sideboard.

"Not a thing," Dez said. "We were just discussing different techniques of lovemaking."

Victoria knew better than to ask.

Kavi cleared her throat. "Is everything ready?" she asked.

"Yes, just help yourselves. Everything is right here, including condiments if you need them."

"I doubt we'll need anything." Abena already had a plate in hand as she turned to Dez. "Just sit your pretty little behind down and tell me what you need. I'll get it for you."

In short order Abena had a bowl of soup in front of Dez. She didn't wait to taste it. The butternut squash soup glowed a pretty golden yellow with flecks of black pepper floating on its surface. It melted over her tongue, setting her taste buds alight with its subtle burn of ginger.

"You're right, Abena. Ms. Jackson is a fantastic chef." The brew was thick, just like she liked her soup and some of her women. She spooned another cube of squash in her mouth and almost groaned as it dissolved in her mouth's heat. Even the temperature of the soup was perfect. "If the rest of the meal is like this, you won't be able to get rid of me." She looked at Mick. The woman didn't seem too happy with that statement.

"You're acting like you haven't eaten in days. Don't your one-night stands feed you the morning after?"

"Usually I don't stay long enough to eat . . . food." She lifted her spoon to Victoria. "Thanks for inviting me over."

"Anytime."

Dez smiled. "Don't say that unless you mean it."

She could tell the other women were growing restless with her not-so-subtle flirting. Dez forced herself to turn away from that charming blush. "So, Abena, do you cook, too?"

Despite the tall woman's knowing look, she responded in kind with a detailed list of all her misadventures in the kitchen, most of which Victoria had had to rescue her from. From the stories, Dez learned that Abena was charming and funny, a shameless flirt who'd been with her lover for almost nine years.

"He hates it when I call him my 'lover,' but who else but someone who actually loves me can take what I dish out in the kitchen?" Abena said. "And speaking of love, this here is the best woman in the universe, you understand." She stared at Dez. "Treat her well."

"I will, if she gives me the chance to."

The second course was apparently Kavi's favorite. When Abena came back with her plate loaded down with the fine Mediterranean couscous topped with the Spanish-style garlic shrimp simmered in red pepper flakes and olive oil, Kavi jumped up from whatever conversation she and Mick were having and took off for the food. Dez watched her as she ate voraciously, barely touching the token amount of roasted winter vegetables—broccoli, carrots, and red peppers—she had virtuously put on her plate. Dez caught Mick's warning look. Did this woman think that she was trying to steal her girlfriend from right under her nose? She was more subtle than that. Besides, she had her eye on more interesting things. Behind the steam rising from her plate, Victoria's face was a sensual dream of red lips and curved throat. Her fingers accidentally dipped into the sauce on her plate and she licked at them, nibbling delicately at the few grains of couscous that stuck to her knuckles. Then she laughed at something Abena said and Dez felt her own mouth curve in response. This woman could easily get her in trouble.

"Are you just waiting on someone to serve you?" Mick asked. "Because that's not going to happen."

This bitch will not ease up off me. Dez forced herself to smile at Mick. "I guess that means you're not going to get me a little something for my parched throat then, either?" Both her wine and water glasses were still full. She could feel the other woman's eyes on her back as she stood up to fix her own plate.

As she sat down, Victoria tapped a fork against her wineglass to get everyone's attention. She had it almost immediately. "I want to thank everyone for coming here tonight. For some it was incredibly short notice." She smiled at her friends. "And for others it was somewhat of a surprise." Her lashes fluttered down to shield her eyes as she looked at Dez, then away. "So, again, thank you for coming to my home and for staying even though this get-together was just another excuse for me to cook." She lifted her wineglass. "So for this, I raise my glass to you, old friends and new."

They all dutifully raised their glasses and drank, although not everyone was happy with the reason for the toast.

"To piggyback on that"—the women looked at Mick as she lightly tapped her own glass—"let's also toast to discernment in our choice of friends. May we always know how to tell the good from the bad."

The women looked uneasy, but Dez put her glass down, not bothering to glance in the bald woman's direction.

Kavi cleared her throat and turned on a smile. "So Dez, how come we haven't seen you around town? I bump into Derrick at some function or another at least twice a month." The long-haired woman lifted a forkful of couscous and shrimp to her mouth.

"My brother and I don't run in the same circles."

"So does that mean you're slumming tonight?"

"Something like that." She smiled pleasantly at Mick before tasting her food for the first time. It was good. Very good. But the company was beginning to ruin her appetite.

"Stop it, Mick. Don't scare her off. Tori likes her," Abena scolded gently from Victoria's side.

"Yes, please. There's no reason to be rude to my guest."

At least not yet. The collective thought hovered around the table but remained unsaid. Dez admired Mick's self-restraint. To make up for the bald woman's hostility, the other women made nice with Dez, joking about what Derrick told each of them about her and applauding her good taste in asking Victoria out.

"To be honest, my brother is the one with the good taste. If they weren't friends, I probably would have never met her." She looked over at Victoria. "That reminds me, do you all go out in town or is this just strictly potlucks and house parties?"

"Sometimes we go out, but we generally stay away from the party scene. Mick has a lot of girl parties at her house on South Beach. When we're not hanging out there, we're at home."

"That explains why after a month of being back I'm already seeing the same faces over and over again in the bars and clubs in the city. You ladies should come out. The place needs some new blood."

"For you to feed off of?"

"If you like." She aimed her teeth at Mick again.

Kavi rolled her eyes. "I know you're probably wondering why my darling here"—she lightly pinched the arm resting near hers on the table—"seems to have it in for you."

"The thought had crossed my mind, but I didn't think it was important enough to ask."

"No, Kavi, don't tell her. That's embarrassing." Abena looked at her friend.

"I think what's going on here is embarrassing," Kavi said. "This woman is trying to take Tori out. Haven't we all been saying Tori needs to go out with a woman with sex on her mind. Well, if everything we've heard about Dez is true, she very definitely has sex on her mind." She glanced at Dez in quick apology.

Dez shrugged to say that it was nothing. Now she *was* curious where this was heading. Beside Kavi, Mick stiffened but said nothing.

"Years ago when Mick was still into the club scene, she met Dez. They had a one-night stand, or apparently Dez thought it was a one-night-only thing, and never called Mick after that."

Dez swung her gaze to Mick. *Really?* She could see it. The woman was attractive, sleek, and flexible-looking. In the months before she and Ruben got together, she'd been voracious in her appetite for sex with women. Back then it had been three girls a day, sometimes scattered between meals, occasionally at the same time. She could imagine being drawn to Mick's hardness in the flashing lights and smoky haze of a club, seeing her dancing, twisting, and shaking to the music and wanting to tame that energy beneath her. The memory abruptly came back to her. Dez's brow lifted.

"You don't even remember me, do you?" Mick's voice was a hard challenge.

"Actually, I just did." Dez rolled her shoulders under the weight of their collective stare. "I never said I would call."

Kavi suddenly looked uncomfortable. Her gaze skimmed over her lover to Dez.

"So is that how you plan on treating Tori?"

"I am still in the room, Mick." Victoria said. "I didn't have this dinner party for you to release your old anger at Dez. What happened between you is in the past. Let's just leave it that way." Still she glanced back at her friend, communicating a look of sympathy and support that even Dez could not miss. Seeing that, Dez suddenly had enough.

She leaned back in her seat. "This has been really interesting. I came here expecting to have a nice dinner with a beautiful woman and instead I end up in the middle of this . . ." she spread out her hands, not even knowing how to describe what she was now a part of. "I'm not sure what you all expected when you came here tonight, but I hope you got whatever it was." She stood up. "I didn't, so despite the fantastic meal, I have to go."

With a quick nod, she retrieved her jacket from the hall closet and let herself out. In the driveway, she saw that two cars had (intentionally?) blocked her in. She shrugged on her jacket and swung her leg over the motorcycle. The grass would work just as well as the drive.

"Wait."

Victoria ran down the front steps, quickly buttoning a long sweater coat over her thin blouse and skirt. Dez put the key into the ignition but did not turn it. Even in the dark she could see the jiggle of full breasts as Victoria rushed toward her.

"Listen, I'm really sorry about that." She put a hand on the handlebars as if that alone could stop Dez from leaving. "Mick was out of line there."

"Don't you think you were a little out of line, too?" Dez adjusted her hips on the bike and crossed her arms. "If you knew your friend had an issue with me, then why invite her, or even me for that matter?"

"You're right. I'm sorry." She looked up into Dez's expressionless face. "Can we just start over?"

"It depends on what you mean by that. I'm not going back in there." She nodded toward the house. "Give me a call some other time if you want. If you don't want, you don't even have to tell Derrick that we saw each other." Her eyes raked the voluptuous body again. And she released a silent sigh of regret. "I'll see you around."

Dez turned on the engine and Victoria's hand fell away from the motorcycle as she slowly backed the bike away from the house. She stepped back as Dez pulled down the drive, slipping through the narrow space between somebody's Honda SUV and a dark Mercedes sedan. Dez rode away but couldn't stop herself from watching her brother's best friend grow smaller and smaller in her rearview mirrors.

Chapter 13

"Fuck . . ."
The steady ringing of her phone woke Dez from a sticky, erotic dream. In the dream, she spooned steaming butternut squash soup down Victoria Jackson's back, watching the sensual mix of colors, her lover's deep gold skin, the paler gold of the squash as they mingled and separated. Victoria didn't seem to mind the heat of the soup at all. If anything, she moaned and wriggled beneath Dez, begging for more. The liquid gathered in the deep valley of her spine, trailed toward the thick mounds of her ass. Dez pressed her mouth against the shifting flesh, tasting the salty and robust flavor that was nothing but Victoria's skin. She cupped the squirming ass in her hands and prepared to slide between the thick, responsive cheeks. Dez jolted awake when Victoria's ass started ringing. She reached blindly for the phone.

"Hello?"

"Desiree?"

"Mom?"

"Come over and help me with the laundry."

At three in the morning? "Okay. I'll be right over." Dez rolled over and turned on the light. She dressed quickly and stumbled to her truck, managing to get to her mother's house, still only half-awake, without getting into a wreck.

The house looked dark from the outside. The sense of déjà

vu shook the last of sleep from her brain. Instead of knocking, Dez used the key and deactivated the alarm from the
panel by the door.

"Claudia?" She called louder. "Mama?"

"Up here, love."

There were candles everywhere. They followed the wind-
ing thread of the staircase, dozens of tealights in tiny glass
cups, glittering and dancing like phosphorescent ghosts. Dez
followed the lights up the stairs and found her mother in the
bedroom, where only a single white candle burned at her
vanity table.

Dressed in a pair of worn, comfortable-looking pajamas,
her mother knelt on the floor in the rubble of dirty clothes.
The pajamas hung from her slight frame. The last time Dez
saw Claudia she had seemed fashionably slim in her jeans
and sweater, but today she just looked tired and too thin.
Almost childlike.

"What are you doing, Mama?"

"Sorting laundry. Don't ask silly questions, love. Put your
things away and come down here on the floor and help me."

Dez looked down at the backpack in her hands, grabbed at
the last moment for who knew what reason. She dropped it
on the bed and went to Claudia. They silently sorted through
the clothes, putting whites with whites, jeans with everything
else dark blue, linens with linens.

"Is everything all right?"

When Claudia only gently shook her head, Dez tried again.
"What are all the candles for?"

"To keep away the darkness inside, of course." Her mother
smiled weakly at her.

"Did something happen?"

"Doesn't something always?" She put a lacy camisole in
the small pile of hand washables. "Your father called me
today. He's coming to see us."

"To see you and Derrick, you mean."

She made a dismissive motion. "He's coming to see us, all of us."

"I thought you and he were such great friends. Aren't you happy that he's coming?" Her tone was less than charitable.

"Dez, don't be unkind." She was quiet for a moment. "He's bringing his family with him."

"I see." And she did.

When her father had left them twelve years ago with the excuse that he felt stifled and should have never been with Claudia in the first place, Dez hated him. She didn't understand why he had to leave them, his family, to move across the country where no one knew him.

"Warrick called me last night." Claudia looked at the clock on her bedside table. "A few hours ago, really. That's when he told me. I thought I was over everything that happened between us. But I'm not." She stood up and hefted a basket of presorted clothes. "Come on. Grab the other one."

Dez picked up the laundry and followed her mother downstairs.

In the laundry room, more candles burned. The dryer and washer were empty, opened and waiting to be filled. She put the basket on top of the dryer.

"Did you know he wasn't in California a month before he started seeing that woman? I tried not to take it personally, but I did. My friends in Berkeley say that she's pretty and young. Somebody from Africa. Her parents sent her to U.C. Berkeley to get a good American education. And he found her. What does a forty-year-old man want with a college girl? Don't answer that." Claudia's neck bowed over the basket of laundry. "I feel like such a fool. An old fool."

Dez looked on, feeling helpless. "It's okay, Mama. You don't have to see them if you don't want to. You can hide out at my house all week if you like."

Claudia lifted her head to reveal a watery smile. "Thank you, love. But I doubt that's going to work." Her body shuddered lightly. "His call just took me by surprise, that's all. I'll be fine."

Right. Dez watched her mother putter around the laundry room, putting clothes and soap in the machine, trying to do the most mundane of tasks to take her mind off her aching heart. After all these years. This was how love could cripple you, turn you into something less than a child even when there were more important things to worry about. Like death.

It was worse back then when he'd left them, so Dez supposed that she ought to be grateful. She wasn't. She blinked against tears of her own and fiddled with the handle of the basket. The washer with its load of whites began its rhythmic growl, but it didn't quite hide the sound of Claudia's crying. Dez made no pretense of paying attention to the pile of clothes under her restless fingers.

Claudia kept to the business at hand, separating the small pile of white delicates from the colors. Eventually she turned away to pour fabric softener in the washing machine, then to clean the dryer's lint trap. Candles flickered restlessly. Dez opened the door to night sounds and stood glaring into the darkness until she felt her mother's presence close behind her. "I don't like to see you like this."

"I'll be fine. Really." Claudia put a hand on her daughter's back and let it rest there with her cheek pressed against Dez's head. "Thank you for being here. I just badly needed your company for a few moments. You're the best daughter any woman could ever hope to have." She went back to the laundry. "Now go. I'll call you later in the week so we can have lunch."

Dez left, but went back upstairs to her mother's bed. She put her backpack on the window seat and slid under the covers. At some point she must have fallen asleep because she never saw Claudia walk through the door, only felt a shifting weight behind her in the bed, then a warmth at her back. Relieved, she fell into a deep sleep.

*   *   *

"Was it the sex?" Dez asked her mother. "Is that why you're still hung up on him?" She took a bite of her butter-and-honey-soaked whole-grain pancake and watched Claudia's face. "I've done a lot of crazy things for good sex, too."

Claudia almost choked on her Belgian waffle. "I don't think this is the most appropriate conversation to be having with your mother, darling."

Dez didn't think so either, but she wanted to distract Claudia. There was still a lot of sorrow on her face.

"But," her mother said with the beginnings of a smile, "since you asked, he was wonderful. I never had anyone to compare him with, but Warrick always made sure that I had a good time."

"Oh." That blew Dez's shit right out of the water. "Okay. Next subject."

Claudia shook her head and laughed softly. "Yes, please."

Dez shrugged. After the misery of last night she had had to get her mother out of the house. The place where Claudia had moved wraithlike about her life's minutiae was not the place to attempt the great cheer-up. In her mind's eye, every-where Dez looked she saw burning candles and her mother's drawn, sad face. The light flickering over its delicately etched lines only made her seem more fragile. So, Novlette's it was. The light, weekday crowd was a nice change from the Sunday crush. Without the tightly packed bodies, it was eas-ier to appreciate the view of the bay and the gold dust sprin-kle of the early morning sun on the water.

Claudia seemed to be enjoying herself. She initially picked at her Belgian waffle with its heavy dollop of whipped cream and thick, sauce-drenched strawberries. Then as her mood lightened, her appetite grew until the gigantic waffle was all but gone and she was reaching over to take occasional fork-fuls of pancakes and eggs from Dez's plate.

"So, with all this hot sex going on at home, were you ever tempted by another man?"

"Darling, please." Another reluctant smile transformed Claudia's face.

"Oh, come on. I just want to know if I got my whorish ways from you or Warrick."

When her mother flinched, Dez could have slapped herself. But Claudia surprised them both with a grim laugh. "I think you got it from my side of the family. Not necessarily from me, mind you. More than likely your grandmother. She loved sex." Claudia pointed her fork, sticky with whipped cream and strawberry sauce, at Dez. "You know, she had at least a half a dozen affairs before Daddy finally got enough courage to throw her out. Not that she stayed gone. Like most men, he couldn't resist her for long. Even after she showed up pregnant with a child that wasn't his." That was Aunt Paul. Granny Martine's love child.

"I know that Granny was scandalous. I was talking about you. Don't think I didn't notice how you avoided my question about the other men."

Claudia laughed. "Look, but don't touch. That's my motto where temptation is concerned. Paulette always said that I was so much into self-denial that I should be a nun, but I don't think that I'm that bad. I'm just not as . . . free with myself as she was."

"Free." Dez chuckled. "That's a nice way of putting it."

"How else—"

"Hey, Claudia, I thought that was you."

They both looked up as a tall, lawyer-looking man stopped at their table. He was handsome enough in his adventurous pink pin-striped tie and a well-cut Italian suit.

"Hullo, Kincaid," Claudia greeted the stranger with a deliberately cheerful smile.

"Sorry to intrude." He propped himself up on an empty chair next to their table.

"It's all right. We won't flog you for it." Claudia turned to Dez. "I'm not sure if you two have already met but, Kincaid, this is my daughter, Desiree."

He shook Dez's hand. "A pleasure."

"Kincaid taught a finance class at school a few semesters ago."

He must be a wild man. Dez smiled, trying to at least pretend that she didn't want him to disappear.

"Well, it's good to see you again. Listen, let's get together and do something soon." He passed Claudia his card. This probably wasn't the first time he was doing that. "I'll leave you ladies to your lunch. Good to meet you, Desiree."

Dez cringed at the way he made her name sound, all feminine and fragile. "Yeah, take care." She stretched her lips at him.

"I hope he's not one of the men you're finally considering," she said when he was safely ten feet away. "He looks too much like Daddy."

Claudia arched an eyebrow in surprise. "You haven't called Warrick that in a long time."

"Sometimes I slip and forget. Anyway"—she waved her hand dismissively—"my point is, you can't go backward. Straight ahead is the only option. Just like *Warrick*, that guy doesn't deserve to eat the shit off your shoe."

"And speaking of eating," her mother made a face around her mouthful of Dez's hash browns. "I am, so hush."

"Fine."

After breakfast, Dez dropped her mother off at Eden's and watched as the two women embraced in the doorway before slipping inside the pretty bougainvillea-covered bungalow. She trusted her with Eden. Dez wasn't quite sure of the nature of their friendship, but she knew that the tall, robust-looking woman would take good care of her mother.

On her way back home, she checked her cell phone. She hadn't answered its persistent ringing all morning and knew there had to be a few messages. She had four—one from her brother asking her to do some stupid thing or other, two from Rémi, and the last from Victoria.

"I don't like how we left things the other night," she said

on the voice mail. "I'd love to make it up to you. Call me."
She left her number.

Dez saved Victoria's message and called Rémi back. After
a brief conversation, the two women agreed to meet up later
in the week.

Chapter 14

"So how have things been for the prodigal?" Rémi turned to Dez. They slouched on one of a dozen benches lining the stretch of beach, drinking vodka from paper-bagged glass bottles and taking occasional peeks at the stars winking above them.

"Do you and Derrick get together and compare notes or something? He called me the same thing not too long ago."

"But he didn't say it with this much love."

"How did you guess?"

The two women laughed. It had been a long night. The other women who had been traveling with them on the night's adventure had long since retired for the evening. Staying out past three in the morning on a school night didn't feature into their plans. Rémi and Dez were danced out, fucked out, and smoked out. Their cigarettes, plain old nicotine this time, dangled limply from their fingers while their eyelids drooped over reddened eyes. But they weren't ready to end it yet.

"What's the matter with that boy anyway? You think by now he'd find the right girl and loosen up. Isn't he about to turn twenty-seven?" Rémi sprawled back against the bench and tipped back the brim of her hat. "If a change is coming, it better come now."

"It might never happen. I mean he's the lawyer, the offspring with the legitimate job, the well-earned money, the platinum life. By all appearances, he's doing everything right. He doesn't need to change. Both he and my mom love him just the way he is." Dez laughed, putting the bottle to her mouth again. "Neither of them gives a shit that he's got a stick up his ass a mile wide and just as long."

"Ouch."

"What? Reliving old memories?" Smoke from Dez's cigarette curled up around her face, forcing her to narrow her eyes against the gray stream.

"Hmm." Rémi smiled in the dark and took a drag of her own cigarette. Then for no other reason than they could, they laughed.

"I've been missing you since you've been away, Nichols."

"I know. It's been the same for me, too, but I couldn't come back yet. Not without a good reason."

"I guess a good reason showed up, huh?"

"Yeah." But Dez didn't want to talk about that now. She didn't want to talk about death or anything else permanent. "Mama called me back and I had to come." That was close enough to the truth.

"Understandable. I wish you'd given my request some priority, too." An ocean of silence fell between them.

"I was sorry to hear that your daddy had passed on, Rémi."

"Thanks."

"Mama told me last fall."

"And I got your card."

But it hadn't been enough, even Dez could see that.

"Eventually it was all right. He and I were never close, and although he disowned me, I still loved him."

"I know. Love is a treacherous thing that way. You don't always love the people who love you back."

"Here, here." Rémi raised her vodka skyward before tossing the last of it down her throat. The bottle clinked when it fell in the trash can a few feet away. With a harsh sigh, she leaned her head back to look the sky full in the face. Her own face was slack from want of sleep.

Dez looked away from her friend's pain and rested her eyes on the horizon instead. In less than an hour the sun would come up. Dawn was a glimmer beyond the stars, a slow graying of black skies, and the most subtle of blushes where the sky met the ocean. She wanted to have been there for her friend, to have been less self-absorbed to see that Rémi wouldn't be merely glad that the man who'd thrown her out of the palatial family home, even erased her name from the family Bible, had died. She'd sent her a card all right. Something breezy and funny that hadn't really captured the spirit of what she wanted to say, but had to do because she had been in a hurry, rushing through some town and high on Ruben.

The sun gradually rose, spreading across the expanse of sky and sea like a lush blanket of grays, then pinks, then a vivid, lush gold that bathed their faces in brilliant color.

"Sorry about how things ended in the desert with Ruben." Rémi's voice was rough from the cigarettes and vodka. "I know it was hard."

"Yeah. I'm sorry too. But I'm more sorry that I wasn't here for you when all that shit went down with your dad and the rest of your family."

And just like that, things were clear between them. They quietly breathed the shared air and stared out to the ocean, letting the old hurts float away with the lifting morning breeze.

Rémi crushed her cigarette out on her boot heel and dropped the butt in the trash. "Let's get out of here and get some coffee."

"What's open at this time of morning except for IHOP?"

"There's a place just off Biscayne Boulevard. It used to be Candy, that boy's club."

"Have I been gone that long?"

"Oh, yes, my friend. You have."

They found a cab to drop them off on the tiny street off Biscayne. Dez stared up at the cheerful two-story house with a balcony ringing the second floor and brilliant fuchsia bougainvillea dripping down its red brick walls. Small tables sat on the porch, already occupied by people watching the day's virgin sun and drinking their morning lattes. A gigantic rainbow flag waved lazily from the front porch just below the sign hanging from the eaves that said VICTORIANA.

"When did all this happen?"

"Two years ago. Just after you left, actually. Sweet, huh?"

Very. When she ran off with Ruben, the city didn't have a gay spot that wasn't a club. Sexy. Smoky. Very nighttime. This place was cute. Inside, Victoriana was light and airy with artfully painted wooden tables scattered around the large space, potted plants near the open windows, and a young cutie behind the coffee bar.

"Jailbait," Rémi warned.

"Doesn't mean I can't look."

They bellied up to order their first round of drinks, then stumbled out to the porch and commandeered one of the tables to recover from the night's excess. Dez rubbed her eyes and hunched over her black coffee. The scented steam bathed her face in heat. Just the mere presence of caffeine was enough to send her body on the road to recovery. The alcohol felt heavy in her system, weighing her body down in the chair. She was getting too old for this. Glancing over at Rémi made her feel slightly better. Her friend looked as exhausted as she did. A quick peek at the clock inside told her that it was just past seven o'clock.

The sound of high heels dancing up the walkway tore her eyes away from her coffee. Victoria Jackson walked toward the building looking fresh and breezy in a knee-length floral dress and a light sweater in the seventy-degree morning. Her luscious breasts bounced with each step, echoing the spring of the loose curls around her face. Was that a pencil stuck in her little updo? With her big handbag gaping open with what looked like books, catalogues, and magazines, she reminded Dez of her high school librarian. Sexy Mrs. Renfroe. Now all she needed were some wire-rimmed glasses and that teasing smile that the librarian always wore when she was suggesting a new book for Dez.

"That woman always looks so fucking good," Rémi murmured. "I would do her in a minute."

"I wouldn't." Dez pursed her lips. "I'd take at least an hour, maybe two. You see her often?"

"Not nearly enough. Running into her at your mom's the other night was definitely not the usual thing. She owns this whole place, although she works mainly at the bookstore upstairs." Rémi's sleepy eyes roamed freely over Victoria. "I always wondered if she was single, but she seemed so . . . reserved."

Dez sat up in her chair. "You mean she's a dyke?"

"If not, then close enough. She and your brother might have had a thing." Rémi waggled her eyebrows at Victoria who was still making her leisurely way toward the building. "I don't mind bi chyks."

Dez didn't either, but it didn't matter. She had enough reasons not to pursue this woman. Still, she *was* nice to look at. "You say that now, but remember that girl you were fucking around with in college who dumped you for that boy?"

"I'm already over that."

"Like hell."

Behind her, Dez heard Victoria's voice, floating out to the porch in warm, indistinct notes. Slouched in her chair, Rémi watched her over Dez's shoulder, her mouth curving up with that flirtatious, lopsided grin that so few women had been able to resist. She sipped her espresso and straightened up in her chair as the footsteps came closer.

"Morning, Ms. Jackson." She touched a fingertip to the brim of her hat, acknowledging the woman walking up behind Dez.

The beige hat and its silver studs encircling the crown

complemented Rémi's olive skin and the shadowed wicked curl of her mouth. Did Victoria like that? Dez felt a momentary surge of jealousy.

"Hello there. Rémi Bouchard, isn't it?"

"Yes, ma'am."

Dez could smell her, like an orchard in summer, floating up behind her. She turned in her chair. "Victoria."

"Dez. I thought that was you over here."

"Yes. Rémi was just introducing me to your place. It's very nice."

"You should see the bookstore upstairs. I'm especially proud of it."

"I will one of these days," Dez nodded. "Thanks."

She was having a hard time trying not to stare. Up close, Victoria's full-bodied beauty played havoc with her senses. Dez remembered kissing her, the taste of her lush mouth, the noises she made when Dez bit and sucked her lips.

Victoria fiddled with the strap of her shoulder bag. "We open in a couple of hours but you can come up and see it now if you like. It's not like I don't have a key to the place." She smiled softly, another kind of invitation.

Rémi seemed to sense her friend's reluctance, maybe even the lingering *something* between the two women. "Yeah, why don't you go on up there, D? I'll be right here when you get back."

"I can just see the store when it's open. No need to break out the special keys just for me."

"When a woman offers to open her special place just for you, you don't tell her 'another time.'" Rémi kicked her under the table. "Go, before I ask to take your place." She delivered that smile of hers again to Victoria.

Dez knew her friend was joking, but she stood up anyway and turned to Victoria. "After you."

It wasn't difficult to follow the gently swaying hips into the café and up the wide staircase to the bookstore. The hardship came with following through with a resolution to cut this one loose and focus her energies elsewhere. By the time Victoria opened the door to the sunlit attic space and closed it behind them, Dez couldn't see the harm in seeing where this could go.

Victoria dropped her bag on a neatly arranged shelf behind the register. "Well, this is it." She spun to indicate the surprisingly large and airy room with its neat rows of bookshelves, lush flowers, and smell of new paper.

"It's very nice." Dez didn't take her eyes off Victoria. "How did the rest of your dinner party go the other night?"

Victoria seemed surprised at the question. She looked around the store, Dez supposed, checking by habit to see if anyone was nearby, then back at Dez. "It went all right. We finished up not long after you left. Abena was disappointed that you had to go."

"I think that she's perceptive enough to realize that I couldn't stay."

"Yeah." Her voice drifted off into apologetic silence.

"Look." Dez stepped closer. "That night's over. Life has gone on since then, so why don't we?"

"Absolutely. I was hoping you'd say that. I still want to make it up to you."

Dez liked the sound of that. In her experience, apologies from truly penitent women were often the sweetest. Her voice dropped two octaves. "How do you plan on doing that?"

Victoria chuckled. "Not *that* way. At least not yet. Why don't we start with breakfast? I'm not sure what you and Rémi have planned, but if you're free why don't you two join me up here for a bite."

"No. Next time we get together I want to have you just to myself."

"Exactly. Next time. But for today, why not? After all, she's your friend, not mine, and so far she seems pretty nice." And there came the teasing smile, a la Mrs. Renfroe. Dez couldn't even breathe, much less refuse her.

Victoria went down to fetch Rémi and breakfast, leaving Dez to her breathing lessons. As instructed, she went out to the balcony to wait. The day was gorgeous. Now risen to full flush, the sun shone brilliantly on another jewel of a Miami winter day, crisp but with the promise of even more warmth to come. The past few days of low temperatures seemed to be over. It might even hit seventy today. The wood of the railing felt warm under her hands, although some of the night's moisture still lingered to tease Dez's fingertips. The foot traffic on the small avenue was picking up. It was mostly people in their workday suits and business-casual Polo shirts and slacks running into Victoriana's for the morning hit of caffeine.

"Here we are. Bagels all around." Victoria walked in with two steaming cups in her hands while Rémi sauntered up behind her holding a tray with their breakfast.

"I was just going to head home when the lovely Ms. Jackson invited me to come up here and dine with you all." She put the tray on the table. "She's very persuasive."

"At least I'm not the only one finding that out today." Dez thanked Victoria for her fresh cup of coffee as she took it off her hands.

"Enough with all this foreplay. I'm dying of curiosity. What's going on between you two?" Rémi looked at Dez just because she didn't know Victoria well enough to interrogate her yet.

Victoria answered anyway. "Nothing. But I'm hoping that something will."

"The way my friend here was looking at your ass you don't have to hope for anything. It's *going* to happen."

"Thanks, Rémi. Now I know why I don't let you help me get girls." At least not girls she wanted to hang around for a while. Dez spread the vegetable-flecked cream cheese on her sesame-seed bagel and took a bite.

"This is for me, baby, not you. I want to know in case the time is ever right for me to toss my hat into the ring."

"Keep that hat on your head, Rémi. The ring is a little full right now."

"Is it?" Victoria smiled.

Dez chose to slowly chew her bagel, saying nothing. Rémi merely looked thoughtful and, as always, amused.

"I think we both have our answer, Ms. Bouchard."

"Call me Rémi, please. Since I suspect that we'll be seeing a lot more of each other."

"Of course. And by all means, call me Tori."

To Dez, she was Victoria. Alluring, subtly intruding into her awareness until she was a firmly fixed reference point. Last night had drained Dez physically. Earlier in the evening she and Rémi seduced a woman, bent her over a chair in her Ritz-Carlton suite. Her body had been so soft, like Victoria's, arching back into her in the smooth, come-fuck-me way she'd imagined Victoria doing many times. Rémi had been content in the beginning to have the woman eat her out as she sat in the heavy, high-backed chair with her eyes closed, lost in her own fantasies. She was easy to ignore. The woman groaned and gasped, wet, eager, and sweaty with the promise of an easy come. Dez pounded into her from behind, grunting in her exertion. Beyond the windows of the hotel suite, the Atlantic spread out lush and blue, peaceful. She wanted to say that the woman's name had been Victoire or Vita or some variation of the woman she'd wanted instead. But she knew that it wasn't.

"So, Victoria." Dez took a sip of her coffee. "What's the story with you and my brother? I never pictured him for running with such classy company."

"Then I guess you underestimate him, don't you?"

Rémi smirked. *Get yourself out of that one*, her look said.

"So my mother keeps saying." She didn't bother to apologize about Derrick.

"I'm curious, too," Rémi said. "Isn't Derrick one of those—what's the polite term for it—homophobes? Now Dez and I find out that he has a dyke for a best friend."

"Derrick isn't like that." Victoria bit into her croissant, then daintily wiped the crumbs from her mouth. "He and I met in school when he was getting his law degree and I was getting my doctorate. He was—still is—very macho, yet sweet. At one point he wanted to take me out but when I told him that I don't date men, he was all right with it. We've had a friendship ever since then."

"He never once tried to get you to change your mind?"

Her mouth twisted at Rémi's question. "Once. But he was drunk and didn't know what he was doing."

"Right," Dez said. She and Rémi shared a cynical glance. "If he's anything like me, he probably thinks about changing your mind about men at least once a day."

"Maybe in the beginning," Victoria admitted. "But we've been friends for over five years now and I like to think that he—we—are beyond that."

She might be right. Dez had no claims to knowing her brother, and definitely not as well as she knew herself. If she had a "best friend" like Victoria around, there wouldn't be a single minute of the day when she wouldn't think of touching her, of showing her just how good she could be. Her heated gaze told the other woman as much.

Rémi chuckled. "Should I leave you two alone?"

Victoria blushed. "No."

"Maybe for an hour or so," Dez said at the same time.

Rémi looked at her. "Can you really go another round or are you just talking shit?"

"You'll never know, will you?"

Victoria looked from one woman to the other. "What are you two talking about?"

"Nothing important." Rémi stood. "Gotta run. I need to power up for tonight at the club."

Dez pushed back her chair, too. Despite the two cups of coffee and the double shot of Victoria, her energy was draining. If she didn't go to bed now, there would be no point in going to sleep at all.

"I know that you have to open up the bookstore soon, so I won't linger either," she said. "Thank you for your hospitality. I'll give you a call soon."

"Why does that sound like a kiss-off?" Victoria put her hot chocolate aside and wrinkled her nose.

"It's not," Rémi said from the sidelines. "She'll probably be calling you sooner than you'd like."

"Shut up." Dez shoved her through the door before turning her attention to Victoria. "I will call. One thing you should remember about me now is that I don't make promises I can't keep." The memory of the dinner conversation with Victoria's friends rose up between them. "Okay?"

"Okay."

Only after seeing Victoria's answering smile did she follow Rémi out of the cozy building and out into the sun. It was time to find some sleep.

Chapter 15

Dez rolled over in her rumpled bed and stared at the clock. Barely ten o'clock. Warrick and his other family were supposed to arrive in town today. She didn't want to deal with them. Not today. Even talking with Claudia on the phone the day before and hearing her stiff-upper-lip act couldn't force her to be in the same room with the man who'd effectively ruined her teenage years with his sudden, post–coming out abortion of her from his life. And yes, Dez knew she was being dramatic, but she was just immature enough to want to indulge herself. Screw maturity for a little while.

Once upon a time she would have been glad to see him. Any smile, any time, he had to share with her would have been more welcome than the sun. When she was younger, she lived all of the father-daughter clichés. She was a daddy's girl and loved it. He came home early from work some days just to take her (and Derrick) to the park; she rode on his shoulders through the crowded streets of Disneyland while the rest of the world passed like a parade before her; he bought and taught her how to ride her first bicycle; Warrick even helped to coach her softball team. From the moment she was born they were a mutual admiration society. In her eyes, he could do no wrong. And Dez thought he felt the same about her. He didn't.

"Your father will only be here for the weekend," her mother said yesterday. "We can all bear his presence for a little while. Right?"

Dez couldn't. She left a message on Claudia's voice mail, some bullshit about her being too busy to see Warrick. Her mother would be able to read through the lines. No need to explain further.

After her workout and a shower, Dez indulged in a leisurely breakfast on the terrace. She savored every bite of her spinach-and-cheese omelet, each sweet mouthful of her fresh strawberry-and-papaya smoothie. With every swallow she teased herself with thoughts of another sweet mouthful she would love the chance to enjoy. While the breakfast plates and pots went through the dishwasher, she dialed a number she recently programmed into her cell phone. She tried for nonchalance when Victoria answered.

"What are you up to?"

"Not much. Making lunch."

"And you didn't call to invite me over."

"I figured you might be busy with one of your women."

"Not at all. Right now I'm completely focused on you."

Ain't that the truth?

"Would you like to join me for lunch?"

Dez laughed. "I thought you'd never ask."

She left the plates to fend for themselves in the dishwasher and went to make herself presentable. Faded jeans, a tight vintage T-shirt, and a big-buckled leather belt replaced the boxers and wife-beater Dez had put on after her shower. Before she left the house, she checked her look in the mirror. Hot. Available. Not *too* hungry. Perfect.

"Hey," Victoria said as she opened her door to Dez's knock.

The tall woman found herself smiling at the vision Victoria made in the doorway, her hair loose, a curling halo around her face and shoulders.

"Come in."

"What's on the stove?"

"Nothing now, but I did make grilled cheese sandwiches and tomato soup. Table's already set."

"The truth is I've just had a late breakfast and am not even a little bit hungry." Dez bit her lip and tried to look charming and forgivable. "But I'd love to watch you eat."

Victoria laughed and shook her head. "Come sit at my table anyway, you shameless flirt."

The house smelled like home, toasting bread, and bubbling cheese, and felt warm in a way that Dez's did not. A radio was playing, an oldies station advertising an old school party at the end of the week. Then George Clinton came on, funking out the beginning notes of "Atomic Dog."

"This song and even your house remind me of my aunt. She liked Parliament, too."

"I don't know whether to be insulted or . . . insulted."

"Neither, please. I was always very comfortable at her house. With her I always felt very wanted."

"Good."

It felt very different sitting at the dinner table with Victoria than with her Aunt Paul. There was that sweet ache in her cunt, for instance. The other woman smiled next to her at the table, sharing her secret to the perfect grilled-cheese sandwich.

"It's in the cheese, of course."

"Of course."

Dez slipped easily into her warm gaze, found herself saying ridiculous things just to hear her laugh. Victoria was very entertainable.

"What are you doing this weekend?" Dez asked.

"Not much. Getting some orders ready for Monday." Victoria paused. "Having a bath or two." She took a leisurely bite of her sandwich.

"Want to go for a drive with me?" Dez watched the slow movement of her mouth around the bread.

"Where?"

"Somewhere close. I can have you back in time for work on Monday morning."

Victoria's brows shot up.

"I promise."

"That's quite an invitation. Do you always ask strange women to go away with you for the weekend?"

"You're not strange, are you?" At the look on Victoria's face, she grinned. "It's not an invitation for sex."

"Really? That was the one thing I was holding out for."

"Very funny." Dez leaned in. "Unless you're not joking."

Victoria chuckled, lifting a spoonful of tomato soup to her lips. "I'm *not* an easy lay."

"I didn't think you were. So will you come with me? I promise to get you back here in once piece, your chastity intact."

Victoria was quiet for a moment. "I'll let you know after lunch."

When Dez pulled up in the truck a little after nine that evening, Victoria was already waiting in the driveway with her duffel bag and backpack. The truck idled as Dez leaned out the window. Victoria sat on her duffel bag, looking comfortable and incredibly sexy in faded jeans and an oversize sweatshirt that advertised her bookstore. Dez stared at the oversize V and A for longer than was really polite.

Finally she cleared her throat. "Ready?"

"Sure." Victoria smiled and stood up. Dez hopped from the truck to pick up Victoria's bag, then walked around to open the passenger door. "May I have the pleasure of your company, young miss?"

"Since you ask so nicely." She took her slow time walking to the truck before doing an odd sort of ass-in-the-air hop and dance to get into the vehicle. "Thanks," she said when she was finally settled in. Dez firmly closed the door.

They drove silently out of the city, each woman distracted

by her own thoughts. An hour into the trip, Victoria looked over and caught Dez's eyes on her.

"Shouldn't you be watching the road?"

"I am."

"Call me crazy, but I don't consider myself a part of the landscape."

"Okay, crazy."

Victoria groaned. "That wasn't very funny."

"Never said I was." Dez laughed.

"So what's on your mind?

"Nothing much."

The silence stretched comfortably between them.

"Just wanted to get away for a while. Then I thought of you."

"How . . . gratifying."

"What?" Dez actually turned around in her seat to look at her.

"I was an afterthought."

"Less and less these days actually."

Victoria looked at her, mouth hanging open. "I guess I should be grateful for your honesty, huh?"

"With me, it's always the little things."

"I'm starting to see that."

An hour and a half later the moon was a gleaming jewel just beyond the truck's windshield. Dez was mesmerized. Not by the moon, but by Victoria, whose voice hummed low and soothing as she spoke of nothing in particular, but moved easily from subject to subject with only a few words from Dez, understanding that she was in a mood to just listen.

"I've been with other so-called feminine women before and it just never worked out for me," Victoria continued. "I'm not saying that I buy into the whole idea of butch-femme, but for me personally, there is just something about a girl with a swagger . . ." she slid her companion a glance. Dez offered a brief smile, but said nothing.

Victoria sighed. "All right, I've babbled on enough. Your turn."

"What? I was enjoying your monologues. Go on."

"I don't think so." Victoria crossed her arms in her lap, hugging herself through the seat belt. "You show up at my doorstep with your big sad eyes and—"

Big sad eyes? "My father is in town with his new family, and I don't want to be there to meet them."

"That's not so bad. Derrick told me your father was going to be here for the weekend. He seemed excited."

"Well, on top of that, my mother could be dying. I'm not handling that very well either."

Dez concentrated on the road in front of her, wondering why in hell she just said that. *Because you need someone who you can be real with, that's why.*

"Why did you tell me?" Victoria turned to look at her travel companion.

"Why not?" Dez laughed. Then the ugly humor faded from her face. "I'm sorry." She prolonged the silence for as long as she could.

"I found out when I was in New Mexico over a month ago." I-75 stretched out distant and dim before them. Other cars sped by, easily overtaking the Lexus's eighty-mile-per-hour speed. "It's not important how I found out, only that it wasn't from her." Dez's voice roughened. "At first I wouldn't believe it. I thought maybe someone was playing a trick on me."

A low-slung sports car zoomed passed, then merged in front of the truck without signaling. *Too close.* Dez tapped on the brakes, then continued speaking as if nothing had happened.

"But it was real." She laughed again.

"Have you talked to anyone else about this?"

"Of course not." Dez's eyes moved briefly from the road to look at Victoria. "Please don't think I told you to get a pity fuck or something. I don't even know why I said anything;

but whatever the reason, you don't have to respond. Don't hold my hand, don't tell me everything is going to be all right, none of that bullshit."

"Do you want to talk about it?" The *it* hovered like a specter in the car between them.

"Not really." Dez managed a quick smile. "Thanks for listening, and thanks for coming with me this weekend. Especially since we hardly know each other."

Victoria nodded. "Just to let you know, you did me a favor by suggesting this trip. I need this break as much as you do."

"Good."

They got to their destination a few minutes shy of midnight, eyes bleary and asses sore from sitting still for three hours. Dez pulled into the drive of her aunt's summer house and the sensor lights caught the truck in their stripping glare.

"This is it."

"Great." Victoria hopped out of the truck. "Where's the bathroom?"

"Inside." Dez tossed her the key. "The code for the alarm is 1980, then press 'enter.' The panel is behind the door. I'm going to the store for some groceries. Make yourself comfortable."

When Dez came back, Victoria was already curled up under the covers. Only her wild hair was visible above the sheets. Her bags were nowhere to be seen. She must have already unpacked and stored them somewhere.

Dez unloaded the groceries, then checked to make sure that everything in the house was just as she left it last time. A woman came by every couple of weeks to make sure the place didn't get overrun by rodents or any other vermin. Except for a light coating of dust, the place was spotless.

This was hardly how her aunt kept the house. Her casual housekeeping style always pleased the child in Dez even long after she stopped being one. Bathing suits strung over the porch railing for days. Ingredients for dinner strewn over the countertops long after dinner had been made and consumed, windows left open at night to let in the breeze off the water. Still, Dez could feel her aunt here, in the safety and warmth she felt walking into the beach house. In the face of her parents' broken marriage, the security of Aunt Paul's love had been a priceless thing, as was her willingness to answer every question Dez asked, no matter how embarrassing or painful.

Dez left the kitchen for the bedroom, feeling exhaustion bear down on her. She brushed her teeth, washed her face, and undressed down to her tank top and boxers before crawling into the bed beside Victoria's very warm body. Before her hormones got the chance to act up, Dez fell asleep.

She managed to keep to her side of her bed during the night. The first thing she saw when she opened her eyes was Victoria's face tucked into the curve of her own arm, delicate and vulnerable. The dawn light slowly shifted over Victoria's hair and face, bathing her in shadowy blues that changed slowly to gray before bursting into amber and orange flames. Victoria breathed softly as the colors played over her skin. She only moved once. When Dez, in a moment of irresistible curiosity, touched her hair, the coils of red and pale and brown crackled, then, as if touched by a current of electricity, curled around Dez's fingers, reluctant to let go. Victoria flinched in her sleep when Dez tried to pull away before being discovered. She opened her eyes.

"Did you sleep well?" Victoria husked, blinking at Dez through her curls. "Or did you spend all night staring at me?"

"I would have loved to spend all night staring at you, but the drive wore me out." Her eyes lingered on Victoria's sleep-softened face and mouth. "We can try some staring and touching games later, though."

"Hm. Sounds tempting."

"But no go, huh?"

The other woman shook her head, but a smile dimpled her cheeks.

"That's fine. I can be patient." Disappointed but not surprised, Dez sat up in the bed. "How about some breakfast?"

"You cook?"

"When it suits my purposes."

Dez left Victoria to use the bathroom. After her shower, she poked through her supplies until she found ingredients for omelets and French toast. She was portioning out their breakfast when Victoria walked in. Dez smelled her first.

"I see you've had a shower," she said without looking up. "Too bad."

"You like me smelling like raw ass, then?"

Dez laughed. "That wasn't exactly the smell I noticed this morning. I'll check for that one tomorrow, though."

She tucked the last slice of toast on a plate and turned around. She was right to wait. Victoria's appearance was a pleasant shock to the senses. Her hair curled loose and damp, exploding around her face very much the way the sunset had this morning. A white dress with tiny straps and a peek-a-boo lace hem that fell just below her knees added to her angelic look. Her feet were bare and the toenails brushed a light shade of pink. As always, *delicious* was the word that came to mind when she looked her fill of this woman. Dez's mouth watered, ready to eat her up.

"May I smell you?" Dez asked. Her nose twitched to get more of that bewitching scent coming from Victoria.

She looked puzzled, but came closer. "Sure."

"Thanks."

Dez had always been a smell-oriented kind of woman. A lover could turn her on or off with a certain smell. And it was never as simple as body odor. Whenever a woman smelled good, it was hard for her to resist, especially when the scent was complex enough that she had to work to name it. Victoria wore such a scent now. Maybe it was her body oil, or even her deodorant. Whatever it was, Dez liked it. She liked it a lot.

"By the way, breakfast is ready." She walked even closer to Victoria, smiling and being careful not to sniff her like a dog in heat. Her hair smelled clean, like shower steam and fresh fruit. Tangerines and honey with a hint of lime. The scent was at the back of her neck, caught in the damp curls that lay against her skin like vines. "You smell really good." She could feel Victoria close her eyes, feel the soft body loosening, feel how easily she could turn into velvet in her arms, her pussy becoming wet and spreading open under Dez's mouth while breakfast lay cold and forgotten on the counter. "May I touch you?"

"No," Victoria sighed the word, like it could very easily turn into a yes.

"Fair enough." She closed her eyes and took another deep lungful before backing away.

"I—" Victoria took a deep breath. "I didn't mean to sound that way, it's just that—"

"You don't have to explain." Dez felt the surrender in Victoria's body. If she hadn't said no, then they would have been sliding around naked on the kitchen floor, fucking like they'd just invented the word. "Where do you want to eat?"

Victoria sighed. "The porch is fine."

The temperature had fallen again, so south Florida was back to its average winter high of sixty-five degrees.

"Go on out. I'll bring your plate to you. Do you want anything to drink?"

"Um . . . orange juice if you have any."

"Of course."

When Dez walked out with the plates and glasses balanced on two trays, she found Victoria sitting on the porch steps leading down to the beach. She stood up to help Dez with her burden.

"Thanks."

They sat down and began their meal in silence. Victoria's eyes widened when she took a good look at what Dez had prepared. She didn't know that this meal of ginger-scented

French toast with mango jam and the thick broccoli, almond, and havarti cheese omelet had once been enough to land women in Dez's bed.

Dez watched Victoria between bites. Despite the superb breakfast, she looked miserable. Still, Dez made no effort to break the awkward silence.

"This is very good toast," Victoria finally said.

"I know. Thanks."

Victoria looked up sharply, only to encounter Dez's teasing smile.

"Can I tell you that I'm sorry again?"

"You can, but there's nothing to forgive. I know me. You did the right thing."

"No, I didn't." Victoria put her toast down, then picked it up again. She dipped it in the small saucer of mango jam and finished it off in two neat bites. "I don't want to be like the others. I don't want to fall for you, fall into your bed, then fall by the wayside on your way to the next conquest."

"And how do you know that's what I'm going to do?" Victoria's look said it all. "Derrick again, huh?" Dez took a careful sip of her water. "I'm not going to make you any promises, Victoria. You're an incredible woman and I'm very attracted to you. We could have a good time together. But if you don't want to do this, just let me know now."

"I wish this was simpler." Victoria brushed the hair out of her eyes with the back of her hand. "Derrick and I have been friends for a long time and I think if I go through with this, then our friendship is going to change permanently. It might even end. This is not something I'm willing to do lightly." She took another triangle of toast between her fingers. "I want you, but I want to be sure."

Damn. Dez nodded at her brother's best friend over the rim of her glass. *Why couldn't I have gotten infatuated with Nuria or one of those other easy, no-hassle girls?* "Fair enough."

"Do you hate me?"

"No. I do like you for your honesty, though. This just lets

me know that I'm going to *really* enjoy you when you're sure."

Victoria shook her head and smiled around her toast. "No comment."

After breakfast, they put on sandals and went for a walk.

"So where are we?" Victoria asked.

"Sarasota. A little snowbird town on the west coast."

"I could tell that from the highway signs. I meant the house. This piece of land."

"Ah. This was Aunt Paul's home away from home. She brought me here all the time when I was growing up. I spent most of my summers with her, either in Florida or traveling to someplace new."

"Sounds fun."

"It was, mostly."

When nothing else was forthcoming, Victoria looked across at her.

"What?" Dez asked.

"Do you deliberately do this mysterious thing or is it just a bad habit?"

Dez blinked. "What are you talking about?"

"Nothing." She laughed and shook her head.

Their walk took them up from the house into the interconnected, bird-named streets that ran through the larger neighborhood. Between the time that Dez's aunt had bought the house and now, the little slice of paradise had become a suburban jungle. Only the fact that she owned an acre of land on each side of the house—including the beach—stopped the suburban termites from getting close.

"This is a cute neighborhood. It has a little bit of everything." As they walked, houses gave way to a circle of shops and restaurants.

Dez's mouth curled with distaste. "Yeah, it does. A little racism here, a touch of homophobia there, with a touch of elitism for spice."

"I thought you liked this place."

"I do. But sometimes I just wish that the people would disappear."

"That bad, huh?"

"It can be." Dez shook her head, dismissing the subject. None of that was worth talking about now "Come on." She took Victoria's hand. "I want to show you something."

It was still early, but there were already a few people about, mostly joggers and the occasional retired couple walking their matched set of French poodles or Great Danes. One jogger almost stepped in a hole while gawking at Dez and Victoria's joined hands. They crossed the street and darted into a well-lit alley littered by flowering dandelions, black-eyed Susans, and smooth stones that were supposed to have made a pathway, but instead made walking in thin sandals difficult.

They left the manicured sidewalks behind and ended up walking in high grass that tickled the backs of Dez's knees and poked under the hem of Victoria's skirt. The high grass cleared at the edge of a retention pond. It was quiet and peaceful with the sound of the ocean breeze racing through the weeds. Dez sat down and pulled Victoria down beside her.

"This is where I played when I was a kid."

The pond water flashed blue with a clear reflection of the sky. Dragonflies played above its surface, dancing between the cattails and tiny mangroves. Dez took Victoria's hands again, this time putting them against the concrete between them. Etched in the surface was Dez's name right next to her aunt's with their matching handprints.

"She was a hooligan, just like you?"

"That's what my mother used to say." Dez chuckled. "Auntie Paul could never understand how she could have such an uptight sister. Her words, not mine. It wasn't until I was almost in high school that Mom started to loosen up and do what she wanted to. It was good to see, especially after the divorce."

"It's hard to imagine your mother not being as free as she is now."

"That's a good thing. Before she was so rigid and judgmental. Everything had to be just so or else."

Why was she telling this woman all this? Dez was sure that Derrick had told her all this and more.

"Let's get going," she said. "There are much more interesting stops on this tour."

Back on Main, they walked past the entrance to a "white store." Victoria peered at the glittering white dresses in the window.

"They sell expensive white clothes and shoes to rich white people after Labor Day," Dez mock-whispered.

Next to an old-fashioned ice-cream and candy stand stood a small door with opaque glass and an innocuous-looking sign that advertised the store simply as THE WOMAN'S ROOM. The windows were opaque, too, but had rich swirls of color, all muted the shades of the rainbow, decorating them. Dez opened the door and held it wide for her companion.

"Come on in." Her grin was absolutely wicked.

"Good morning," the woman at the counter chirped as they walked in. She was thin and boyish, with dark brown hair spilling down to the middle of her back in shiny waves. Her face, the same shade as honeyed chamomile tea, broke into a smile when she got a good look at who just walked into her store. She jumped from behind the counter to hug Dez. "Jeezus! It's been how long since I've seen you?"

"Too long, Trace. What's going on?"

"Nothing much, as you can see."

The store was empty except for two employees bent over open boxes, restocking the shelves. One of the girls looked up and waved at Dez as her giggling coworker looked on. Dez smiled back.

"Trace, this is Victoria Jackson. She owns the indie women's bookstore in Miami."

"I've heard of your place. It's called Victorian or something like that."

"Victoriana," she corrected with a smile. "Good to meet you." The two women shook hands.

"Victoria, meet LaTracia Delgado." Dez grinned. "She's the owner and proprietress of this lovely den of decadence."

For the first time, Victoria seemed to realize what sort of place they were in. The area where they stood could have been the hallway to any number of homes she'd been to before. But that was where the similarity ended. Off to her left and going deep into the store was a space made up to look like a sitting room, complete with a mock-up of a burning fireplace, a high-pile Persian rug, and at least a half dozen inviting, burgundy cushions on the floor. Each wall was covered by dozens of shelves that were neatly stocked with love oils, potions, toys, and even edible panties. The room beside it was made to look like a kitchen, with a sink, a bar with two stools, and more shelves. It was a cozy kitchen, one more intimate than most with its cozy blues and yellow, and the tile-work around the "appliances" decorated with yonic flowers in various stages of bloom. Instead of spices and groceries, the shelves here held self-heating lotions and oils, honey dusting powder, battery-operated cucumbers, and various other erotic delights. Next to the kitchen was the bedroom. Sumptuous shades of plum and lavender decorated the walls and four-poster bed with its gauze drapery and thick pillows. This room had even more shelves than the other two.

"Welcome to my pleasure palace." Trace waved her hand around the store. "Would you like a tour?"

"This place is amazing." Victoria walked with Trace into the bedroom. "I thought about adding a sensual aid section to the bookstore a few years ago, but it just seemed like too much trouble. Don't you ever have frat boys and cops come in here trying to harass you?"

"Yeah, a few, but nothing too serious. This is a great location. The college girls love it. It's a place where they can come without being stared at and made to feel strange for wanting to control how they get off."

Dez thought Victoria would be offended, but instead she laughed, putting a hand on Trace's arm. "That's great." She turned to look back at Dez. "Thanks for bringing me here. This is fabulous."

"Yeah, it is." She left the women to their shoptalk and made her way into the "parlor," a small room at the rear of the store with sofas and magazines and other miscellanea for the weary shopper.

A display of harnesses and dildos caught her eye. The leather harness she'd used for years was comfortably well-worn and supple from her own body's oils, but there was always room in her treasure chest for new equipment. She fingered one that the label described as "The Pony."

"Shopping?"

Dez turned to face Victoria.

"*Window*-shopping, yes. Did you find anything you like?"

"Oh, yes. Trace has some things here that I've never seen in Miami."

"True that. I always buy my Kama Sutra stuff from her. She has the best selection outside of the Internet that I've ever seen."

"So that means you come here often?"

"I used to, but it's been mail order the last couple of years. Got to support the independents, you know."

Dimples appeared in the curves of Victoria's cheeks. "I'm sure she appreciates your business."

Behind them, Trace stood talking with some customers, a group of hippy-ish young girls with shy smiles. When she was done, she came back over to Dez and Victoria.

"So, what else can I show you two?"

* * *

"After all that, I need to cool off," Dez said as they left the store. Victoria nodded. They bought ice cream from a nearby Ben and Jerry's and walked back to the house, this time taking the long way up the sand dunes that dumped them out on the beach in front of the house. Lost in their separate thoughts, the women walked silently under the afternoon sun, eating their ice cream.

Derrick is going to kill me, Dez thought as she looked over at Victoria. In the store, she had wandered from shelf to shelf, her imagination on fire with thoughts of using everything—oils, whips, dildos—with Victoria. While her hand hovered above a mocha and chocolate swirl silicone toy, in her very vivid imagination she felt herself slide into Victoria, felt the arch of the other woman's back under her belly.

Trace had been called away to help more customers, so Dez left Victoria's side to keep from propositioning, or worse yet, begging her. She turned around to see Victoria only a few steps behind her, tapping her finger against her mouth as if considering one of the toys. Immediately Dez wanted that finger inside her pussy, that mouth on her clit.

Taking Victoria with her to Sarasota wasn't the best idea she ever had. Still, the pain of wanting her was sweet. Sweeter than any sexual satisfaction Dez had experienced in a long time. When that thought seared through her mind, Dez knew that she was in trouble.

Next to her, Victoria was having troubles of her own with the giant waffle cone of cookies and cream and strawberry ice cream she'd bought. She bit at the oversize mounds of ice cream, but still they melted, dripping red and white and dark streaks down her fingers.

"Need help with that?"

"I think I just might." Victoria licked at the bottom of the cone, trying to catch the cream before it dripped down to her wrist. She didn't have much luck.

Dez wasn't much of a cone person. She had her Cherry

Garcia and White Russian mix in a modest-sized bowl and was already half-finished. "Come over here."

She bent her head under Victoria's cone. "Try not to poke my eye out, I'm doing you a favor here." With smooth, steady strokes, she licked the bottom of Victoria's cone until it was as clean as when she first got it—if a little bit soggy. Then she started on her ice-cream-painted hands. She moved her head as she licked in long, rhythmic circles down and between the soft fingers. She licked until the fingers were clean and wet from her tongue, until her clit was fat and thrumming in her pants. The ice-cream cone almost fell from Victoria's hands.

By the time Dez was done, Victoria's back was to the empty lifeguard's tower and they were both breathing heavily.

"Let's get going." Dez's voice was rough. What she really wanted to do was lead Victoria back to the cottage and sink between her thighs. Since that absolutely was not going to happen, Dez needed to walk it off.

She spent the rest of the afternoon on the porch, stretched out on the hammock, watching the waves crawl up on the sand. Victoria came out and joined her, but she respected Dez's need for silence and space, and sat a reasonable distance away on the lawn chair with a book and a glass of lemonade.

Then she spoke. "It's okay not to get what you want right away."

Dez stirred from her contemplation of the backs of her eyelids. "Will I eventually get what I want?"

"Maybe."

She closed her eyes again and settled deeper into the hammock. Victoria went back to reading her book. When night fell, they retreated into the warmth of the house. Dez started a fire in the hearth and lay down on the rug a few feet away from the flames. Nearby, Victoria sat in an overstuffed chair and continued to read. That was how morning found them, softly snoring in the early dawn light next to a fire that had long since burned down to nothing.

"So what was yesterday about?" Victoria murmured from beneath her blanket in the chair. Her serious brown eyes blinked down at Dez from behind a curtain of curls.

"Sulking." The cushion Dez rested her head on exhaled the artificial scent of green apples as she stretched. "Don't you know me by now?"

"No, but I wish I did."

"Good. I don't want to ruin the mystery just yet." She rolled over to stare briefly out of the window. "I am sorry, though. Sometimes I'm like a little kid with none of the cuteness."

"I wouldn't say 'none' exactly." Victoria wrinkled her nose and poked Dez lightly with her toe.

Dez yelped and scooted a few inches away. The other woman giggled. As she turned her head against thc back of the chair, something caught her eye.

"Hey, is that you in the picture?" She gestured toward a large photograph suspended from the ceiling and hanging in front of the window. Its frame was stained glass, a rich and vibrant blue shot with golden stars and a sliver of a moon. It glowed in the early-morning sunlight.

"Yeah, I'm the little one." Victoria shot her a "no kidding" look. "The lady next to me is my Aunt Paulette."

"She's gorgeous."

"Yeah, she was." Dez turned her head to look at the photograph. Aunt Paul had hung it there at her request almost sixteen years ago. Never mind that at certain times of the day it was hard to see exactly what was in that pretty frame. "For a long time she was my favorite person in the whole world."

"It looked like she felt the same way about you."

Dez laughed. "She spoiled me."

"The first of a long list of women to do that, I bet."

"Hardly." She paused. "When my parents divorced she took pity on me. She noticed that I was a wreck and, essentially, took care of me and helped me to realize that the divorce wasn't my fault. I was very grateful." She shook her head as if to wake herself from a dream. "Not that Mom wasn't there for me, but I was a handful back then and Aunt Paul was the only one who could handle my fits. She treated me like an equal, but never let me run over her. I learned all about women from her, how to love them, how to charm them." The suede pillow with its scent of factory fresh apples briefly comforted Dez as she pressed her face into it and swallowed past a lump in her throat. "She died when I was twenty." Her voice thickened. "For better or worse, she's the reason why I'm able to live the way I do. Money hasn't been a problem for me for a long time. Even now she's spoiling me."

Dez lifted her head once more to look at the photograph. In it, the eight-year-old Dez was happy, leaning into her aunt's chest with a cheeky grin. Paulette, at a robust and gorgeous twenty-nine, straddled her motorcycle, one hand at rest on the handlebar, the other on her niece's shoulder.

Victoria's toe touched her again. More gently this time. "How about I make us breakfast today?"

"Fine by me," Dez said, breathing through the resurrected ache of her aunt's loss. "I'm ready to be your kept woman."

Victoria smiled but made no move to get to the kitchen. If anything, she snuggled more deeply beneath her blanket. Her eyes, thoughtful and gentle, watched Dez.

"When's that breakfast going to come?" Dez's tone held a distinctly childlike whine. The subject of Aunt Paul and her leaving was finished; now it was time for food.

"When do you want it?"

"Now?"

"How about later? Come on the porch with me."

"I have to warn you, I get grouchy when I haven't eaten."

"I'll take my chances." Victoria tugged Dez to her feet and

out to the porch. "I like you. But I love your brother. This is going to be hard."

Victoria stretched into the mild chill of the Sunday morning. Her sweet sleep scent enfolded Dez as Victoria stepped closer, linking their fingers. Sunlight fanned across the sky, filtering through her hair and across the seawater stretched out before them, bright like the flicker of a million fireflies.

"You're like that ocean out there, Desiree Nichols. So amazing and beautiful that it hurts my eyes." Victoria pressed her cheek into her shoulder. "I don't want you to hurt my heart, too."

Dez didn't know what to say. Part of her wanted to blame Derrick. After all, what kind of shit did her brother tell Victoria that the woman was so convinced that Dez was about to rip her heart out and piss in the gaping hole? But the other part of her knew how easily she could take everything Victoria had to offer, then leave her with nothing but sticky sheets to remember her by.

Dez loved sex. She loved the power. She loved the noises. She loved the sweat. And that was all her relationships had truly given her in the past, even the one with Ruben, although in the beginning she'd sworn that it was more. That's all she'd ever wanted from most of her partners. But Victoria needed more than that.

Victoria released her and turned to go back inside. She followed silently behind, thrown off balance by a woman for the first time in her life. *Did she really want to pursue this?*

Victoria tackled breakfast while Dez went to take a shower. When she walked back into the kitchen, their food was laid out on the breakfast island, with two stools sitting side by side.

"Eat up." Victoria licked her finger and snapped the lid shut on a container of cream cheese. "You're going to need your strength today."

Dez perked up at the promise in Victoria's smile. "You don't need to tell me twice."

They left the house to see the rest of Sarasota. Dez played tour guide, showing Victoria all the museums and stores and little neighborhoods she thought were interesting. In the small downtown retail district, Victoria's jaw dropped at the size of Mansell's, the Main Street bookstore. Dez didn't bother telling her that this was the best place in town to girl watch. The college girls came here. Though young, they all looked delectable in their lowrider jeans and tight little shirts. Mansell's also had a mammoth selection of coffees, teas, and pastries.

"I am *so* jealous. This place is huge."

"Go ahead and explore. I'll be in the coffee shop."

"You sure?"

"Yes. Go." Dez watched her disappear up the wooden staircase to the bookstore's crammed loft space, noticing that she wasn't the only one checking out the view. Dez threw the boy behind the cash register an irritated glance, then turned away, laughing at herself. *It's too soon to act like that territory is yours, Dez.*

She wandered into the coffee shop to browse among their magazine and postcard selections. As she spun the white wire rack, a card with a full-color scene of a lavender field in Provence caught her attention. Her mother loved lavender. When the twins were twelve years old, she and Aunt Paul took them to France to play in the vast fields of purple-blue flowers and hunt truffles with funny little grunting pigs. The water of the Mediterranean had been so bright.

Dez found a quiet corner and called her mother. "Hey, Mama. How are you feeling?"

"No complaints." Claudia's voice sounded strong. "Your father isn't here yet but Derrick invited me out to lunch. We're just now leaving my house." Dez could hear the faint purr of a car's engine in the background.

"Sounds good. Who's driving?"

"Your brother. He bought himself one of those little sports cars like mine. It's very cute." Derrick said something that made their mother laugh. "Oh, sorry, darling. It's actually nothing like mine. According to your brother, it is the Lexus SC hardtop convertible, the sexiest machine ever made. Personally, I don't think it's anywhere near as hot as my vibrator."

Dez chuckled, glad that her mother was in good spirits despite Warrick's impending visit.

"You should come see it—the car, not my vibrator."

"I will as soon as I get back into town."

"Where are you? Somewhere interesting, I hope."

"Aunt Paul's house in Sarasota."

"Isn't it a little cold for the beach?"

"It's a *lot* cold for the beach. But I'm not going swimming anytime soon." Dez crossed her booted foot over her knee and leaned back in the chair. "Just enjoying the sun and showing a new friend around."

"A new friend? Is it serious?"

Dez laughed. "How come I called to talk about you and we end up talking about me?"

"Because you brought it up?" Claudia answered Dez's laugh with one of her own. "So, is it serious?"

"I don't know. Probably not. It's fun, though."

"As long as she knows that it's only fun."

"We've already had that talk, Mama."

She heard Derrick say something in the background, but Claudia shushed him. "Just be careful, darling."

"I will."

"I love you."

"Love you, too."

Dez breathed a quiet sigh as she hung up. Claudia was doing much better than the last time they talked, but that would no doubt change once she saw Warrick. And there wasn't a damn thing Dez could do about it. She plucked a magazine from a nearby shelf and sat back to wait for Victoria.

Two hours later, she looked up from the magazine in her

lap when Victoria sat down next to her, struggling into the seat with an armload of books.

"Restocking your store?"

"Nope, just my personal library. This place is great. They have an amazing selection of out-of-print books here. I would much rather live here than Miami."

"You think so?" Dez stood to help her with her books.

At Dez's telling glance around the store with its homogenous, pale-eyed crowd, Victoria grimaced. "Maybe not."

"Maybe not." Dez led her toward the register to check out.

The rest of their afternoon passed in a blur of shopping and sightseeing until Dez pléd mercy and demanded that Victoria take her to dinner as a reward for all her hard work.

"I'm too old for all this exercise," she complained, throwing their latest round of purchases in the back of the little SUV.

"Come on, wimp. Let's go feed you before you collapse."

"Finally," Dez firmly closed the back of the Lexus. "My two hours of begging pay off."

"You think *that* was begging? Wait until we get to know each other better." Victoria walked off, leaving Dez to mull over that one.

"*This* is the best part of Sarasota."

Dez reached over to steal a bite of Victoria's neatly cut steak. The other woman gave her a mean look, but she ignored her, forking the tender piece of filet mignon into her mouth. Its aromatic juices flooded over her tongue as she chewed. Dez looked across the water at the slow dying burn of the sun across the sky.

"Is food all you think about?"

"Not at all." Dez gave Victoria her best dirty-old-dyke look. "It's definitely in the top two, though."

Victoria laughed. "Why am I not surprised?"

"You're a smart woman." She nodded as the waiter reappeared to refill their wineglasses, then disappeared again. "Let's drink a toast." Dez raised her glass. "To uncharted territory."

At Victoria's questioning look, she shrugged. "Any excuse to lift a glass." But Dez's eyes were wicked and hungry. They both knew what "uncharted territory" she wanted to explore next.

Dez cleared her throat. "How long have you owned the bookstore?"

Victoria allowed the less-than-smooth segue. "It's actually the other way around. Victoriana has me. Six years now."

"Six? You weren't on Biscayne when I left two years ago."

"The store used to be in a smaller space before we were able to expand and move to the upper eastside."

"I never figured you for a bookstore-owning type."

"What did you think I was? A stripper?"

Dez choked on her laughter. "Not exactly. I never thought of you doing much of anything beyond having lunches with beautiful women and entertaining strangers for the weekend."

"A society honey?"

"If you want to call it that, sure. Those hands of yours don't look like they do much work. They look like mine."

Victoria made a show of examining Dez's hands. Finally, she said, "If you look closer you'll see six years' worth of paper cuts and staple puncture wounds," she said. "Before that I was a full-time student. I had to quit the school game after they gave me my Ph.D."

Dez was intrigued. *Dr.* Jackson. She vaguely remembered Victoria saying something about a doctorate before. "How old are you, anyway?"

"Older than you, I bet."

"Come on, stop playing games and answer my question."

"I guess you're the only one allowed to play, huh?"

"We can play together anytime you want, Victoria." Dez poured raw seduction into her voice.

"Thirty-six."

"Seriously?" She raked Victoria with her gaze.

"The women in my family age very well." It was Victoria's turn to raise her glass.

"And what about your parents?" Dez asked.

"Both alive and happy." Victoria traced the rim of her glass with an index finger, smiling. "They're in Toronto still running the antique business they started before they had me."

"You're very lucky," Dez said.

"Yes, I am." Victoria murmured. "So are you. Both your parents are still alive. Cherish the fact that your mother is here now and still able to tell you that she loves you."

"All that, huh?"

"Yeah. All that. I lost my brother while I was in college. I know."

She squeezed Victoria's hand, felt the empathy well up inside her, but said nothing. Anything she said would seem trite and ridiculous. In the face of that real loss, her situation was nothing. Dez squeezed her hand again, then pulled back to reach for her wine.

Dez had never made any effort to get to know someone outside her established circle of friends without the eventual goal of getting them into bed. Had never wanted to. But she wanted more than that with Victoria. That much was obvious by now. She didn't know if she'd have let herself pursue the woman without that being true. Derrick would never forgive Dez if she treated his best friend like all the others. But she had no experience with this, didn't even know how to proceed.

Victoria called her name. "Tell me about your aunt," she said.

"Really?" Dez cocked an eyebrow at Victoria. The other

woman nodded, seemingly giving permission for the old memories of her favorite and only aunt to bubble up, warm and bittersweet. Dez smiled. "There's not much to tell, actually. She was a lot like me. Or, more accurately, I'm a lot like her. She didn't have to work. Her father was some kind of a doo-wop singer back in the day, and he had a couple of hit songs that they always play on certain stations and at certain times of the year. Although she was his love child, she was also his only child. After he died, she started getting royalty checks from his music. Because her lifestyle was pretty modest, she invested most of the money. Her only luxuries were women, her bike, and good food."

"Yeah," Victoria chuckled. "She sounds a lot like you, all right."

"Except I have a few more essential wants than she did."

"I can imagine." She met Dez's eyes across the small table. Her look said that she imagined all sorts of things where her dining companion was concerned; things that she wasn't quite ready to share yet. Victoria cleared her throat. "Would you like dessert?"

They left that evening, packing up the remains of their weekend in silence. Dez would have liked to put her mind on the next day, on the possibility of finding her father in town and protecting herself and her mother against him, but her preoccupation with Victoria wouldn't let her. On the drive back to Miami, she asked the question that had been burning her tongue for hours.

"If all I had to offer you was sex, would you take it?"

Victoria looked at her. "*Is* that all you have?"

Dez shook her head. "I'm not sure, but I don't want to commit to something and end up breaking you when I can't do it. And I don't make promises when I'm not one hundred percent sure." She briefly met Victoria's eyes. "What I am sure of is that I want you. You know that. When we talked you said you don't want to ruin your relationship with

Derrick. Fair enough. But what if you just experiment? Try me on for size, so to speak. And if it turns out that you only want me for sex, then we can get that out of our systems and no one would even have to know about it. Once that's done, you can go on being Derrick's friend. No harm, no foul, everyone gets satisfied." Dez grinned wolfishly.

"Are you joking?"

"Why would I be? I never joke about something this serious."

"Sex?" Victoria's tone was incredulous.

"Yes."

"Have I ever told you what a bad woman you are?"

"Yes. And you can keep on telling me." Dez's voice dropped to a deep rumble. "All night. For as long as you want." She turned back to the road. "Think about it. I can get you off however you need, whenever you need it. No complications."

Chapter 16

"I had fun this weekend." Victoria turned around with her duffel in hand. She moved it behind her and it made a noise as it scraped against the door. She dropped it on the step and moved toward Dez. "Thank you."

"Anytime. I enjoyed your company very much." Dez brushed her fingertips across the other woman's cheek. "Let's . . . get together again. Soon."

"Yes." The air from that simple word brushed Dez's lips as they came closer to Victoria's. They hovered then, at no sign of resistance, made contact.

Christ! Wetness flooded down, coating her swollen pussy lips. *And all I did was kiss her.* She felt Victoria's hands on the back of her shirt, pressing into, then under the cotton. They both trembled.

"Can I come in?" The heat in Victoria's mouth and hands made Dez feel feverish. And horny as hell.

"No."

She used her tongue to try and make her case, licking at the full lips before diving in again to taste every corner of her mouth. Then her hips came into play, pushing and gliding against Victoria's, even holding her against the door and promising a taste of something she'd never had before. But what she had really wanted all day long was to know the shape of that ass, to feel it move under her palms, to squeeze its firmness. And she did so now.

"Fuck," a voice breathed.

Who said that? It didn't matter. They both wanted it. But they also knew what was on the line if Victoria let Dez in.

"You have to go." Victoria pulled away. Her mouth was wet and slightly swollen. "I'll call you later." She stumbled inside and closed the door in Dez's face.

Dez stood outside the house, burning. There were so many things she could have done, would have done, if so much wasn't at stake. She leaned her forehead against the door.

"Victoria?" Her voice was hoarse.

She felt her through the door, a faint conflicted presence.

"Tonight, I'm going to be thinking about you." Her fingers curled against the wood. She fought the urge to say something else, to tell Victoria how good she could make it, how she would come for hours, how Dez would fill her up, make her scream with pleasure—if only she'd open the door. She swallowed. "Call me soon."

Dez felt restless. Pent up. On the drive home, images of Victoria, sweating and hot, pressed against her own front door arching her wet pussy for Dez's mouth, tormented her. It was dark. There were high bushes to shield the yard from the eyes of passersby. No one would see. And even if someone could see, so what? Victoria had been so close to giving in. So close. Dez felt like she'd wanted this woman forever. This waiting shit was for celibates and fools. She pressed her hand against her aching clit through her jeans and groaned.

As she was pulling into her driveway, the cell phone rang.

"Your father just got in tonight," Claudia said after Dez's hello. "He wants to have drinks with all of us tomorrow."

Shit. "Fantastic. Tell him I can't make it."

"Darling, please. Derrick will be there. You should, too."

Not fair. Not fair at all. "All right. I'll come. Where is it?" She parked the truck in the garage and turned off the engine.

"Their suite at the downtown Hilton. Seven o'clock. Call the hotel to get the room number. I can't remember it right now."

Claudia probably barely remembered her own name right now. All because of that asshole ex-husband of hers. "I'll be there."

"Thank you." She heard a smile in her mother's voice. "I owe you one."

"You owe me several, but who's counting? See you tomorrow." She closed the phone and tucked it in her pocket.

The next day came much too quickly. So did the night. She rode up in the mirrored elevator at the Hilton, sneaking occasional peeks at her reflection. If she didn't know better she'd say that she looked nervous with her tight mouth and darting eyes that couldn't stay on any one thing for long. *Fuck him for doing this to me.* With a deep breath, Dez forced herself to calm down. She consciously relaxed her shoulders, loosening everything inside her—except her bowels— before looking back in the mirror. This was better. She looked arrogant and cocksure again, her preferred façade whenever she was out in the world. Besides, it was the one that got her the most pussy. And speaking of which . . . a woman two bodies away was also giving her reflection the eye. Reflexively, Dez winked. The woman, peach-colored and pretty in a farm girl kind of way, blushed and looked away. A bell signaled the fifteenth floor.

In honor of the occasion, Dez had worn black, appropriately funereal slacks, a button-down shirt, and her favorite leather jacket. As she got off the elevator, she felt the woman's gaze on her ass. She strutted down the hall to give the farmer's daughter an eyeful. It wasn't until she was halfway down the hall that she realized that she was going the wrong way. At least the elevator doors had already closed. Dez doubled back to find the right room. Warrick came to the door when she knocked.

It was easy to forget that it had been almost five years since they'd seen each other. That time had been good to him. If anything, he looked more prosperous and more handsome than the last time. A few more flecks of gray dotted his thick hair, only adding to the already "distinguished" look. His smile was wide and white and the body beneath the charcoal gray suit looked trim. The lawyering business must be good out in California.

"Desiree. Look at you!"

And look at you, you smug asshole. Dez served him up one of her own bullshit smiles and stepped inside the suite. "How's it going?"

Warrick seemed taken aback by her casual greeting. She didn't know why. It wasn't like they were long-lost friends or anything.

"I'm doing well," he said. "Come on in. You're the last to arrive."

Good. She shrugged off her jacket and hung it on the coat rack by the door.

"So how are things in your life, Desiree?" He closed the door and adjusted the drape of her jacket on the rack. The tiniest sneer in his voice betrayed that he had his assumptions about Dez's life and didn't care to hear her version of things.

"Same as always, Papa. Real good." She bowed, a mocking tilt of her head that she knew reminded her father of Aunt Paul.

Warrick had never liked her aunt and liked her even less when Dez had turned out to be a dyke, too. As a child, Dez had gotten used to his offhand, and often unkind, remarks about Paul. They were easy to ignore because Paulette had given less than a piece of rat shit what he thought. But she never thought that one day his cruel remarks and disgusted looks would be directed at her. Dez learned the hard way.

She came out during her arrogant phase. Even when she knew that her father couldn't deal with what he scornfully called her "alternative lifestyle," Dez still brought a girl home. Someone sweet and feminine, undeniably gorgeous with her big Afro and pillowy body; but still a dyke. Mia was sixteen and had already been plucked several times before the fourteen-year-old Dez got a hold of her. Dez had boldly walked her into the family's house, shared peanut-butter-and-jelly sandwiches and giggles over the dining table before taking her up to her room for the sticky, teenaged version of "show-and-tell." When the two girls emerged, breathless and glowing almost two hours later, they humped into Dez's father. Warrick's nostrils flared, like he smelled the dyke on them. Then he walked past as if Dez wasn't even standing there. Her stomach and her face fell, but she turned to Mia with a carefree smile and asked the older girl if she wanted to go for a dip in the pool.

She ran to her aunt later that day, finally giving into the tears that had threatened at that one poisonous look from her father. Paul patted her shoulder then made her a root beer float. When Dez could finally speak without dissolving into hiccupping tears, her aunt made a simple offer:

"If you want to hang out with your girlfriends, bring them here. You know that you have the whole attic to yourself. Just give me some warning so you don't give this old dyke a heart attack when I hear strange noises over my head."

The teenage Dez had shuddered. "As if I'd do anything with a girl when you're in the house. That's too weird."

Her aunt only laughed. Not long after that, Dez wanting to bring girls home wasn't an issue anymore. Her father filed for a divorce and moved out.

"Mama. Derrick." Dez greeted her family with a properly somber nod.

Her brother and mother stood next to the high window with drinks in their hands, like someone had just finished making yet another inane comment about the view of the city and they were looking at it just to be polite. Claudia's face was slightly pinched, but she looked like she was handling the situation well enough. Derrick nodded at his sister, but said nothing. It was probably better that way.

Dez smiled at her father's wife who sat on the couch watching their exchange with calm eyes. Tall and elegant, she could have been any society woman Dez encountered on the streets of Miami. Her skin was pale, like milky tea, but she was still beautiful with her high, wide cheekbones and straightened hair that fell just beneath her breasts. Like her husband, she wore a suit. A Chanel in burnt gold that made the best of her complexion and mirrored the color of her eyes.

"Desiree, this is Sushaunna. My wife."

"Pleased to meet you." Dez bowed over her hand, lightly kissing the scented skin. "Sorry about my slight tardiness. I had something come up at home."

"You weren't late at all," Sushaunna said in her slightly accented English. "We were all just getting to know one another." Her smile was a gentle appeal for friendship. "And please call me Susha."

Dez smiled back. "Great. Then let's get this party started."

"We're going to be over here in the parlor," Warrick said. "After you."

Dez brought up the tail end of the procession to the pretentious little sitting room with an expansive view of Biscayne Bay. Lights glittered off the water. A table sat prepared with platters of finger food—cheeses, fruit, vegetables, even caviar and crackers. The tall bar opposite the gigantic window seemed fully stocked. There were enough chairs in the room to accommodate everyone and then some.

"Help yourself to anything you want."

This is too fucking weird. Her father walked around like some benevolent patriarch while his family seemed perfectly willing to go along with it. Dez poured herself a hefty glass of scotch.

"Would you like me to freshen your drink for you, Mama?" she asked from the bar.

"Yes, please."

She took her mother's glass of white wine and topped it off.

"Before you got here, darling, your father was just telling us how he wanted to give Sushaunna a tour of the city. She'd never been here before."

"It's a nice town. I'm sure you'll love it," Dez felt obliged to say to her stepmother as she passed Claudia her wine.

"To tell the truth it reminds me a little of some California cities I've seen. I'm sure there's not much difference."

Derrick grunted. If Miami were a woman, he would have married her by now. He loved the city with a passion that few understood. To him, La Bonita was like no other city on earth. "I wouldn't say that," was all he said.

Dez chuckled from behind her glass. "So, Papa. What brings you to our fair city? I thought you were done with us forever."

Warrick glanced at his daughter, her spectacular height and handsome, dykey looks, and hated her. Or at least that's what Dez thought. "I could never be done with this place," he said. "After all, my children are here. And Claudia, the woman who I considered my best friend for a long time."

"Hm. I guess I wasn't clear enough." She swirled the pale amber liquid in her glass. "What are you doing here and why did you want us all to come?"

"Isn't it enough that I wanted to come?"

Dez shook her head but forgot to smile.

"I'll not stand here and be interrogated by my own daughter." Warrick finally put away his fake smile.

Susha spoke up. "Rick thought it was time that I met his first wife and his other children. The twins' grandparents are in town for the week and could babysit for us, so it was the perfect time for Warrick and me to come see you."

There was a new set of twins. Dez hadn't heard that. They,

she and Derrick, had been replaced, too. She noticed the faintest twitch of Derrick's jaw but knew the fucker wouldn't say anything.

"And," Susha continued with a faint lowering of her voice, "he told me about your being ill, Claudia. I wanted to tell you in person that if there's anything that I can do for you, just ask it."

"Thank you." Claudia's mouth tightened. "But God willing, I won't be needing anyone's help with that for a long time, if ever."

He talked about his old wife with his new one. Yet hadn't said a word to Derrick or Claudia about these twins—only that he had new children now and he was well and truly settled in California. Bastard. Claudia must be aching.

Dez's phone rang. She fumbled in her pocket for it, answering without checking the caller ID. Whoever it was, she would talk to them. It had to be better than this farce playing out in front of her.

"Hello?"

"Yes. Let's do it."

"What?"

"If that's all you have to offer, I'll take it. The ride could be fun."

Victoria. A puff of breath, thick with relief and anticipation, left her mouth. Dez made brief excuses to her family as she turned around and left the room. "All right. Can I come over tonight? I'll bring a copy of my STD test results."

Victoria laughed. "No. It's not going to work that way. How about dinner? Maybe some dancing. A little wooing first. I know it's just fucking, but let's not dispense with the foreplay."

Dez laughed at herself. "You're right. Um . . . tomorrow after you close up. I'll meet you. We can go out after."

"Okay. See you at the store." Her giggle flirted with Dez through the phone. "We can trade test results then."

She took a deep breath before going back inside. The

Nichols, old and new, were getting along splendidly. No one seemed to even notice that she had stepped out of the room. Susha and Claudia sat closely together on the couch talking like old school chums while Derrick and their father stood at the bar refreshing their manly drinks and talking shop. Lovely. Dez picked up her glass of scotch and walked to the window.

Beyond the blue-tinted glass, city lights beckoned. They made her long to be outside, away from this generic hotel suite and the fake smiles and awkward silences. Was she the only one who wondered why they were all here in the first place? What was Susha thinking here in this hotel room faced with her husband's old family? Did she have doubts about Warrick? Did she wonder if he would leave her, the mother of his new set of twins, for someone with a firmer belly and more looks than sense? Dez would never do that to anyone. Despite what her mother said, that was one thing that Dez did not share with her father: If she made a promise, she didn't turn around and take it back later on. She avoided that trap by never making any at all.

She deliberately shook off her grim thoughts and turned her attention back to the conversation going on in the room. Claudia said something about Susha's children, connecting them to Dez and Derrick in a deliberate and cheerful way. It literally made Dez ill to see her mother be nice to this . . . man.

"Desiree, darling."

She looked at her mother.

"Susha was just wondering where the best places are to go couture shopping in the city. What do you suggest?"

"That depends. Is Warrick paying?" She shoved herself off the wall and went to join her family.

After too many hours of small talk and strong drinks, Warrick's old family left him to it at the hotel. Under her children's watchful eyes, Claudia called some of her friends to meet her at a cocktail party nearby. She said that she needed something cheerful after the dismal gathering she'd just left. Dez saw her off with a frown.

"I hope she's all right."

Her brother wasn't worried. "Mama will be fine. She's a lot stronger than either of us gives her credit for."

Dez made an uncertain noise.

"Come out for a real drink with me. I need to wash the taste of all that bullshit off my tongue."

She looked at him in surprise. Did Derrick just offer to spend more time in her presence? Willingly? "Sure."

They went to a bar nearby, a straight one, of course, that had enough eye candy to keep Dez entertained. Cigarette smoke curled in the air around them, snaking into their clothes and hair. At their quiet table, Dez sipped her rum and Coke and watched the parade of scantily clad women with surprisingly little interest. Her mind strayed to Victoria, lingered on the memory of her mouth, her lush breasts. No one in the bar seemed nearly as fuckable. Ah well. She turned to her brother. Derrick moved his tumbler of scotch around on the table.

Dez suddenly realized that she could count the facts she knew about the adult Derrick on one hand: He could have damn near any woman he wanted. Claudia trusted him and, as if that wasn't enough, he was brilliant. Fresh out of law school and having aced the Florida bar exam, he got hired by one of the top firms in Miami and was already their golden black boy. If she cared enough, Dez could have been jealous. But there was only one thing she cared about now.

"Your daddy is a serious piece of work, isn't he?"

"Tell me about it. He's changed." Derrick chuckled, but it was without any real humor. "I used to want to be like him in the worst way." *No shit, Mr. Lawyerman with the penthouse suite and thousand-dollar suits.* "But tonight when he flaunted his new life in front of us, his new twins, his gorgeous new wife with the Berkeley education and the foreign accent, I wanted to kill him. I've never seen Mama look so hurt."

"Where the fuck were you when he dicked us over the first time? Did you forget the divorce? Him leaving us?"

"Shit, Dez, we were just kids. Besides, even then I knew that things happen between a married couple that aren't necessarily any one person's fault."

She wouldn't know about any such complications between couples. Dez couldn't rightly remember ever being part of one. The thing with Ruben didn't count.

"Shit." He sighed. "The reason I asked you out today was to talk. Seriously I was watching you tonight. Watching us, how we all were with one another. Like it or not, all we have is each other. We can't afford to be at odds."

"I didn't start this, little brother. At least I don't think I did. I'll be damned if I even know what happened to make things so bad between us."

"Puberty."

"Probably." In the two years she'd been gone, Dez had almost forgotten about the animosity between her and Derrick. She'd certainly forgotten the cause. He was her brother. Warrick preferred him to her. She'd lost a girl or two to him growing up, just as he had to her. All these things were nothing. They were adults now. Or so she thought until he attacked her on the afternoon they picked Claudia up from the McAllisters'.

She cleared her throat. "So, how's Trish?" That seemed a safe enough topic.

"Still fuckable, so you can't have her." Derrick smiled weakly.

"Then what are *you* doing with her?"

"Very funny."

"I thought so." Dez signaled the roving waitress for a refill.

Once the woman had come and gone, leaving a nicely topped-off glass of Appleton Estate and Pepsi, it was Derrick's turn to clear his throat.

"I'm sorry about the shit I said to you the other day." He looked at his sister with dark eyes. "Mama always liked you best," he said. "And I didn't think you loved and cared for her the way that she obviously loved and cared for you." He played with the condensation on his glass. "I always felt that you were selfish and completely undeserving."

"So what made you change your mind about my selfish ways? Daddy showing us what a great life he has without us? Or was it just an epiphany, like lightning striking out of the blue?"

"I knew that you wouldn't make this easy for me."

"Mom's always saying that nothing worthwhile is easily gotten."

"Sounds true enough." He drank down his scotch and put his empty glass on the table. "Listen. Not very much has changed. I still think that you've had it too easy. You've never had to work for anything. Not your grades, money, or even Mama's love." Derrick's look was matter-of-fact. "You're a spoiled, selfish brat, Desiree. But you really love our mother. And sometimes I think you even love me, despite everything. You're my blood." He smiled weakly. "I've been a shit, and I'm sorry."

Would he be saying this if he knew about her and Victoria? Dez didn't let herself ponder the question for too long. She needed this reconciliation as much as he did. "Insult-apology accepted." She finished the rest of her drink. The tumbler settled heavily on the table between them. "Now, are you going to buy us another round?"

Chapter 17

Victoriana's coffee shop hummed with hectic late-evening activity when Dez pulled up at ten-thirty. Cruising was still going along full speed with the baby dykes and old-timers alike giving one another the eye. Even the rich dykes in their pinstripes and designer glasses were getting in on the action. Dez spied one or two that seemed to be just there for the libations, but they were few and far between. She nodded to the girl behind the bar before taking the stairs up to the bookstore.

Through the small glass opening in the front door, she could see a lone figure moving around behind the cash register. Dez knocked.

"Hey." Victoria gestured her in and locked the door behind her. Dez's flesh started to simmer. She leaned back against the door.

"Are you done for the night?"

"Yes," Victoria said, stepping back behind the counter.

"Are we alone?"

"Yes."

Dez relaxed into a sigh, closing her eyes as her body made firmer contact with the door. "Come here."

"We're going out, remember?" Victoria said, but came anyway, walking toward her with slow deliberate steps.

"After," Dez said, reaching for what she wanted.

Victoria's mouth tasted of "yes" and "right now," flavors that made Dez's knees weak and her underwear sopping wet.

"Do you—shit!—do you have a couch or something?" She gasped when Victoria's cool fingers touched her breasts, inciting her nipples with delicate pinches. She pulled her mouth away. "Tell me," she swallowed. "Is there anything that you don't want me to do?" It seemed the easiest question to ask.

"No dildos," Victoria breathed in her ear. "I don't want you to fuck me with anything but your fingers and tongue."

Dez felt the strap-on cupped in the seam of her button-flies droop in disappointment. Maybe this wasn't going to work. She tried to pull away but Victoria licked Dez's mouth and drew the full lower lip between her teeth.

"Chicken?"

Dez laughed, never one to back out of a dare. "No, that's not what I want to eat right now." She reached under Victoria's long skirt to cup that sweet ass she'd been thinking about for so long.

"What, you want to toss my salad?" Victoria nibbled her lips. "I'd suggest something more substantial if you were planning on staying at my house all night. We wouldn't want you to pass out from lack of proper nutrients."

Dez chuckled. "Fine, you win." She slid her fingers in the back of Victoria's panties for one last squeeze. "We have reservations for eleven o'clock anyway."

Dez took her to Anansi, a late-night restaurant that didn't close its doors until two-thirty in the morning. She and Rémi had been here a time or two, solidifying their friendship over a bottle of expensive wine and a well-prepared meal. The tuxedoed host escorted them to a secluded table, weaving them through the crowd of wealthy night owls just beginning their evening's pleasure. Dinah Washington's "Call Me Irresponsible" crooned from the restaurant's hidden speakers.

"This is an interesting place. I've never been here before."

"Good." Dez guided Victoria to her chair with a possessive hand at the small of her back. "I hope to introduce you to a lot of new experiences before we're through."

The host hid his smile as he placed menus on the table in front of them. "Enjoy your meal, ladies."

Dez dismissed him with a nod. "The desserts here are fantastic. I usually make sure to save room for some."

"I'll take that under advisement." Victoria murmured as she opened her menu. A smile played at the corner of her mouth.

Anticipation slowly uncurled like a fanged snake in Dez's belly as the evening progressed. She didn't want to eat, at least not food. Victoria's face captured her attention and held it. The full curve of her mouth, her throat moving as she swallowed her food, the nervous fire in her eyes. Dez couldn't remember being this anxious to have a woman, to have anything. When the waiter came back, she ordered wine for them both, toasting Victoria's beauty and her good judgment in saying yes to Dez's proposition. She wanted her to say yes again, say it later when she had the soft woman spread out under her on the bed, when she had those legs in the air, those thighs clasped around her ears. She forced herself to calm down. At this rate she wouldn't last more than five minutes in Victoria's bedroom. She felt like a horny teenaged boy. With a hand that shook, she lifted her glass of wine.

When their dinner came, she couldn't eat. But Victoria didn't have that problem.

"You really enjoy your food, don't you?" She smiled at Victoria's half-finished plate of pasta. *Just keep talking. If I keep talking then I won't be able to think so much about fucking.* Victoria licked a spot of Alfredo sauce from her bottom lip and Dez clenched inside her jeans.

"Yes." The other woman looked suddenly bashful. "I told a lie the other day when I said that I liked to cook more than I like to eat."

Dez's raised eyebrow begged her to continue, anything to keep her from thinking about licking a different kind of cream from a different set of lips.

"I like both. Very much."

"Ah. I never would have guessed."

Victoria blushed and smiled when it became obvious that Dez wasn't making fun of her appetite, was in fact pleased by it. Very pleased.

After the main course was finished, they ordered dessert to share. Two forks and tiramisu. Victoria's preference. She ate while Dez, the happy voyeur, watched and took only occasional bites of the rich and creamy cake. While they talked, Victoria gestured with her fork, tapping it against her mouth, pointing it in the air, but always licking it clean after each bite of the tiramisu. Her lipstick was long gone and her mouth shining wet and slightly pink in the dim, low-hanging light when Victoria pushed the half-finished dessert away with a sigh of deep satisfaction. Dez reached for her cigarettes.

"Mind if I smoke?" She was already taking one from the pack.

"Yes, I do." Victoria leaned across the table. "You have to know that smoking—no matter how expensive the tobacco"— she made a dismissive gesture at the slim green box—"is not good for you."

"I do, but I like smoking." But she put the cigarettes away.

"There are much better things to put in your mouth."

"I wouldn't deny that." Whatever game this was, she liked it already. "But this is all I have right now."

Victoria dipped a finger in the remains of the tiramisu that sat between them. "Here," she said and leaned across the table toward her dinner companion.

Intrigued and suddenly in desperate need of a fix that had nothing to do with nicotine, Dez pushed her wineglass aside to brace one arm against the table. She opened her mouth. Before the finger could touch her lips, her tongue snaked out to lick its underside. She pretended not to hear Victoria's quick intake of breath. Her tongue curled around that finger, licking catlike at the sticky crumbs before pulling the digit into her mouth. Unseen, her tongue worked vicious magic, dipping into the flesh between Victoria's fingers then retreated, only to begin a suggestive suck and release motion. The crotch of her briefs was wet. But that happened the moment she saw Victoria get out of the truck and begin her slow ascent up the restaurant steps. Now it was much worse. She was soaking in her own juices, legs splayed wide under the table, and the seam of her pants tight against her clit.

"Do you want to continue this elsewhere?" Breathless anticipation made Victoria's question a demand.

"No." Dez released the finger and sat back in her chair. "I would have enjoyed my cigarette here. Why not this?" Her voice deepened. "Come closer."

Victoria started to lean across the table again but Dez shook her head. "Here, next to me."

Their table was intimately placed, blocked from most of the restaurant by several large plants, but they weren't completely hidden from view.

Victoria didn't seem to care. "Where do you want me?"

"It doesn't matter. I work well with both hands." And she wanted them both on this woman right now. She wanted to feel the slide of her wet pussy, to curl inside Victoria and hear her gasp. When the chair moved next to hers, she sighed with anticipation.

Under the cover of the tablecloth, she started to lift Victoria's skirt. "May I?"

"Please." Her voice trembled. "Please do."

That was all she needed. Dez traced a finger along the smooth skin of her thigh, lifting the skirt as she went. "I would rather have your creamy little pussy as a second dessert." Her fingers found the damp crotch of silk panties. "But this will have to do for now."

A low moan came from Victoria's throat when Dez touched her.

"Remember, you can't be too loud. We are in a public place after all." Then she proceeded to test her self-control.

Dez would have liked to see Victoria's breasts, the hardening nipples with the pucker of raisins, the taste of sweet milk. With a quick flick of her fingers, Victoria loosened the first button of her blouse, then a second. Dez held her breath and slowed the downward stroke of her fingers. A third button, then the silk bra with its lush weight teased Dez's eyes and brought sudden moisture to her mouth. She unconsciously leaned forward and bit her lip.

Now it was Victoria's turn to laugh. "We're in a public place, remember?" The last word was barely whispered before Dez's fingers continued their dance. They slid between the slick petals, around her clit, alternatively stroking and pushing until Victoria's breath came in little gasps. Her hand clutched the white tablecloth and spilled the rest of Dez's water into the unfinished dessert, sending the glass rolling from the table to the rug on the floor. They both ignored it. Victoria's thigh, pressed alongside Dez's, began to shake.

"Uh uh. It won't be that easy." She slowed her strokes then pulled back until her fingers were barely touching Victoria.

"What?" The trembling at her thigh gradually faded as Victoria opened her eyes. "What are you talking about?"

Dez didn't know. She had every intention of teasing, of bringing Victoria to the very edge, then pull back just before she could fall over. But those bowed lips were pussy-wet, teeth marked from her self-control. And she didn't look happy. *Neither would I,* Dez thought. She reached out again and whispered something she hadn't said to anyone else in a long time.

"I'm sorry."

Victoria came all over her hand, dripping come into the crevice between each of Dez's fingers, even splashing the

prominent veins in Dez's wrist. At the last moment, Victoria
bent into her and bit into the soft skin where her neck and
shoulder met in an effort to stifle her moans. "Thank you,"
she muttered hoarsely when she could, then straightened in
her chair.

"You're welcome." Dez didn't try to disguise the tremor in
her own voice.

Victoria sat, dreamy-eyed in her chair, mouth full and passion-
bitten, her blouse still unbuttoned to allow a glimpse of sweat-
dampened cleavage. Dez dropped money on the table for a
check that hadn't come yet.

"Are you ready?" Desire clawed under her skin. She didn't
want to play games, didn't want to force Victoria to admit
who was running the fuck. Her old impulses had resurfaced,
then, thankfully, died a quick death. Beside her, Victoria
blinked and nodded slowly. She cleared her throat.

They were silent as they stood on the curb waiting for the
valet to bring Dez's truck around. Silence reigned still as they
drove through the nighttime glitter of South Beach, past the
midweek partiers, the beautiful people on their way to the
next beautiful place. In Victoria's driveway, Dez set the alarm
on the truck and walked her date up the cobblestoned walkway.

"It's been an interesting evening," Victoria said. She stopped
Dez at the door. Her eyes were no longer dreamy and unfo-
cused.

"I know what you were doing tonight and I didn't like it."

The awareness that the night wasn't going to end where
she wanted it, where she hoped it would, settled into Dez like
a lead weight.

"I want you, but not like this." At Dez's silent look, she
continued. "I won't play power games and I certainly won't
play by your rules." She put her key in the door and turned
it. The look she leveled on Dez let the taller woman know

that she was not invited in. "Besides I have to be at work early tomorrow. This . . . thing we're doing is about pleasure. Mutual pleasure. I think you've had your fun for the night. Call me tomorrow."

And for the second time in their short acquaintance, she closed her door in Dez's face.

Chapter 18

D-day. The day for Claudia's doctor's visit. Almost ten o'clock in the morning, usually too early for Dez to be up, but she was wide awake, dressed in freshly pressed khakis and a Polo shirt like she was going to visit older relatives. She ran her hand over her hair for what seemed like the fiftieth time in the last hour and stared past the windshield at the innocuous-looking building with its red brick and plain glass door.

"Are you going to let me out of this car or am I going to have to fight you?" Claudia sat in the passenger seat looking as reluctant as Dez to get out of the truck.

Dez's finger triggered the automatic locks again. Accidentally. "Sorry." She let out a deep breath and unlocked the doors.

They stepped out into a gorgeous day. It felt like spring in New Mexico with the crisp breeze and the sound of leaves washing above them like rain. Sunlight turned even the staid brick building into something of beauty, bathing it in liquid gold. Dez hoped that was a good omen. She opened the door of the building and waited for her mother to step through. The receptionist already knew Claudia by name, greeting her with a smile and some comment about the weather. She spared Dez a brief but friendly glance before letting them know that the doctor would be able to see them in a few minutes. Dez barely got the chance to appreciate this new level of nervousness—stomach tied in knots, being unable to stand still—before the doctor made an appearance and ushered them back to her office.

Dr. Charles wasn't what she expected. Short and round with big hips and her graying hair tucked back in a neat bun, she looked like somebody's Italian grandmother.

"Claudia, good to see you again." With a chart in her hand, she turned to Dez. "And this must be the baby you were telling me about." She held out her hand and dimpled at the younger woman. "You never said how pretty she was."

Is this woman flirting with me? Dez shook Dr. Charles's hand nervously, barely able to muster up a polite smile. The woman patted her arm sympathetically before turning back to Claudia.

"It's going to be a pretty short visit today, Claudia. The tests all came back negative. You are completely cancer free."

From the corner, seated in her uncomfortable thick chair, Dez jumped, like someone had jolted her with electricity. "Are you shittin' us?" At the doctor's look, she shook her head. "Seriously?"

"Are you sure?" Claudia's face was an echo of her daughter's. Her eyes were shiny with surprised tears.

"Very. The last operation was a complete success. We scraped everything out that we could find, and then some just to be on the safe side. I want to keep seeing you for the next few months to monitor your progress and be absolutely sure."

"Oh my god." She sagged against the doctor as if finally she could stop being strong. "Oh my god." And her tears started to fall.

Dr. Charles made low comforting noises. "I know, honey. It's a big shock." She rubbed Claudia's shoulders as Dez watched, still somehow uncomprehending. "But at least it's a good one."

Claudia pulled back from the doctor, tears streaking her face. "You're not going to call me back in a few days and say this was a mistake, are you?" Her mouth trembled. "Just say you're not going to take it back."

"I won't take it back. As far as I know—and I was very thorough—you're fine. You're free to live your life however you like."

Claudia laughed and fisted her hands in the doctor's neat white coat. "Thank you, Felicia. You'll definitely be on my Christmas list this year."

The gray-haired woman chuckled. "Now that's the best news I've gotten all day. I've heard how generous you can be."

The rest of their conversation floated away from Dez as she watched her mother's tearful face, stripped of makeup but still beautiful. She nodded at something Felicia Charles said, smiled, and then laughed outright. This was what Dez had been hoping for, the thing that she prayed to her aunt's god, weeping, for. Breath fluttered in her throat. She felt like she would pass out from the relief of it.

"Here's a tissue, dear."

Dez didn't realize the doctor was talking to her until she tasted the salt of her own tears. She reached out for the Kleenex with shaking fingers. "Thank you."

Once they got outside, Claudia couldn't stop smiling. Her tears were gone, mopped up and tucked back behind her eyes where they belonged. Still, she blinked in the brightness of the day like a child waking from a long sleep.

"Well, that was—" she broke off and arched her neck to stare at the sharp sky. Her mouth stretched wide and screamed, a long and wrenching cry that flew out of her mouth and filled up the morning air, expanding, rising, cathartic.

A woman walking from the parking lot clutched her gangly wide-eyed child more securely under her arm and gave Claudia a wide berth. Dez ignored them. Her mother leaned back against the hood of the truck and rapidly blinked her eyes as she crossed her arms tightly over her chest.

"After the operation they told me that the procedure had been successful. All the cancer cells were out, but there was also one final test." She uncrossed her arms. "That was it. I can't believe this. After living with this for what seems like forever. And now . . . now I hardly know what to do with myself."

"I'm sure you'll figure something out."

They both would know that the waiting and dread were over. She hugged her mother tightly, pressing her fragile bones to her, felt her deep grateful breaths, and was happy. They drove back to the house, talking softly about nothing in particular while Claudia's favorite seventies station played in the background. When they got to the house, Claudia put out her hand to stop Dez from turning off the car.

"You go on, Desiree. I'm going to celebrate." Claudia said.

"You don't feel like some company?"

Claudia grinned at her daughter. "The kind of celebrating I have in mind isn't something I can do with my child around."

Oh. "Sounds scandalous. Please be careful."

She hugged her good-bye in the driveway and got back in the truck. Although she hadn't shared it with Claudia, she felt deflated, like all the energy that it took to be angry at the universe for making her mother sick, for being strong for both of them, was suddenly gone. There was no reason for any of that now. Dez was limp. She needed someone to hold her up. Without giving herself time to rethink it, she called Victoria's bookstore.

"Good afternoon. Victoriana Books, may I help you?"

The cheerful young voice on the other end of the phone wasn't Victoria's.

"Is Miss Jackson there?"

"No. Today is her day off. She should be at home."

"Thank you." Dez did a U-ey and headed for Victoria's house.

Because her mama taught her never to show up unannounced, she called from the driveway. Victoria's surprised voice greeted then welcomed her into the house.

"Are you all right?" she asked when she opened the door and saw Dez.

"Yeah. Never better."

"Do you . . . do you want something to drink?"

"Um. Something hot. Tea, or whatever you have."

"I have Mexican hot chocolate. Is that okay?"

"Yes. More than." Her mind tumbled into the news from earlier. And she smiled. "That's perfect."

She followed Victoria into the kitchen, watching her, still smiling. Today she was wearing a dress, a peach-colored cotton thing with straps that lay on the full curves of her shoulders like pretty enticements. As she bent to open a cupboard, the cloth of the dress stretched over the smooth valley of her spine, the curve of her ass, and thighs.

Victoria straightened with a tin of chocolate in her hand. "You're freaking me out."

"I'm sorry." Dez opened the refrigerator then closed it again. "My mother's going to be all right. She got the last test results today."

Breath left Victoria in a rush. "That's wonderful." She put the chocolate down, then walked hesitantly toward Dez. Her arms fluttered in the air before settling finally on Dez's shoulders. "What a relief. I'm so glad for you and Derrick."

She gladly fell into the comfort Victoria offered. It was exactly what she had come here for, to bury her fingers into the springing curls and inhale the sweet honey scent of her. Monday night's misstep was forgotten. She needed this. It wasn't like she couldn't get it from some other woman, she could. Rémi, Sage, even Nuria. Any one of those women would have done fine. But Victoria lived closer. And she smelled so much better.

"I don't want any hot chocolate," she murmured into the soft, springing hair.

Victoria didn't ask what it was that she wanted instead.

She rubbed Dez's back in slow circles, soothing the bunched muscles, and turning her into freshly churned butter. The comforting hands dropped lower and Dez's breath deepened. This was where everything got started that first time. Here, in the kitchen. This time, Dez was on the receiving end of a kiss, and being pressed gently against the counter as Victoria's fingers slowly unbuttoned her shirt.

"Come with me."

Victoria's bedroom was wet with light, the sheets of the bed pleasantly rumpled as if she'd lain back down after making it, unwilling to leave it without the imprint of her own body. The impression of warmth and welcome followed Dez down into the sheets as Victoria's body followed hers, mouth tender and hungry as she told Dez with teeth and tongue, wordlessly, of her desire, of what she wanted to do with her unexpectedly yielding body. Dez approved. She wanted to give up her control, better yet, have it taken from her. The past month had been all about control—how to stop from breaking down, from being a fool in front of her father, from falling completely into the caricature of a person who she was before. She didn't want that control anymore.

Above her, Victoria was a lioness, with her fall of varicolored hair, wet mouth, and the hands that touched her with tenderness allowed her mind to roam beyond the fierce bounds of her desire to the press of cotton sheets against her back, the feel of the rest of her clothes leaving her body in one voluptuous fall after another. The room was cool. Her skin was hot, a searing counterpoint to the eyes that watched Dez again like a lioness stalking her prey, calculating the next move. She slipped her hand over Dez's breast and waited for a response, gauging it, then when pleasure seemed like the result, did the same to the other breast, rolling the tips between her fingers, then pinching gently until sensation licked down Dez's body to the blood-flushed flesh between her thighs. She arched under her, like a cat herself, for more of the cool hands that staked their claim with no apologies. Those hands gathered up her breasts like candy and held them ready for Victoria's mouth, the tongue that was rough and soft by turns, prodding her nipples into tight buds of arousal. Desire tightened the muscles of her belly, made her breath harsh and quick. Victoria's hair tickled her throat and slid around her fingers like clinging vines as she pressed her closer, demanding more.

The fingers caught her unaware. They slipped between her thighs to stroke her thick and yearning clit. Her breath hitched. Victoria laughed against her skin. She didn't have to ask for anything. The long fingers glided over her wet pussy, gathering juice to lave her clit. Each stroke brought Dez higher until she was gasping for breath, her attentions fully claimed by the mouth pulling at her breasts and the fingers strumming a wild flamenco between her legs. She gripped the back of Victoria's head as her legs fanned wide and flexed against the bed. The syllables of her lover's name tumbled from her mouth in harsh, separate pieces as she lost every single one of her senses to Victoria. Orgasm tumbled over her like a merciless wave and left her shuddering, gasping, and weak.

When she floated back to earth, Victoria was there, kneeling beside her on the bed. Smiling. She was still dressed.

"You look sleepy."

"No," Dez murmured. "I'm ready for round two." But her eyelids felt so heavy and the sheets were divine under her skin.

Victoria tucked the covers up and around Dez's shoulders. "Maybe *I'm* not ready for round two." Dez kissed her fingers before they floated away and felt herself begin to slip gently into sleep.

"Thank you," she mumbled, already gone.

"Claudia is the strongest woman that I know. When my father left her she didn't lose her shit. I did." Dez's voice was a ragged whisper in the warm bedroom. "She made sure that most of our routine stayed the same after Warrick left. We still went on vacations, we went to the markets, we had family time. Not once did I see her break down after the man who promised to spend forever with her decided that forever was too long and he had better things to do with the rest of his life. Well, the other day she finally broke down in front of me. After thirteen years, she cried over this man on my shoulder. And while I was hoping that I would never be hit with a love like that, I was happy that she finally showed me how his leaving had hurt." Dez turned from her unblinking stare at the ceiling. "Isn't that fucked up?"

Victoria shook her head. "Not every love ends up like that, you know?"

"Yeah. Some end up worse." An image of Ruben walking away came unbidden to her mind.

"I didn't realize that you were such a cynic."

"I'm not."

Victoria made a noise of skepticism and settled more comfortably against the pillows. The scent of her was close and warm, sun-blushed sex that came from her hands and between her legs. Dez suddenly remembered that Victoria hadn't been satisfied. She kissed the other woman's hands and invited her without words to come closer and straddle her relaxed body. Victoria came, smiling. "You don't have to do this, you know."

"I know." She pressed Victoria's palm to her lips, smelling herself on those soft fingers, watching as above her she unwrapped a slow, teasing smile while the sun shone through her hair, haloing her in gold. Her breasts, framed in the neckline of her dress, trembled and came lower.

Dez released her hand. "Take off your clothes."

Victoria's coy smile hinted at a refusal, but she sat back on her heels, unzipped, and pulled the sundress over her head, revealing a utilitarian black bra and the flesh of her belly, the subtle rise of her ribs under butterscotch smooth skin. An elegant movement of her back against her bed released her from her white half-slip.

"The bra and panties, too." Dez's voice was thick with want.

"Those you have to come get yourself."

Dez smiled and reached for her. The vision came, pulled in by the tether of her fingers, soft in the dark underwear and smelling of the afternoon sun and tangerines and Dez's pussy. With the ease of long practice, Dez unsnapped her bra and tossed it aside. Now, Victoria hovered over her, waving her thick, tempting nipples above Dez's mouth, just out of reach. Her thigh slid over and between Dez's, her arms made indentations on the bed near the taller woman's ears.

"I'm here. Now what?"

The tease. But Dez knew how to get what she wanted eventually, even when she was flat on her back and feeling lazy and horny at the same time. Her hands traveled the length of Victoria's back, cupped the ass in their panties and pulled her up and closer. Perfect. The breasts came, all her warm skin came, snuggling against her face and she licked the brown sugar swells of flesh. She took the nipple between her teeth, heard Victoria moan above her, softly, reluctantly even. Dez loved breasts. It was her shame and her delight. Everywhere she went she stared like a schoolboy at half-mast at all the breasts that bounced, jiggled, swayed, and sailed by. After all these years of looking, she just might have found the perfect pair. Her mouth made hungry suckling noises as it explored its newly found treasure.

Victoria tossed her head back and hummed in pleasure as her entire body vibrated above Dez. Her smile was pure temptation. Dez maneuvered off the black panties, then sighed, riding happily through the feeling that all the rewards of heaven were heaped on her. Victoria made herself more comfortable, kneeling over her, offering her breasts to Dez's mouth and her wide open pussy, wet and succulent, to her hands. But she didn't touch it, she was having too much fun watching Victoria's arousal and the groans she made from just having her breasts played with. *So damn beautiful.*

It didn't take long for her to realize what Dez was doing and take matters in her own hands, straddling her lover's belly. She sat down and started rubbing her wetness on Dez's hard belly. Her pussy was both soft and rough on Dez's skin. She groaned from the distraction of wanting it on her mouth, to feel those bristly hairs under her nose, the slippery cunt-flesh around her tongue. Victoria laughed and arched her back, pushing her breasts more into Dez's face and sliding her pussy in long strokes on her belly.

"Do you know how badly I want to eat you right now?"

"Apparently not badly enough. Your mouth is in the wrong place." She wiggled and slid up Dez's body again. Her mouth went slack with sensation. Dez grabbed her ass cheeks, held them wide, and slid her fingers between her flesh and Victoria's body. Victoria hissed as the fingers moved inside her.

"Yeah, it is." But she liked to delay her own pleasures. Instead she fucked Victoria slowly with her fingers, watching her move above her, hands anchored on Dez's shoulders as she massaged her clit on Dez's belly.

Her mouth went dry staring at this woman. At the deep inhalations that lifted her breasts to heaven, her face beatific in its concentration on pleasure, the black hair between the legs, the fat clit peeking out, intent on its mission of bliss. She could watch her all day and not get tired of the sight. Well, maybe not all day. She abruptly took her fingers away and, with a hand firmly on Victoria's ass, flipped them over on the bed.

"I'm suddenly not so lazy anymore."

She hitched Victoria's knee high on her hip bone. Victoria chuckled, then arched her neck as Dez's fingers slid inside her again, deeper. "Hm, I'm very happy to hear that."

Then she couldn't talk, she couldn't seem to catch her breath, couldn't stop coming with Dez fucking her, legs spread wide on the bed, Dez's fingers in her mouth, sucking on them as her pussy sucked on the fingers of Dez's other hand, pulling them deeper with each spasm. She floated down the peak of her come. Dez pulled her fingers from Victoria's mouth now, dragged them down her chin, to her throat. Sweating and limp with hair clinging to her face and mouth, Victoria rolled over and stared at the ceiling. Dez's heart beat deep and loud in her chest, keeping time with the throb between her legs. She wanted to touch again. She wanted to come again. But she loosened her thighs and leaned back in the bed to watch her lover instead. Her mouth was slack and full, beautiful in the aftermath of her orgasm. Dez had never seen a more desirable or delectable woman. Victoria stirred, then turned to look at her.

"Is it true what Derrick says about you?"

Dez watched her with lazy eyes. "It depends. What does my handsome and talented brother say about me?"

"That you . . ." she smiled, pressing the backs of her fingers to her mouth, and turned again in the sun. "That you've had many women, many ways. That there's nothing you don't know about sex."

"Damn. I didn't know I had it like that." Dez had to laugh at her brother's exaggeration. What was he doing speculating about her sex life anyway?

"I think he's a little jealous of you sometimes. Even when you were away he couldn't stop talking about you."

"And my sex life, too, apparently."

Victoria looked delicate and young, barely like the thirty-six-year-old that she claimed to be as she stared at Dez from behind the curtain of her hair. "I've never been very adventurous. The women I've been with have been a lot like Derrick, I'm a little ashamed to say."

Not unexpected, though, Dez thought, tracing the fine skin over Victoria's ribs with her thumb.

"They've been very reliable. Very sweet. Good in bed, but nothing—" she blushed. "—nothing to scream about."

"And you think I'll be any different?"

"So far, you have been." She rolled over on her stomach and looked beyond Dez to the window. "You make me want to try things. *Be* different."

Dez chuckled and ran her hands over her lover's ass. "I can't promise you anything new, baby. I can only be me."

"That's all I want. I just wanted you to know that you don't have to hold back with me. I can take it, whatever you want."

"Really? That's not what you said to me the other night at the bookstore."

"That was for our first time. It's different now."

Dez breathed in the knowledge of her surrender. It left a pleasant feeling in her, something tingling and warm that she didn't want to look at too closely.

"All right. I don't think that I'll invite you into anything you can't handle. But if I do, I want you to tell me to stop."

"Of course I will." Her tone was playful as she rubbed herself against Dez.

"I'm serious. Take a safe word. Please." Dez tried to think of the least sexual thing to Victoria, something that even in the midst of pain, she would remember. "Veronique. That's what I want you to say, if." She gathered a handful of Victoria's hair and gently forced her to meet her eyes. "Understand?"

Victoria quieted. "I understand. And what about you? What word will you use?"

Dez laughed. "I won't need one. Anything you can dish out I can take."

"Sure of yourself, aren't you?"

"No. Not really." The truth surprised Dez into a moment of quiet. "Especially not where you're concerned."

"Good." Victoria brushed her fingers along her sides, prompting another burst of laughter. She drew back, surprised. "You're ticklish?"

"No."

She tickled her again. Dez's laughter erupted, uncontrollable and deep. She knew that at any moment she could stop Victoria, could clasp her wandering hands together and imprison them against her chest. But she enjoyed the feel of the full naked breasts against her own, the slide of her skin and effervescent laughter. Victoria proved herself to be merciful and ceased her tender torture. They lay close, each breathing heavily, legs tangled together. Dez kissed her slightly parted lips. "Cancer," she breathed against her mouth. "My safe word is cancer."

Chapter 19

"Sage isn't half-bad," Dez said, sizing up her friend as the smaller woman sauntered across Gillespie's main stage, her Jamaican accent lost in the bluesy strains of "Me and Mrs. Jones."

The lights sought out the tattoos curling up the side of Sage's neck each time she turned her head. Like most things she wore, the black Armani suit and silk shirt fit her well, flowing over her muscles and taut skin.

"Shit. She's fucking amazing." Phil lounged back in her chair, arm spread out behind Dez as she watched her lover with a cat's-creamed smile.

"I just can't believe that you two are together."

"Sometimes I can't believe it either. She was right under my nose all these years and I had no idea," Phil said.

The woman at a corner table in the club, the one who was the "Mrs. Jones" of the moment, flashed her gaze over Sage like the Jamaican woman was something forbidden, thus completely irresistible. Her man was oblivious.

"And this open relationship thing actually works for you?"

"Yeah, why wouldn't it?" Her friend looked at her in surprise. "I can have any woman I want, anytime. But I also have this gorgeous, sexy beast of a woman at home waiting for me every night. We only have one rule: If I call, she drops whatever sex thing going on and comes home. I do the same thing for her."

"I think I'd be too jealous in something like that. I like to have exclusive rights to the pussy."

"Which is why you and I aren't fucking."

Dez laughed. "Too right."

Onstage, Sage slowly dropped to her knees, spreading her thighs wide and showing off the subtle bulge of her dick.

"She is *so* wicked." Phil giggled and leaned closer to the stage. Her lover winked at her.

Sage didn't sing often, but when she did she liked to do it onstage where everyone could see. If possible, she was even cockier in the spotlight, all strut and butch appeal, flirting with dykes and straight girls alike as her girlfriend watched and admired from her choice seat. Everyone at their table, and maybe others, knew that Sage had fucked the slim woman with the long legs and acres of hair weave. According to Mrs. Jones, it hadn't been half-bad. She and Sage had taken her out for a long test drive together.

The final notes of the song tapered off amid the crowd's enthusiastic applause. Sage grinned and tried to look humble. She and Phil smiled at each other across the crowded club and she rolled up her sleeves, laying bare tattoos and muscle and the shaky heterosexual status of some women in the place. Her next song was "Fever."

Dez had to laugh. Sage was wicked, but that was one of the reasons she got so much pussy. She nodded at Rémi as her friend sat down. The club owner was working tonight, cultivating her exclusive clientele by sitting and chatting with some regulars and anyone she recognized as new at Gillespie's. With a low sigh she dropped her hat in the middle of the table and stretched out her long legs.

"It's nice and packed tonight," Phil said.

"Like damn near every night." Dez lifted her beer in a silent toast. "Excellent investment idea, man. Excellent."

"Of course. Although sometimes it does get a little tiring."

"Maybe if you weren't up all night fucking, you'd feel more rested," Dez grinned.

"Hm. Good point."

Phil chuckled. "Very good point." She briefly looked at the waitress who was setting down their various refills before turning her attention back to her girlfriend on the stage.

Dez salted the back of her hand and downed a shot of tequila. The liquor rubbed against the back of her throat as it went down smoothly like warm silk. She was taking it easy tonight. Beer and tequila, that was it. Her blood felt pleasantly fizzy and, while she wasn't drunk, everything was *very* all right with the world. It had been almost a week since that amazing morning at Victoria's house. Since then, they'd been together over a dozen times, whenever the bookstore owner could spare time in her schedule for a long, leisurely fuck. Dez didn't quite like the idea of a quickie with her—everything with this one needed to be savored—but she wouldn't rule out the idea if it was her only option.

"Oh, there's a cute one," Rémi nudged her. "I bet she likes to wrestle."

She turned in her chair to look where Rémi had indicated with a jerk of her chin. Dez took in the bald head and tall lanky body just making its way into the club and nodded in agreement. Then she saw the woman's face. *Figures.* Just her luck, the woman turned and saw Dez checking her out. Never one to back away from even a potential challenge, Dez winked and pursed her lips at Mick. She knew Victoria's little friend wouldn't appreciate the gesture, but what the hell?

"You know her?" Rémi asked.

"Something like that."

Phil joined in the conversation. "Was it worth it?"

"Not really." Especially not with the bullshit she put her through at the dinner party a few weeks ago.

"Too bad," Phil said.

"Yeah." Dez stood up. "I'm heading to the ladies' room. Be right back."

*   *   *

Dez wove through the crowded club to the relative quiet of the back hallway leading to the bathroom. She felt a presence behind her but paid it little attention. As she hesitated at the left turn into the bathrooms, someone pushed her past the toilets to the vestibule farther down the hallway that led to the club's back exit. Dez grunted as her back hit the wood-paneled wall. *What the fuck?*

"You don't fool me, you little bitch." Mick pressed against her, breath hot against Dez's mouth. "Sniffing after Tori like you're just filled with good intentions."

"Obviously you don't remember a thing about me." Dez grinned. "I'm not 'little' anywhere." She held her arms flat against the wood paneling of the hallway, not touching Victoria's friend. "Go home to your girlfriend." Dez moved her arms, a subtle demand for release, but Mick apparently wasn't ready to leave.

"Why don't you leave Tori alone? She's a nice girl who deserves better than anything you have to offer."

"I'm not in the mood for this." Dez abruptly brought her thigh up, firmly between Mick's legs. "Why are you all in my shit? Kavi not giving it to you good at home? Does she fuck you so good that it makes you cry? Like I did." Rough breath jerked against her face as Mick twitched against her then backed away. Dez chuckled. "Mind your own fucking business, *Michelle*." Then she shoved her off. The woman's back hit the wall on the other side of the hallway, but she immediately bounced back and came for Dez.

"Don't do it, little girl." Her glance flickered down the hall with its steady trickle of female patrons trying not to look their way. "I won't play nice with you this time."

Mick stopped. Her eyes scraped Dez with a look, then she backed off, walking back down the hallway from where she came. Dez leaned back against the wall, looking after Victoria's friend and watchdog with a frown. *Women. Jeezus!*

Chapter 20

"**Y**ou are without a doubt the best fuck buddy I've ever had." Victoria panted from the rumpled sheets.

Dez pushed herself off the bed and stood up. With not-quite-steady hands, she tucked in her shirt, pulled up her zipper, buckled her belt and smoothed the phantom wrinkles from her pants. "And you've had how many?" A smile misted across her mouth.

With her body bare and glistening from the sweat of their sex, Victoria lay beautiful and replete in her bed. The damp sprawl of her thighs exuded its tempting, briny scent, a scent that still lingered on Dez's mouth and fingers. She licked her lips and something in that action reminded Dez of last night. She hadn't bothered mentioning the scene with Mick at Gillespie's to Victoria. If the bald-headed woman never said anything to her friend, why should she?

"Just you, but I'm very sure that you'd have been exceptional even if there had been twelve or twenty."

"I'm flattered."

"Don't be. You know it's the truth. You're good at what you do."

She stopped in the act of reaching for her keys on the floor. "You make me sound like a whore."

"Nothing so common, love." Victoria slid up the bed and collapsed against the pillows. "Never anything so common."

Then she saw the look on Dez's face. "What? Does that offend you? It shouldn't."

But Dez was. Granted she was the one who'd suggested this arrangement. And so far it was working out for them both. Sex nearly every day without the lurking specter of commitment and enough spicy encounters to keep Victoria's appetite for variety satisfied. But she didn't sign on to be the disposable stud service. "It's not simply about offense—" The doorbell interrupted whatever she was going to say next.

"Who on earth is that?" Victoria sat up in the bed. "I'm not expecting anybody." She stood up and put on her robe. "Don't go anywhere. I want us to talk about this."

Dez watched her go. Victoria had called an hour earlier sounding urgent and sexy as hell, her voice low and rough. "I need you now." She murmured something about her fingers and being wet, but Dez didn't need to know any more. She was already cutting across three lanes of traffic and heading for Victoria's house. She had been on the way to meet her mother and Derrick but called them quickly to let them know that she was going to be a few minutes late. Dez rang the doorbell, intrigued but hardly expecting Victoria to drag her inside, pull her pants down, her mouth already open to feast on her pussy. She hadn't been surprised like that in a long time. And Victoria was very good, eating her pussy past the first orgasm into a second, then dragged her, with her pants still pooled around her ankles, to the bedroom. It was then that Dez took control, filling the drenched woman with three fingers and latching onto her clit with a dry mouth that hungered. And because she had come when she called, Victoria called her a whore.

She pocketed her keys and left the bedroom. Downstairs, Victoria stood in the hallway talking to her visitors. Her normally low and melodious voice was high with surprise.

"We can finish our conversation later," Dez said, walking past her and two older women in the sunlit entranceway.

"Oh . . . um . . . don't . . ." She cleared her throat. "Okay. I'll call you later on."

"Did we interrupt something, darling?" one of the women asked.

"No, Mom—"

"Of course we did. We can just get a hotel or drive around for a while until you finish up here." The second woman stared at Dez with open curiosity. When she saw that no one was going to begin introductions, she extended her hand. "I'm Delia, by the way, Victoria's mamá. This is my wife, Veronique."

Victoria looked even more uncomfortable. "Sorry. Mom, Mamá, this is Dez. A friend."

Dez looked at the women for the first time. Amazingly, they both looked like Victoria. Delia was fine-boned and tall, with her mocha skin, straightened black hair and a white linen trouser suit that made the best of a rail-thin figure. The other was plump and pale with green eyes and a scattering of strawberry freckles across her nose and cheeks. An attractive couple that complemented each other's unique looks. Dez put on her most respectable face, the one she imagined that parents liked to see on the women fucking their daughters, and shook Delia's hand.

"Pleased to meet you both."

Veronique kissed her lightly on both cheeks, then pulled back to look Dez full in the face. "It's good to meet you, too. We've heard a few things about you over the years."

She couldn't hide her surprise. "Have you?"

"Oh, yes."

"But Dez has an appointment somewhere else." Victoria gripped the edges of her robe. "Don't you?"

Dez's smile turned playful. "Unfortunately, I do." She nodded to the women as she turned to go. "See you soon, though."

"Soon" turned out to be later that night when Dez called from outside the door demanding to be let in.

"You've told your parents about me," she said the moment Victoria was close.

"No, I haven't. At least not like that."

"What does that mean?"

"I . . . might have mentioned you a couple of times before we formally met. You know, as Derrick's sister."

"Uh huh. Then why did Veronique look like she wanted to see my innards roasting on a spit when you told her who I was?"

"I have no idea."

"So you don't think of me as your whore, then?" She linked her fingers above the high curve of Victoria's ass and pressed their bodies closer. "Or maybe I'm the whore you mention to your parents on a regular basis."

"Stop saying that. You know I don't think of you that way."

Dez captured her fist and kissed it. "I know. Sometimes I can get a little sensitive."

"No kidding."

The sound of laughing voices came from somewhere in the house. Victoria closed the front door and stepped outside, pulling Dez with her.

"You have to go now. My parents are in the guest bedroom upstairs."

"So does that mean you're not in the mood for a little quickie?" Dez nuzzled at her throat and slid her thumbs over Victoria's nipples that were already stiff from the cool night air.

"No, that's—" she groaned and arched her breasts toward Dez. "Stop. I mean it. Now go home."

Dez chuckled. "I'm going. Call me later. If your parents' visit is going to dry up my action, then I want to know as soon as they leave."

"Have I told you how awful you are?"

"Not recently."

A smothered giggle tickled Dez's neck. "Go." She smacked Dez's jean-clad backside and pulled away. "I'll call you."

"Yeah, I've heard that before," Dez muttered. But she went anyway, sauntering down the driveway to her bike without a backward glance.

Chapter 21

"Hey, Ma." Dez looked past Claudia to see her brother's lean form spread out on a deck chair by the pool. He was all oiled up and sleek in tiny Speedos and sunglasses reflecting the glare of the sun. "I didn't know you had company."

Dez was restless today. Her mother's company was just what she needed to calm her down, but a family reunion wasn't what she had in mind.

"Your brother isn't company, darling. Come in."

Claudia closed the door and started back toward the sliding glass doors leading outside. "We're having margaritas, do you want one?"

"Sure, why not?" She walked in past her mother, past the Anita Baker and mellow saxophone and past the sunshine that spilled into her house to the pool where her brother looked so comfortable. He didn't quite sneer at her presence but close enough. Dez jerked her chin his way in greeting.

He nodded back, then she saw the occupant of a nearby deck chair, the girl from Claudia's birthday party. What was her name again? She did look nice in a bikini though, with her belly ring, prominent abs, and pert little A-cups in some sort of push-up contraption. Trish, that was her name.

"Good to see you again, Desiree." Her teeth were small and cute, like a little girl's.

"Likewise." She would always mind her manners for a beautiful woman. "You all make me feel overdressed." Dez gestured to her leather jacket, jeans, tank top, and boots. Motorcycle riding gear.

"Then get comfortable, darling. You know where every-thing is." Claudia handed her a salt-rimmed glass only half-filled with a frozen margarita. "You're riding that thing home, I don't want you to get too tipsy and fall off," she said by way of explanation for the small portion. "I'd like to keep my daughter for a few more years."

"You and me both." Dez pulled off her jacket and boots, propping them on an elegant little glass table, before claim-ing a deck chair. She put her drink on the ground next to her.

The sun burned through the gray tank top, warming her chest and belly. What would Derrick say if he had been the one to come over unexpectedly and see her laying out here in the sun with Claudia and Victoria? If she were to introduce the bookstore owner as her girlfriend? He'd probably lose his shit.

"So are you two living together yet?" She looked from her brother to his girlfriend.

"Of course not," Trish glanced at her lover and giggled.

At the same time her brother made a strange noise, some-thing between a growl and a snarl and said, "None of your business. You don't see me asking about your sex life, do you?"

"Not right now, but I hear you've been talking about it with other people."

"That's hard to believe," Derrick said.

"No shit? Well, somehow I believe the source."

"I wouldn't. None of your little friends strike me as reli-able types."

"I won't fault you for that." She licked at the salt on the rim of her glass and grinned at her brother. "You've always been a shitty judge of character."

Claudia looked up from her laughing conversation with Trish to chide her daughter. "Desiree!"

"It's true, Ma. Remember that girl he took to the prom thinking he was guaranteed to get some ass right after—"

"Oh my god, I don't think I want to hear this story," Trish said, but perked up in her seat anyway.

Dez's cell phone vibrated in her pocket, cutting off whatever she was going to say next. Rémi's number flashed on the tiny screen. She answered it. "Hey, what's going on?"

Her friend's voice bled through the background of hard thumping bass. "We're trying to have a four tonight with that girl from Sage and Phil's party. You should come."

"What girl?"

"Remember the one with the coke and the hungry ass."

"Oh, yeah." That had been a nice little party, but the hangover the next day had been its own kind of hell. Not worth a round two, that's for sure. "You go ahead and handle that by yourselves. I'll sit this one out. Call me after."

"Yeah, we'll save the tape for you."

She laughed. Rémi wasn't joking. "Nice."

As Dez slid the phone back into her pocket she bumped into her brother's disapproving sneer.

"Another sex party?"

What happened to their truce? "Excuse me?"

"Isn't that all you and your lazy friends ever do?" Derrick asked. "You all have a rep for that kind of shit. If it wasn't for Tori and her friends I'd think that all lesbians do is fuck anything with a pussy and get high."

"Derrick!"

"I'm not saying anything you don't already know, Mama."

"Maybe so, but I think you may be scandalizing your girl just a little bit." Dez turned to Trish. "You ever heard him curse and carry on like this before? In bed doesn't count."

Claudia looked at her. "Really, Dez. Don't you ever talk of anything but sex?"

"Of course, but most times those things aren't worth mentioning."

"Jesus!" Derrick said, as if that proved whatever point he was trying to make. "I'm just glad that Tori isn't caught up with anyone like you."

"Anyone like me," Dez mocked. "Do you actually think that I would corrupt your sainted Tori?"

"I don't think, I *know* so."

"Shit, I'm sure you don't know half the things your little darling is up to."

"I'm in a better position than you to know any of that, that's for damn sure."

Dez smirked. "You think?"

"All right, that's it." Claudia shook her head and held up her hands. "Desiree Paulette Nichols, stop provoking your brother. And Derrick, please be nice. I wanted to have a relaxing day at home. This isn't it."

"Sorry, Ma," the twins chorused like they'd done a thousand times before. They glanced at each other and shrugged. Dez stood up.

"I'm gonna get a swimsuit from inside. Anyone want anything while I'm up?" When everyone shook their heads, she turned to walk inside the house. "I'll be a much nicer person when I get back. And, if we're all lucky, Derrick will be, too."

He wasn't, neither was she, but they managed not to kill each other in front of their very amused (and sometimes appalled) witnesses. Dez left them to their party of three a few hours later. Maybe it wasn't too late to get in on that foursome Rémi mentioned. Or she could just sit and watch, perhaps even whisper the details of the fuck to Victoria one day when she wanted the bookstore owner to get off by touching herself. It was a nice thought.

Chapter 22

It had been a whole week and three days since Victoria's parents came. And they were still here. Dez wasn't complaining. Much. She and her lover still managed to talk on the phone although Victoria refused to give herself relief with a little harmless phone sex.

"My parents are in the house!" she'd hissed when Dez suggested it.

Now Dez was well into the second week of forced abstinence and she didn't like it at all. She knew that she could get it from somewhere else, had even tried it a couple of times, but it wasn't quite the same. No one could moan quite the way Victoria did, with that sexy sound low in the back of her throat that built into an explosion from her wet mouth. Dez squirmed in her chair at Novlette's Café and forced herself to pay attention to what was going on around her.

The restaurant was packed, as usual. Lazy weekend chatter along with the playful squeal of babies and their goo-goo talking minders jostled the air, giving the late Sunday morning just the right amount of restorative energy that Dez and her friends needed.

Of the five women, only Rémi was missing. She was out of town for the weekend, wrangled against her will to some family thing that she hoped wouldn't blow up in her face.

Still, she'd been cheerful when Dez dropped her off at the airport on Saturday night.

Nuria tapped Dez's hand. "You still with us, baby?"

"Where else would I go?" Dez murmured.

Last night, Nuria had followed two rough-looking butches home to their dungeon in Buena Vista. Today she oozed pure sexual contentment in her loose-fitting silk pants and thin, low-cut blouse that did nothing to conceal her bruises. Good for her, Dez thought. Every few minutes Nuria would smile at nothing, especially if that nothing was in Dez's direction.

"Good question," Nuria said just as softly.

Sage was telling a story to the table at large, something not very funny about her latest escapade, but Sage, with her wildly gesticulating arms and exotic tattoos, was simply fun to watch. She was like a dragonfly—quick, beautiful, and ravenous. Between every other word she stabbed food on a plate—sometimes her own, other times not—and wrestled it into her mouth. Then something distracted Dez from the story. A smell. That distinct combination of citrus and honey that meant only one thing. Or more specifically, one person.

She looked up in time to see the curve of Victoria's ass disappear around the corner to one of the quieter dining areas. Veronique and Delia were nowhere in sight. After ten minutes, a more than respectable amount of time, she thought, Dez stood up.

"Excuse me, ladies. Piss stop."

Phil sent her a wry look. "Thanks for the visual, Dez." Sage stopped her story long enough to grab something from Dez's plate and smile around a mouthful of food. "Hurry and come back, man. It's just getting good."

It didn't take her long to find Victoria. She sat at a large corner table with half a dozen other women, perched in her chair and leaning toward a squat woman in a pink dress. The woman shook her head at Victoria and pointed at the notebook in front of them. Dez walked past the table, pausing just long enough to brush Victoria's shoulder and let her know with a tilt of her head where she was going. She didn't have to wait long.

"This is a nice surprise," she said when she met Dez in the bathroom a few moments later. Her lover pulled her into an oversize bathroom stall. Dez touched her throat and her waist, reacquainting herself before slanting her mouth over Victoria's.

Victoria made a small noise, parting her lips that tasted of cold orange juice. Their mouths and tongues slid together in a deep kiss that drove Dez's hands seeking under her dress. Victoria gasped and hooked her knee on Dez's waist.

Dez slid her panties aside and slipped a finger into her wetness. "Damn . . ." She groaned into Victoria's mouth. "You feel so fucking good."

She dropped to her knees and swept Victoria's knee over her shoulder. The shorter woman's back hit the delicate wall of the bathroom stall and her panties ripped. Her mouth found Victoria salty and slick. She made needful noises in the back of her throat before she recalled where she was. Dez was a pro at illicit sex. She knew better than to make noise. She palmed the heavy globes of Victoria's ass, pressing the heat of her lover's pussy against her face as she swept her tongue inside her one last time before feasting on the fat clit that was begging for attention. Dez sucked it into her mouth, caressing it with her tongue in long, hard strokes. Victoria liked that. She gasped Dez's name and pushed her legs even wider apart. Her pussy danced against Dez's mouth, snaking faster and faster until Victoria was bucking, a wild ride that Dez had to get a tight grip on or fall off.

The trembling started in the thighs pressed against her cheeks, her ass shuddered with the impending come. Dez worked her tongue faster and the shudders increased. Over the liquid noise of her tongue lapping at the sweetly weeping pussy she could hear Victoria's gasping breath, the pre-orgasmic pants that shook her body. She hoped to God there wasn't anybody else in the damn bathroom. But she was fast approaching the point of not giving a shit. Her pussy was swimming, wet and hot and fucking ready to explode inside her pants. She wanted to touch herself, slide her fingers past her open zipper and fuck herself to where Victoria was now. But her lover wasn't finished yet.

Dez felt Victoria's fingers curl into the back of her head. Half moons of pain waxed beneath those desperate fingers. She slid two fingers inside her lover and gasped as the contractions started, sucking her fingers deeper in, and squeezing them like a vice. Cream rushed over her chin in a flood. Victoria's thighs relaxed as she collapsed against the stall. Her ass twitched in Dez's hands.

"Damn. I wasn't expecting that." Her voice shook on the last word.

"You should know better after leaving me to stew in my own juices for over a week." Dez kissed her thigh and stood up. "Thanks."

Victoria rolled her head against the gray partition and licked her lips. Her hands tugged open the belt at Dez's jeans, and eased the zipper down. The pants slithered down her ass and caught at the widest part of her thighs. "What can I do for you, baby?"

Dez growled when those seeking hands found her drenched cunt. "Not a thing. You already did it." She readjusted Victoria's skirt and started to pull away. "I have to get back outside."

Victoria's hands stopped her. "Are you sure you don't have time for—"

Electric fingers nudged her clit. Dez's legs widened despite her resolve, giving the other woman better access. Victoria kissed her cheek and nibbled on her jaw line.

"Don't be selfish, Desiree." Her tongue stroked Dez's lips and chin, licking away all traces of wetness from her face.

The last thing that she wanted was to be selfish. She wanted to share all this, the liquid fullness of her pussy, her clit fat and hard under Victoria's clever hand, the tingling rush of arousal, the hum of the blood through her veins. Her hips arched up to meet each stroke of her lover's fingers. Dez's eyes fell closed to hold the sensations closer, to slip her entire consciousness into the fever of desire raging through her body. This was like no other quick fuck she'd ever done. Each moment was a slow revelation of feeling. This was her nipples stiffening, peppering against her shirt into tight little buds of almost-pain, her breath shallowing in her throat, eyelashes fluttering beyond her control, and the jump of her pussy like a fish snapping for a bite of the dangerously forbidden. She groaned.

Victoria heard her wordless plea and filled her, two fingers in her pussy, one in her ass, her thumb hard against her clit. She had learned Dez well in the last two weeks. Her fingers played her in tandem, strumming her clit, stroking her hard and deep until she couldn't focus. She forgot the bathroom, forgot the need for quiet. Thunder rolled inside her head, tumbling through her body until she shook with it, her body rattling the gray partition. Dez came so hard she bit her lip.

"Fuck!" Her hips trembled out of control, thrusting and shivering against her lover's hand. A long while later, she drew a deep breath in Victoria's hair. "That wasn't very nice."

"Oh, but it was." She kissed Dez quickly on the mouth. "Now I have to get back."

Dez waited until Victoria had already washed up and left before she tumbled out of the stall. She washed her face and hands, rinsed her mouth before heading back to the table.

"We were about to send a search party in there for you," Phillida said.

"But then I told her that unless she wanted to see you bare-assed and fucking some anonymous girl, then it's best to wait it out." Sage grinned.

"That true, Dez?" Phil's look was incredulous. "Did you get lucky in the john?"

"Of course not. Just, you know, a shaky stomach. I mixed up a bad batch of piña coladas this morning." She sipped her lemon-spiked water, then winced at her sore lip. "So, what did I miss?"

Chapter 23

Finding pleasure was something that Dez had always done very well. When she was fourteen and her life at home was falling apart, she'd forced her raging insides to a sort of calm when she dragged herself and her friends to the amusement park and lost herself in the adrenaline rush of the fastest roller coasters, the most gravity-defying rides, and every calorie-rich, grease-laden foods that the park had to offer. Around the same time, her good looks started to blossom, becoming noticeable despite the perpetual scowl on her face, or perhaps because of it. Older women started to make offers that she eagerly accepted. Then she was introduced to other pleasures, instructed on how to eat pussy, to finger fuck, and the proper way to wear and use a dildo. She was a good student. In a few short years she'd discovered many ways to please her senses—food, drugs, sex, exercise, adrenaline.

Fucking Victoria was a new pleasure in itself. The taste between her legs was addictive. She found herself wanting to feel the wet, undulating pussy under and around her tongue all the time. She wanted to hear the music of her moans, the high, choked cries of her reaching orgasm, to feel the tense line of her damp calf draped down her back. Her senses sharpened when Victoria was near. She smelled her, could hear and anticipate her breath. Her own pussy opened and swelled, her mouth went dry at the thought of tasting her. Being with her was like free-falling—breathless wonder, a tilted world, awareness sharp, the feeling that she was ready for anything, yet when *it* came she found out that she wasn't ready at all.

Of course, she couldn't tell Victoria any of these things. This was only a fuck thing, after all.

Chapter 24

"You look like you're getting yours from somewhere on the regular."

Sage jerked her chin at Dez over their breakfast. Phil glanced at them from behind her dark glasses and sipped from her usual cup of Jamaican Blue Mountain dark roast.

"You sure do," she said in her gravelly morning voice. "Anybody I know?"

"Better yet, anyone you want to introduce us to?" Rémi's look was merciless. "The last time a woman had that much stamina you weren't shy about sharing her with us. Want to do it again?"

She knew damn well there was no way Dez was going to share Victoria with anyone. Rémi also didn't see the point of Dez keeping her new fuck buddy a secret from everybody, but that was a whole other, private, discussion.

"Are you sure it's only one girl?" Nuria murmured. "*If* it's a girl."

Sage pointed a strip of turkey bacon at Dez and wagged it at her friend. "How long has this been going on?" Her teasing tone said she was only mildly interested. After all, what else was there to talk about at eleven on a Sunday morning when half the women at the table were barely awake.

"It's been at least three weeks," Phil answered for Dez. "Remember the first time she came in here all smiley-smiley. I thought it was just a great lay the night before, now I see it's been three weeks of great lays."

"Look at her face," Sage grinned. "I think we just found our girl out."

"Did she make it into your bedroom yet?" Nuria glanced around the table with a raised eyebrow and a smile. "You know if she's still fucking her in the guest room that it's not really serious."

Dez shook her head, but said nothing. The waitress came back just then with Rémi's extra order of honey-almond pancakes and whipped cream. She bobbed between Dez and Rémi, smiling nervously even as she deftly slipped the plates in front of the muscular, bare-armed woman. Rémi had that effect on most women.

Dez's eyes automatically dropped to the waitress's modest sized bosom beneath the yellow "Novlette's Café" lettering stitched on her red blouse. Nice, but no contest where Victoria's succulent C-cups were concerned.

"You didn't find out anything." Dez said after the waitress left. "Can't a woman have a good time without getting the third degree from her friends?"

"Only when the friend isn't hiding anything."

"I'm just seeing someone new." Dez made a throw-away motion. "Nothing too serious, but it's fun. We're going to keep it that way and under wraps for a little while."

"Why? You think one of us will take her away from you?" Sage smirked, looking at Rémi.

The women had played so many games in the past, it was sometimes hard to keep track of who was and wasn't for sport. In college, they often played seduction games with one another's girlfriends, betting who could steal a girl the fastest. Usually they had to put it out there early on if the woman they were seeing was not part of the game. Did they really have to do that now? They were grown women now, for chrissakes, not kids with toys. But . . .

"This one's all mine, ladies. Hands off."

Dez didn't want to share Victoria. No one else was going to feel the slack weight of Victoria's body, damp and heavily scented after orgasm, the slow aroused smile that sometimes greeted her at the door, the pillows of her ass resting against Dez's cheeks as she took her from behind and heard the moans that left Victoria's body as her control began to give way.

"If we don't know who she is, how can we tell her no when she comes sniffing around?"

Dez aimed a glance at Phil. "Trust me. You'll know."

"All this secrecy is making me very curious," Nuria said.

"It's not secrecy, it's caution. Just give me a little time, will you? If this thing doesn't work out, then she won't want it to get out that we even knew each other."

"Really?" Rémi perked up. "Is she slumming?"

The corner of Dez's mouth quirked up. "Yeah."

"Well, that wouldn't be a first. Remember that girl from Morningside who had a fiancé?"

Sage grinned. "Oh, yes. She definitely didn't mind being shared."

The women laughed. They remembered the girl well, especially since she gave them all crabs. It was only funny in retrospect.

After they left the restaurant, Dez called Lady G's and asked them to deliver a box of dark chocolate–covered strawberries to Victoria. For reasons she didn't feel like exploring at the moment, she needed to know that the other woman was thinking about her. Dez stepped into the bright afternoon and sighed deeply at the warmth of the sun on her face. She briefly thought of smoking a cigarette then, remembering Victoria's distaste, decided against it. Intent on nudging Victoria out of her thoughts, she allowed her friends to talk her into extending their Sunday outing. They drove to the beach in Phil's Mustang convertible and spent the rest of the day spread out on blankets, drinking, smoking, and reeling in any woman who happened to glance their way.

At sunset, Dez was the only one of the five friends who didn't have someone to occupy her hands or her attention. Sage and Rémi took their oversize blanket some distance down the beach to entertain a greedy college girl who insisted on having them both. Phil and her new friend, one with a penchant for fast cars and girls in high heels, held hands and snuggled close as they walked on the sand. Nuria had offered to keep Dez company, but when Dez kindly refused the offer, her friend went skinny-dipping with the Queen Latifah–looking "straight girl" who'd followed them from the restaurant. Nuria made sure that Dez saw the way that her white thong and wispy bra clung to her body before she ran into the water with her new butch. Subtlety was never quite her thing. Dez ignored her, snuggling deeper into her mound of blankets, and tried not to think of Victoria.

Chapter 25

"Can I spend the night?" Dez asked Claudia over the phone, her voice still groggy from the previous night's sleep.

She wanted her mommy. Simple really, and not the most mature of feelings, but that was what she needed and she needed it now. The girl was confusing her. She was confusing herself over the girl. Nothing was clear to her. The simplicity of her mother's company, the certainty that she loved her and wanted nothing in return was what Dez needed right now.

Of course her mother said yes, and she went about the business of her day floating on the warm pillow of anticipation and relief that she would see Claudia again. The day lasted longer than she had expected, ending too late at a party in Palm Beach that she'd been too sober to enjoy. At three in the morning, she showed up at her mother's house, stinking of other people's excess. Dez felt so tired that she trembled with the effort to stay upright. After giving her daughter a worried once-over, Claudia dragged her inside and put her promptly to bed.

In the morning, Dez felt human and alive again. She yawned, popping the gaping hinge of her jaw as her bare feet hit the bottom stair, then stopped short. Her mother was humming. The tune sounded vaguely like the one coming from the local jazz station—Winton Marsalis—and blended strangely enough with the scent of the garden just beyond the screened window, jasmine and peonies, blooming beneath the harsher smells of nail polish and nail-polish remover.

"Good morning, love." Claudia screwed the cap back on the bottle of nail polish and set it in a neat row with her other pedicure paraphernalia on the coffee table. "Restful night?"

"Very. Thanks for tucking me in." She brushed her lips across her mother's forehead and sat down on the couch. "You look like a regular lady of leisure."

"I *am* on sabbatical, you know. At some point I'll get back to writing that book, but for now I'll just enjoy not feeling sick and not doing a thing I don't want to." She reached for a box of cotton swabs, sliding Dez an impish look.

Claudia glowed, as if the news that she was better had freed her to be beautiful again. Even her hair was regaining its old thickness, though the salted black curls were straighter than they used to be. Soon it would be time for another haircut.

"It's cool." Dez held her hands up. "Don't get excited. If anyone can appreciate the fine art of doing nothing, it's me. I'm sure the university can go another semester without you if they had to. The kids will be starved for that sexy version of French lit that you teach, but they can wait."

"They will, and the school will wait, too," Claudia said. "By the way, there's French toast and scrambled eggs in the kitchen if you want some. Strawberries and yogurt, too."

"Thanks." Dez watched her carefully clean off the excess polish with a cotton swab, tracing around one toenail then another. It triggered an old memory. "Remember when Aunt Paul used to get her nails done?"

Claudia looked up, tilting her head to one side. "Oh, yes." She laughed. "I used to wonder what those girls did besides sit around in little shorts and paint her toes."

"She was a femme who loved femmes."

"I think she was a bit of a slut. Not unlike you, my love."

Dez looked at her mother, at the old teasing smile then the glint of silver from the ring on her toe. "Oh, please. If you looked this good you'd spread it around, too. Aunt Paul knew what she was doing. And so do I."

"I'll take your word on that one."

Claudia finished the ritual with her toenails then held out the bottle of nail polish and an upraised hand, wordlessly asking Dez to paint her fingernails the same sparkling shade of green as her toes. Dez draped her offered fingers over her upraised knee and unscrewed the bottle.

"What was it like being in love with Warrick?" she asked. The question came out of nowhere, catching them both by surprise. But Dez didn't take it back.

Her mother looked at her quietly, as if gauging the sincerity of her question.

"Painful," she said finally. "But in the beginning when he loved me too it was perfect. As clichéd as it may seem, we fit together like pieces of the same puzzle. Are you—?"

"No. She and I are just hanging out." Dez looked at her mother and raised an eyebrow for emphasis. "Casually."

Claudia gazed down at her nails, watching the color bleed from the tiny brush her daughter wielded. "I was actually going to ask you about Ruben. But that answered my question, too."

Dez felt herself flush under her mother's laughing gaze. She snapped the cap back on the bottle and gave the polish an unnecessary shake.

"Who is she? Someone you shouldn't be messing with?"

"Mom, please."

Claudia laughed again. "Fine. Just don't smudge my nails. You'll only have to redo them later."

"Don't worry. That won't happen." Dez finished up the second coat of polish and put the bottle away.

The soft, translucent ovals of her nails looked harder beneath their coat of war paint, their frailty brushed away by the green-tipped brush.

"Ruben did to me what Warrick did to you." She took an experimental breath. "It was hard at first, but he doesn't exist to me anymore." The coldness of her voice surprised her. It seemed too final. But mentally probing the edges of her wound, she realized that it *was* final. It was over. Her Ruben pain had healed, leaving behind only a faint tenderness. She pushed it aside.

"You look all shiny and new with your polish." Dez admired her handiwork in the light. "Come for a ride on the bike with me. You can't keep all this loveliness to yourself."

"Don't be ridiculous. I'm not getting on that thing." But her voice lacked the same conviction it had two years, or even two months ago. She giggled, actually covering her mouth with her hands, as Dez waggled her eyebrows and grinned.

"Come on. Whatever happened to seize the carp and all that? Or was it just talk?"

"Of course it was."

But she allowed Dez to drag her off the couch and upstairs to zip into something a little less comfortable. They left the house, breakfast uneaten and, after much laughter and "wait, I'm not ready" and "quit messing around" and other assorted teasing, they hopped on the black cherry Ducati and roared off into the city. Claudia's surprised laughter fanned out behind them in the breeze.

Later that night, she sat with her foursome at Gillespie's, letting the night's goodwill put her nicely out of her head. Though Nuria's smart-ass comments were starting to nudge her into the opposite of a good mood.

"So exactly who is this girl you're fucking?" Nuria asked. "She can't be any better than me," she added, ignoring the fact that she and Dez had never had sex.

Dez took a bite of her calamari and glanced around the bar, ignoring Rémi's amused look. Nuria's red mouth plumped into a pout when she murmured, "How can you be so sure?" in response to her comment.

"Dez, isn't that your mother?" Phil asked.

Their whole table turned to see Claudia and Eden with a group of people that none of the girls had ever met. The three men in the group were Claudia's age, well-groomed and successful-looking, while the other three women looked like real classy pieces, gorgeous and refined, if you liked that type.

Rémi looked across the room where her friend had discreetly nodded. "Yeah, that's Claudia. I didn't know that she was dating anyone."

"Me neither," Dez said.

Across the room, Claudia laughed and put her hand on the shoulder of the man closest to her. He looked familiar. Something Dez did must have drawn her mother's attention, because in the next moment the older woman excused herself and made her way over to their table.

"Hello, darling." She bent down to brush her cheek against Dez's. "I didn't know you liked jazz."

The other women at the table quickly made room for Claudia, urging her to sit down. Sage held a chair for her.

"I didn't know you liked that sort." Dez nodded her head at the group her mother just left.

"Very funny. They're more exciting than they look." Then mother and daughter laughed, leaning in toward each other like young girls. "I know they seem boring, love. But they wanted to come here and see what all the buzz was about. You remember my friend Kincaid, don't you?" Dez nodded, suddenly recalling their brief meeting at Novlette's a few weeks ago. "Well, he said this place has been the *It* spot for the last year or so. I think he brought us here to show us that not all bankers were boring."

Dez chuckled again. "Of course they aren't."

"So now that you're here, what do you think of the place, Mrs. N?"

"It's nice. Not bad. The crowd is fun and eclectic, not what I expected at all. And the music is wonderful." The last notes of a moody guitar solo tapered off to the heartfelt applause of the audience. "Do you girls come here a lot?"

"We do, but we don't really want to. Rémi forces us to come here at least twice a week and spend all our hard-earned money."

"I'm sure you noticed how they're all hurting for cash and a good time." Rémi turned her crooked smile on Claudia.

Dez watched their byplay with amusement. If her mother wasn't straight and didn't know better, she'd worry about her falling for Rémi's charm.

"Your little club is not all that," Sage said. "I'm sure Miami dykes and their friends could find somewhere else in this town with hot women, strong-ass drinks, and a fuckable local celebrity for an owner." She looked around the table. "And make sure you gals tell me when you find that place." Her friends laughed.

"This place is yours, Rémi?"

"Yes, ma'am. With a little help from an investor or two." Her gaze moved briefly to Dez.

Claudia's surprised smile widened. "I see."

When the waitress bent over the table with her full tray, Sage switched her empty martini glass for a full one and slipped the D-cup server a twenty-dollar tip.

"You keep that up and you'll buy *her* for the night," Dez murmured, watching the girl walk off with a come-fuck-me sway to her hips. Then she remembered that her mother was there.

Claudia's eyes twinkled. "Is that what you spend your money on?"

Dez shook her head. "I don't have to pay for mine, Ma."

Her mother laughed outright then. "Let me go before you girls scandalize me any further." She stood up. "By the way, Rémi, please pass on my compliments to your chef. The calamari is absolutely beyond compare. The best I've had in a long time, if not ever."

"I'll let Rochelle know, Mrs. N," Rémi said. "Thanks."

They watched Claudia go in silence. Dez had told Rémi about the cancer a few weeks before during one of their quieter moments. She smiled at Dez. "Mrs. N looks great."

"Of course, she's my mother."

Nuria made a laughing noise. "That's our Dez, modest to a fault." She sipped her margarita to hide the not-so-nice look she shot Dez. She was jealous. Maddeningly and incomprehensibly jealous, just because Dez wanted someone who was not her. It was driving them both crazy. Dez could count on all her digits and appendages the times she'd told Nuria that nothing would ever happen between them. They were friends. She did not fuck her friends, no matter how hot and willing they were. This "conversation" had been happening since college and things weren't going to change now. Nuria liked her sex with a little spice, and if half the things she told them about her escapades were true, she and Dez would have gotten along very well together in bed. But it was never going to happen. Nuria, however, was persistent. For a cynic, she really was very hopeful.

Dez finished her scotch and signaled the waitress for another one. It was going to be a very long night.

Chapter 26

"I've been thinking about you all day," Dez whispered into the springy nest of Victoria's hair.

She chuckled and slid her palms up under the back of Dez's shirt. "It's barely two o'clock. You've been up for what, an hour already?"

"But it's been a very long hour." On the way over to Victoriana's she'd called herself all kinds of stupid for wanting to see the bookstore owner so badly, especially knowing that she probably wouldn't be able to get anything more than a hug. But her body was glad she came, especially after the night spent in Nuria's snarking company. Her friend's comments—a constant reminder of how much Dez wanted Victoria and not her—released her from the self-imposed exile. She wanted to be with this woman, so why not?

Dez sniffed appreciatively in the front of her blouse, inhaling the subtle mixture of baby powder, tangerines, and sweat between her breasts. Beyond the closed office door, the bookstore buzzed on with its steady stream of Sunday customers.

"I know that I can't have you for too long. I just wanted to give you this." She pressed a package of still-warm zucchini muffins in her hand.

Victoria chuckled. "You're going to make me fat."

"I like to see you eat." She nuzzled her throat and pressed her fingers into the curve of Victoria's waist. When she pulled back, the other woman looked warm and bothered with her nipples rising up behind her cotton blouse and her eyes half-closed. Her mouth begged to be kissed. But she was wearing lipstick. So Dez settled for a few more seconds at her throat. She honestly just wanted to sink inside her and never move again.

"Meet me at my house tonight. I have a surprise for you."

Victoria purred and leaned even closer. "I like surprises."

"Good." She palmed her ass through the skirt. "Now get back to work before I change my mind about being good."

Laughter bubbled up in Victoria's throat as she turned from Dez to open the door. "See you tonight."

The woman behind the counter, Marta, Dez thought her name was, spared them a brief glance as they walked out of the office together. Dez waved good-bye to Victoria and dodged the bookstore full of women in various stages of browsing and headed for the stairs. She felt like whistling.

"Hey, Dez. Where you heading off to in such a hurry?"

For a moment she froze, guilt making her go fifteen degrees colder. She faltered on the stairs with a hand on the banister. Then she chided herself for acting like the other woman in some trashy hetero drama. She'd been caught in worse situations than this and acted more innocent.

"Hey, Derrick. What's going on?"

Her brother, who looked nothing like a lawyer today in his baggy jeans and a designer T-shirt, stood a couple of steps below her on the stairs. "Not much. Just coming by to see Tori. I didn't know you knew about this place."

"Well, you know, unlike your kind, dykes don't have many places to go in this town."

"Hey, calm down. We called a truce, remember?"

A woman slid between them on the stairs. "Excuse me," she said, giving them a censuring eye.

"Sorry. Old bad habits and all that."

He shook his head but didn't seem offended. "I came to

take Tori to lunch. Do you want to come with us? There's always room for one more."

Generous. Unexpected. "No." Then she remembered herself. "After the way we acted when she saw us last together, I doubt she would appreciate my presence."

"I know an excuse when I hear it. You don't want to come and that's cool." He turned to walk up the stairs. "See you around."

Shit. "Then again, since you asked so nicely." She jogged up behind him. He turned to her with a look of surprise and a smile.

"What?" she asked. "Changed your mind already?"

He chose to ignore that. Dez bounced up beside him as he approached Victoria, then waited respectfully while his friend helped a customer find a book. With the crisp smell of books and the prim way the blouse fit over her breasts before falling over the waistband of her skirt, Dez was reminded powerfully of that first fantasy of Victoria she'd had, of pushing her against the back wall of a library and fucking her until her hair flew out of its pins and her blouse drooped off her damp shoulders. She shifted in her jeans and turned to look elsewhere.

"Derrick. You're just on time, as usual." She brushed his cheek with a light kiss. "Let me get my bag." Then she noticed Dez. Before she could speak, Derrick did.

"You remember my sister, don't you? I invited her to come with us. I hope you don't mind. She won't make trouble like last time." He glanced at his twin. "Right, Dez?"

"Trouble's no friend of mine." She slid her hands in her back pockets and looked back at Victoria. "I'll be on my absolute best behavior." Her lover blinked.

Derrick took them to a little restaurant not far from the bookstore, a place she'd been before and came to regularly when she was in the mood for seafood. With the stirrings of irrational jealousy, Dez watched as Derrick held Victoria's chair for her and sat down at her right side. The brunch crowd was just beginning to taper off and some of the waitstaff looked a little tired from the rush. They weren't seated at the table long before a waitress, a perky little thing with short, muscular legs and wire-rimmed glasses perched on her nose, came over to take their order. She flirted shamelessly with the whole table, especially Derrick who tried to look humbled by her attention.

"The seafood here is good," Victoria said after a long silence, seemingly resigned to being trapped between the Nichols twins.

"But the dessert is even better." Dez happened to look up past Victoria then and caught their waitress's eyes on her. She smiled then deliberately turned her gaze away.

"Really? Do you come here a lot?"

"No. Once or twice. Nothing too regular."

"Do you know our waitress?" Why the hell would Derrick ask her that question now?

She made a vague noise and moved her sweating glass of water two inches to the left.

"What do you mean? You've known her once or twice?" Derrick asked. "Nothing too regular."

She felt her face warm under her brother's laughing regard.

"If Dez weren't so finicky about her hygiene and health I'd worry about her and all these women she runs around with."

She was careful not to look at Victoria. "Let's not talk about me right now, Derrick. That's obviously a boring subject."

"No, no. I'm very interested." Victoria smiled at her best friend before turning to Dez. "Go on."

Dez cleared her throat. "There's nothing to tell. Tales of my sexual appetite have been greatly exaggerated." Then the waitress came back, liberally sprinkling her sexy bookworm charm over all three occupants of the table. When she leaned over to serve Victoria's frittata and salad, Victoria put a hand on the girl's arm. "Tell me," she said with a warm smile. "Have you slept with Dez?"

The girl looked surprised. "Dez?"

"This one right here."

"Oh." Her eyes met Dez's and her small shrug seemed to apologize beforehand. "Just once. But it was ages ago." She finished serving their food and sashayed off to another table.

"Well, that answers that question." Dez cleared her throat again and reached for her water. "Now let's move on to something else."

"I don't think I've ever seen you blush before, Dez."

"And you won't live to see it again if you don't quit busting my balls." She pointed her knife at Derrick before cutting into the long strands of linguini in cream sauce on her plate.

He let it go, reluctantly. Victoria's eyes flickered to Dez as she ate, but were unreadable. Was she hurt? Upset? There was no bargain between them, and Dez had made it clear in the beginning that their relationship was about sex and nothing more. Then why did she feel like apologizing? The girl was over a month in the past, a fun quick lay to get through one boring Saturday afternoon. Nothing special. Why had she decided to come here again? Oh yeah, that devil and the urge to meet her brother halfway in this. His friendship bid. What did she think, that Victoria was going to tell all about their arrangement then declare her undying love for Dez so they could go back to her place and fuck? Who the hell knew? Certainly not her.

Dez pried apart her clams, sucked the succulent salty flesh into her mouth while her lover and her brother talked about who knows what nonsense concerning only the two of them.

"I'm thinking about having a birthday party at the beach. Will you come?"

The resulting silence let Dez know that someone was talking to her. "What?"

Her brother repeated the question.

"Sure, I'll come. After all, it's my birthday, too. Isn't it a bit soon to be planning for it?"

Dez poured out the extra cream sauce from her still-steaming plate of fettuccini into a separate bowl, then dissolved a pat of butter into it. She stirred it with a spoon. Derrick shook the pepper shaker over the brew a couple of times.

"It's already February."

"Seriously?" She did a quick count of the days. Spring *was* coming soon. And their birthday usually fell around the first day of the season. March twentieth. "I guess it just goes to show how much I've been paying attention."

"You forget your own birthday?" Victoria smiled, watching Derrick, then Dez, dip small ovals of toasted bread into the small bowl of buttery cream sauce.

"Not often." Dez bit into her bread and chewed slowly, rolling the creamy sauce and doughy honey wheat bread over her tongue. "But don't worry, there are certain things that I never forget." She fell naturally into flirt mode, even with her brother sitting there.

"Like . . . ?"

Dez licked her lips and smiled. "Like what a particular woman likes and how she likes it."

"Leave Tori alone, Dez. She's not your type."

Both women looked at him. "What exactly is my type?" Dez asked.

"Easy."

A burst of startled laughter escaped her. It was true. Usually if a woman wasn't willing after a certain amount of time, she moved on to one who was. Dez was never one to like a challenge. She left those difficult women to Rémi. "True enough." Her smile became positively lecherous. "But it doesn't hurt to look."

"Look somewhere else. Tori isn't interested."

"I like how you're answering for me like I'm not here, Derrick," Victoria said.

"What? I'm just stating the obvious. Am I wrong?" He looked from one woman to the other. "Nothing against my sister. She's a gorgeous woman—good looks run in the family after all—but I can more easily see you with a man than with Dez."

"Damn, Derrick." Dez didn't know whether to be insulted at the disparaging remark against her character or pleased that she'd managed to wear down Victoria's apparently legendary virtue. Her lover was paying close attention to her meal, delicately picking through her frittata for pieces of spicy chorizo that she slid past her speechless lips. "I'd hate to think of what kind of woman you think deserves my attention."

"For a long time I thought you and Rémi would end up getting together."

"What?" Dez chuckled at the thought of her and her best friend in any sort of relationship. They'd probably spend most of their time trying to out-fuck each other. "I'm surprised you get laid as often as you do for someone who knows so little about women."

Victoria snickered around her fork. "Stop it, you two. Let's move on to more interesting topics of conversation. Please."

Dez obliged by smoothly asking about the state's current policy on gays and adoption, a topic that all three had strong opinions on and took them all the way through the rest of their meal and the car ride back to the bookstore. In the parking lot, Dez left them to enjoy the rest of their day, claiming exhaustion as her excuse.

"I hope to see you again soon," she said to her lover.

Victoria smiled.

At nine that night, Victoria called. "I'm sorry, Dez. I can't come over tonight." Her voice sounded weak.

"You all right?"

"Yeah." An awkward laugh floated over the phone lines. "My period started this evening."

"Cramps?"

"Yeah. A little. Actually a lot. I just took something. Right now I'm waiting for it to kick in." Sheets rustled in the background.

"Hm." She glanced at the table set for two with its candles waiting to be lit and the gift-wrapped red leather bustier and matching panties she'd picked up earlier that day. "Listen, I'm coming over. Leave the door unlocked for me. I'll be there in fifteen minutes."

Between pulling her pants on, putting the food away, and grabbing the necessary supplies from the kitchen and bedroom, it actually took her twenty minutes to get to Victoria's door.

"I'm here," she called out before locking the door behind her and heading into her lover's kitchen.

After putting the kettle on the stove, she went upstairs to find Victoria.

"Hey, there."

Victoria sat by the window in a white wicker chair with a blanket pulled over her hips. Her multicolored curls floated around her face, framing its vulnerable softness. The book in her lap fluttered closed when she looked up. She didn't bother to keep her place, just rested a hand lightly on her belly and leaned back in the chair to watch as Dez came closer.

"I can't believe you're here. This is not the sexiest way to see me."

Dez smiled as she knelt by Victoria's chair and took her hands. She placed warm kisses in both her palms. "I'm sure you didn't know this, but I actually have a bit of a fetish for bleeding women." Her smile turned positively rakish, and Victoria laughed weakly. "How are you feeling?"

"Better. The pills are doing something, but I still feel like shit. At least I don't feel like an elephant is trying to pass through my tubes."

"I have the perfect remedy for you. Get in bed. I'll be right back."

Downstairs, she made a pot of raspberry tea sweetened with honey and filled the hot water bottle with water. Her mother did this for her when she was young and it never failed to make her feel better.

"Here, drink this." She wrapped Victoria's hands around the warm mug of tea.

Dez sat on the edge of the bed and checked the water bottle to make certain the cap was secure. Victoria sniffed the steaming brew before touching her pursed lips to the rim of the mug. She took two long sips, then a third before sitting back against the plumped pillows.

"This is very good. Thank you."

"And now for the other," Dez said. "If you'll allow me."

Victoria watched her before nodding to give permission. Dez lifted the T-shirt away from her belly, baring it to her gaze. Victoria's eyes fluttered closed, but she said nothing. When Dez put the bottle across her bare stomach, she jumped.

"Is it too hot?"

"No, it's . . . it's just a bit of a surprise." A smile drifted across her face and she relaxed even more into the sheets. "God! It feels *really* good."

Dez laughed. "Then my job is done." She sat back in the chair that Victoria just vacated and put up her feet. "Lay back and drink your tea. I'll leave after you fall asleep."

But Victoria did not sleep. She finished her tea and sank deeper and deeper into the pillows. "This was very unexpected, you know." She smiled. "It's almost better than what we had planned."

"A hot toddy and bed rest are better than sex with me?" Dez rolled her head to look at Victoria's soft form on the bed. "Don't say that too loud. I have a reputation to maintain."

"I said 'almost.' It's a very far second." She put her empty teacup on the bedside table. "But it was exactly what I needed. Thank you."

"You're welcome." The words were a low hush that vibrated deep in her chest. She had been anticipating their lovemaking all night, and her body was primed for sex. Washed. Shaved. Oiled. Ready. And while Victoria's pain made her go all mushy inside, it made her wet, too. The woman was beautiful, just the scent of her made Dez react. It had never been like this with anyone else. Never. Not even Ruben, who'd made her explore the limits of her sexuality and move beyond them. The unexpected thought of him brought a melancholy droop to her mouth.

"Are you all right?" Victoria stirred in the bed and stretched out her hand toward Dez.

"I'm fine." She moved from the chair back to the edge of the bed to take Victoria's hand. "How are your cramps?"

She smiled. "Almost gone, thanks to my miracle worker."

"Miracle worker. I like that." Dez touched her face, chasing after its softness with her fingertips and dipping into the deep dimples that briefly appeared out of hiding. Victoria's mouth was delicate under her thumb. It was the most natural thing in the world to kiss her; separate from her desire for sexual contact was her desire for her. To taste her, to have her close, and closer. The wet cavern of her mouth, her slowly awakening tongue, the scrape of her teeth against Dez's lips. She pressed her into the pillows and Victoria arched up against her, hands on Dez's breast and throat. The agitated breath in her chest produced a low, desperate noise. Victoria pulled away, breathing deeply.

"You know we can't . . . go any further . . . the blood . . ." She wet her lips, knowing that Dez wanted to get inside her and needing it, too.

"It's okay. I'll take care of it." Dez kissed her throat. "I'll make it good for you. Works better than aspirin for cramps." She felt incoherent with her need. Her fingers touched her lover through her shirt, stroking the hardening nipples and the full weight of her breasts. She bumped the water bottle out of the way. When she arched against her, kissed her back as deeply as Dez kissed her and tugged at the buttons of her shirt, she pulled away.

"I'll be right back."

She grabbed two thick towels out of her duffel bag and slid them under Victoria's hips. Without giving her lover a chance to realize she'd planned for this, planned her seduction and her surrender, Dez slipped the white shirt off, then the bra.

"Tell me if I do something you don't like."

But it wasn't that simple. She knew that some women didn't like to be touched when they were bleeding like this—shit, she was one of them—but Victoria smelled so fragile and sweet and she wanted her so much that it almost didn't matter what she had liked before. She wanted to give her this pleasure now and Victoria would take it.

She kept her clothes on—black jeans, red shirt, boots, and socks—as she sampled her body, smelled the woman-scent dripping through her pores, the smell of leaking blood and open pussy and possibility. Victoria lifted her breasts to Dez's mouth, scented skin, berry hard nipples and a low voice filled with need yet no suggestions of how Dez could fill it. Her fingers clung to Dez's head, shaping it as Dez pulled down and off the oversize panties and sank—finally—between the heavy thighs with its heavenly treasure of clit, mound, and vulva. Dez burrowed for the tampon string, found it and tugged. Victoria gasped and her fingers dug into the back of her neck. Blood smell sparked in the room, filled it. And Dez feasted on the bare nipples, licking and sucking in the rhythm that her lover liked until she forgot the feel of the tampon leaving her and pulled Dez's head closer, her voice an uneven melody of moans and whispers.

She felt red and perfect and home, and Dez clenched tight deep inside from just that feel of her around her fingers. Her own skin felt hot and tight, like it was too small to hold her body, this thing intent only on pleasure. Dez felt the fingers on her face, gentle and insistent, pulling her gaze up.

"Look at me." Breathless whisper. "Look at me."

Her face was flushed and wet, faint beads of sweat transforming her from fragile to radiant to sexy. She panted. Open mouth. Intent eyes. Hair around her face limp with sweat. Dez's fingers slid deep into her wet, then deeper still. Their eyes locked, then Victoria pulled hers away. She stared at Dez, made her feel the touch of her gaze through the thin black shirt, over her breasts, and the ridges of her belly. Her hips rocked in time with Dez's slow, deep thrusts and her body moved snakelike and slow over the bed. She licked her lips. And moaned. A soft "oh," then her eyes fluttered closed. The tight clench of her body around Dez's fingers.

Her hands fell away from Dez's face to clutch the sheets. Another "oh" and she turned her face away into the pillow. Her body shuddered and Dez's trembled in sympathetic pleasure. Flushed and wet and close. Victoria's neck tightened and stretched and her hips surged hard against Dez's hand. A luminous moment of non-motion suspended them, Victoria, bare and lovely, sweat and light gilding her face, the wet mouth, trembling throat, the eyes heavy-lidded and staring at nothing. Breasts and belly shuddering with impending delight. The red smell flared up as Victoria came, gasping into the pillow.

Only after all the tremors died away did she pull her fingers from their resting place, painting the soft thighs red as she withdrew. She kissed Victoria's belly, breast, and mouth before getting up to go to the bathroom. She came back a few minutes later with a basin full of warm water and a towel. With slow, gentle strokes, she washed her thighs, put her shirt back on, and swept the bloody towels away. Dez went downstairs to get a cup of tea while Victoria put in a fresh tampon. When she came back, the other woman was sprawled in the bed, barely two breaths from sleep. Dez put the tea on the bedside table.

"I'm going to let myself out, all right?"

"All right." Victoria smiled up at her, eyelashes already fluttering against her cheeks. "Call me tomorrow."

"I will."

Dez left the house feeling alert and faintly buzzed, like she'd been sucking on caffeine all night. Her clit had long ago subsided to its normal size and her pants had that post-come cooling moistness that she loved. Part of her didn't really understand what just happened, didn't want to, truth be known, just wanted to roll with the unexpected energy that fucking Victoria on the bloodstained towels had left behind. She called Rémi and Sage.

"Want to come out and play?"

Chapter 27

The noises of the bar—trance music, rising and falling laughter, the clink of glass upon glass—washed over her as she walked in. Rémi and Sage had agreed to meet her for quick drinks and something extra later on, but she was early. After Victoria, she couldn't go back to her house and wait. She needed to spend her energy somewhere, needed to feel it coming off other people. So here she was at The Palladium. Energy here was the low-level kind, the preparty, not quite main-event kind. People came here to get a buzz, not to get drunk.

"Hi, Dez."

She paid respect to the vaguely familiar face and smile of greeting, nodding politely at the curious new ones as she moved through the glass and chrome club. As Dez walked by, a buff boy bent over for his entire table of six, showing off the tattoo growing up from the small of his back. His friends groped, gasped, and stared, all the while throwing their laughing admiration all over his perfect bronze body. One of them, she couldn't tell if it was a boy, girl, or neither, glanced up then to stare at Dez as she passed.

A quiet waterfall set up behind the bar added to the Zen-like quiet of The Palladium. It was a place where she could either pick up a woman, be alone, just bullshit with her friends, or take a date for a nightcap. There was no place like this in all of Miami, not even Rémi's club with its gorgeous clientele and inventive drinks. Dez slid up to the bar next to a couple of posturing lesbians, New York–looking types with pierced faces and dark lipstick.

"A Long Island iced tea, Grace." She waited while the young-looking bartender made her drink and the three other orders thrown simultaneously at her. Grace was seal-slick in her tight black PVC and the short, spiky hair that surrounded what, under different circumstances, would have been a plain face.

"Thanks." She dropped a twenty on the bar and turned away with her drink.

"You look good, Dez."

She was glad that she had a firm hold on her glass; otherwise the entire bar would have seen her surprise. Dez forced herself to take a sip of the drink and moisten her dry throat. Her first instinct was to walk away like she had a few weeks ago, but in here he would just follow her.

"Ruben."

She turned back toward the bar and put her drink down. The mirror above them cast their reflections back at her, showed her blank face and Ruben's beautiful one. They looked like they used to together—a pair of pretty opposites. She was slim and hard in the three-quarter-length black leather coat, black jeans with its heavy belt and buckle, and the deep red button-down shirt that echoed the natural color in her lips. Ruben was all pretty and sweet in pale blue lowrider jeans and a white muscle shirt. Caitlyn was nowhere in sight.

"Aren't you hot in all that leather?" he asked.

"No." Her eyes swept over him again. "What do you want?"

For a moment he looked hurt, like he had no idea why she would talk to him like that. Then his face smoothed.

"You look real good," Ruben said again, eyes taking in the fit of her pants, the slight swell of breasts under her shirt. He winked.

She didn't want to hear that, especially not from him. Dez took another sip of her drink and waited.

"I forget how mean you can be to people on your shit list." He smoothed his eyebrow with his index finger and thumb—a nervous habit she had once found endearing—then seemed to make a decision. "If it's an apology you want then dammit, I'm sorry. Can't we . . . can't we be like we once were, Dez? Friends?" Ruben made a sudden motion toward her, then stopped himself. "What do you say?" He winked again.

She knew he was joking. He just had to be. Then Dez noticed that he was a little drunk. The incessant winking and the yeastlike scent of his breath should have tipped her off right away. To fill the space in the silence, Ruben signaled Grace with a languid wave of his hand. The bartender nodded and smiled when she saw him, then made his drink without asking what he wanted. He had his usual. At a gay bar.

"Where's Caitlyn?"

He seemed startled by her question. "At home."

Ruben got his cocktail and took a deep drink. Against her will, she noticed how his mouth fit neatly on the rim of the glass and how the long pink tongue caught an errant drop of the gold liquid and snared it back into his mouth. Dez moved back to give him some room.

"Remember how you used to tell me about those married girls you'd fuck on the sly? Remember? Can't I be like one of those girls?"

Although their end of bar was far from private, he followed her body with his and slid a hand under her jacket, gripping the smooth muscle of her shoulder through the black shirt.

"I missed you," he said. But Dez also heard the words he'd thrown at her in New Mexico. "I don't want you anymore." She remembered clearly how his pretty face had flinched and twisted when she'd blinked stupidly at him, the clichéd "why?" trapped behind her heavy tongue. There could be no reason for him to hurt her like this.

"Really?" she asked, trying to ignore the press of his dick against her thigh.

She used to love the way he bent under her, always willing to take what she could give, arching his back up into her, pushing and moaning. His trust in her seemed absolute then, nothing was too strange, or too rough, or too sweet, or too tender. Her love for him was like the rush of coke through her system, overwhelming and immediate. It took a little bit longer to wear off, but looking at him she realized that it truly had. Dez had thought she was over him before, but this was the true test: his tempting beauty flush against her, his mouth saying yes.

"Remember the last thing I said to you in the desert, Ru?"

He shook his head, but she could see that despite the alcohol and whatever else he was on, he did remember. She put her hand on his chest, spacing her fingers wide. And pushed.

"Fuck. You." Dez punctuated each word with another hard push. "Don't *ever* come up on me like this again."

She picked up her drink and went to another part of the bar to wait for her friends.

Chapter 28

Dez was obsessed. There was no other word for it. Thoughts of a certain woman crowded in on her at the most inconvenient times—in the shower, riding her bike through thick rush-hour traffic, getting ready to eat a meal she'd spent hours anticipating. It would be easier to take if they were just thoughts about fucking. After all, that was their arrangement, right? But it was Victoria's smile, the way she wrinkled her nose at something Dez said. Sometimes it was her smell. She wanted to talk to her, ask how her day was going and, if it was going badly, help to make it better. Dez brushed her hands through three months' growth of hair, a knotty bush she was starting to grow fond of, and walked through her kitchen to pick up the keys to the truck.

Dez found herself standing on the same precipice where she had stood with Ruben over two years ago, only back then she hadn't hesitated to jump. Despite everything that her father had taught her about fidelity, she had jumped. And now . . . she didn't want to be hurt again, she didn't want to end up alone at the bottom, shattered beyond repair. No, she didn't need that feeling again.

The lunch traffic rush was almost two hours away so she made good time to the bookstore, all the way ignoring the trip-hammer rhythm of her heart that sped up the closer she got to Victoriana.

Victoria stood behind the counter with one of the younger girls who worked with her. Her hands floated in the air as she talked, a balletic counterpoint to her intent voice describing something that Dez didn't know anything about. *Endcaps?* The girl smiled and nodded, punctuating Victoria's words with the occasional "absolutely" and "you're so right."

The girl noticed Dez before she got the chance to speak, looking over her boss's shoulder for just a moment too long. Victoria turned around to see what had taken her previously rapt audience away.

Dez tried to look apologetic. "Excuse me, ma'am. May I steal a moment of your time?"

"Are you sure that a moment is all you want?"

Dez's smile widened as she noticed the two pencils and a pen tucked into the neatly scraped-back and bunned hair. "That's not all I want, but I'll take what I can get."

The girl glanced from Dez to Victoria with a look of naked speculation before moving from behind the counter to give her boss some privacy. Her magenta-streaked Afro bobbed behind her as she walked away.

Victoria leaned her arms on the counter and brought her intoxicating scent closer. Tangerines, baby powder, and her morning coffee. The motion of her arms squeezed her breasts together, plumping the soft flesh up and above the neckline of her blouse.

"What can I do for you this morning?" A smile toyed with the full burgundy curve of her mouth.

Dez leaned onto the opposite side of the counter, dipping down low until they were at the same height and their lips were mere inches apart. "Drop everything and come play with me for an hour."

"Oh, is that all?" Victoria's lips pursed, bringing them just a few breaths closer. Then she smiled. "Let me just tell Shelly that I'm leaving." Her ass wove and shimmied under the thin skirt as she walked away, putting a little extra in it just for her lover's benefit.

"Tease," Dez called after her.

A few minutes later, Victoria got in the truck without comment, arranging her legs demurely under Dez's watchful gaze. The assorted pencils and pens were gone from her hair, her makeup freshened, and she carried a tiny nothing of a purse. Her smell, the look of her, and the low melody of her voice all plucked an answering string in Dez's resistant soul. This is *just* a fuck thing. This is just a fuck thing. Maybe if she said it enough times, then it would become true.

"Don't worry," she forced herself to say. "I didn't take you away from your pride and joy just for a little afternoon delight."

"Then just why did I leave the shop?" She pouted then laughed at the look on Dez's face. "I'm joking."

"The seats fold back if you want me to fuck you here." Dez upped the stakes for the morning. Her fingers floated to Victoria's thigh. Maybe if she fucked Victoria, then she wouldn't have to think about her other feelings, the swirl of ambiguities, or the need inside her. "I have wipes in the glove compartment. Rubbers, too."

And she was instantly there, swimming in images of licking the crotch of Victoria's thong, pulling at the material until the little string slipped between the swollen lips and her tongue was tracing that line, licking flesh and cotton, sucking at the wet cloth, at the wet pussy, as Victoria bucked against her face.

Dez swallowed. "We can do whatever you want."

Victoria shook her head. "Let's . . . let's keep our clothes on." But her thighs widened and Dez's hand seized the opportunity to slide between them and find the gratifyingly wet panties.

"We can do it that way, too." Her fingers proved her point, moving the damp material out of the way to stroke Victoria's thickening clit.

Her lover shuddered. Her head fell back. Her eyes closed. "No, I—" But her hips were moving against the leather seat, her pussy already coating Dez's hand with sweetness. Desperate to feel more, Dez slid deeply inside her.

"Do you want me to stop?" Her fingers moved steadily in their warm sheath, curling in the slick, tight cunt, giving the pleasure slowly.

"No, oh—" Victoria's hand curled fast around her biceps. "But . . ." The breath left her again. Dez knew what she was going to say. They were still in the parking lot of Victoriana's and, despite the truck's tinted windows, anyone who really wanted to see inside could.

"I'll make this one quick." She hauled her lover's hips closer, over the armrest and gearshift, all without taking her fingers from inside the velvety pussy. Dez leaned closer, suffocating in sweet citrus and powder and aroused sweat, to nuzzle the hard-tipped breast out of Victoria's blouse, and sucked the nipple deep into her mouth, hollowing her cheeks, licking its turgid warmth between the pincers of her teeth. Dez squirmed in the seat and her clit slid wet and swollen against the seam of her jeans.

"Baby . . ."

Her thumb flickered over Victoria's clit while her fingers delved deeper, faster. Then her lover was coming, clutching Dez's fingers tight, sucking them farther inside her with each moan and hitch and gasp. As Victoria's breath calmed, Dez still licked her nipple and breast, slurping like her lover was a really good mound of ice cream she was afraid was going to melt.

"Hmmm. . . ." Her hands roved over Dez's hair. Then with a low sigh she released the other breast from her blouse. Dez pounced on the newly exposed skin with her hands and mouth. Her pussy was drenched and tight inside her jeans.

The sound of her zipper going down filled the truck. She just needed one more second. Dez fumbled past the opening in her jeans and plunged her fingers into her own pussy. Her thumb flicked against her throbbing clit. All she needed was—"Fuck!" Once, twice, then she was coming hard against her own fingers with her mouth fastened to Victoria's nipple. Her ragged breathing gradually slowed. She lifted herself from Victoria and arranged the other woman back in the passenger seat. Dez's back and the hollow between her breasts slid wetly with sweat.

"Okay, now I can concentrate."

Victoria chuckled, moving in slow motion as she slid her shoes back on. "Speak for yourself. How can I go back to work like this?"

"I'm not done with you yet. Relax. I meant what I said about an hour. That was barely fifteen minutes." She released another breath then started the car. "Seat belt, please." And they were off.

Dez took her to the pier. It was very seductive at night, but in the day it was only a little romantic with the seagulls pitching to and fro just above the waves and the constant flow of pedestrians on the sidewalk barely ten feet away. The seat they finally settled on was at the end of the long strip of cement benches, practically sitting in the water. It was the only bench facing east and that, along with its close proximity to the high splashing waves, afforded them some privacy.

Victoria looked around. "So, why this place?"

"I want to sit and spend some quiet time with you." Dez's glance lingered on her face, watching for any sign of unease. She felt like she was confessing some filthy little secret.

Victoria smiled and snuggled back into her arms. "That's nice." She fit her back against Dez's belly and breasts, and wrapped the taller woman's arms around her own middle. "I like it when you're nice."

Dez made a noncommittal sound as she laid her chin on top of Victoria's head. She'd used some type of hair gel. It wasn't bad, just different, with its faint smell of apricots.

"You don't do anything with your days, do you?" Victoria asked suddenly.

"I think about you," Dez murmured, slipping a hand under her blouse to touch the powder-smooth belly. A light spray off the ocean flew up above the railing and washed over them. Victoria snapped her eyes closed with a soft scream and whirled around to bury her face in Dez's shoulder.

"Feels good, doesn't it?" Dez laughed.

The flecks of water deflected the day's heat, rising up as steam from her flesh in a thin vapor.

Victoria's only response was to burrow deeper into her lover's skin and laugh. "So you don't have a hobby or job?"

What happened to their nice, quiet time? Dez had heard this before from various people she'd encountered in one town or another. Typical proletarian types who believed that the road to riches, or heaven, was paved with the sweat of one's brow and a little blood thrown in for good measure. "My hobby is actually enjoying myself. And I do it quite well. I've never been one to need manual labor to instill character in me. All that stuff is overrated."

She looked down at Victoria's abrupt stillness. "What?"

"Don't tell me you've never had a job?"

"All right, I won't tell you."

Victoria shook her head. "I don't know why that surprises me."

"Me either. Now shut up and enjoy me. You only have twenty minutes left."

Thirty-five minutes and a long kiss later, Dez dropped her off at the store with a promise to call. Rémi and Sage had a few things planned for the evening, so that call would probably not happen until a *very* long time later.

That night, she put on the leather, the white muscle shirt, and the thick black dick in her pants, ready for whatever her friends had planned. But she ended the pretense by calling Rémi and Sage to tell them that she couldn't come with them to the party, even if every girl there was Tina Turner fine.

After she hung up the phone, she walked the length of the house, staring up through the stained glass at the moon and the flotilla of clouds trailing below it. Dez still carried the phone in her hand. She knew what she wanted to do, but waited until she was about to jump out of her skin to do it.

"That is a nice surprise," Victoria said when she answered the phone.

"Good. Does that mean you'll come out with me to South Beach if I ask nice? I'm sure you know that Derrick's out of town."

Laughter gurgled at her from the other end of the connection. "Yes, I will and I do. Is there a particular dress code?"

"Nope. Just sexy enough to turn me on. And a little easy access would be nice."

The laughter came again. "I know just the outfit."

"Good. I'll pick you up on the bike in an hour."

By eleven they were speeding across the bridge heading for the beach. Victoria clung to her from behind, softly scented and touchable in a way that made Dez ache. She'd followed through on the outfit, guaranteeing with just a few strips of cloth and a cheeky grin that Dez *would* be hot for her all night. The tall woman said as much, eyeing her new toy with undisguised lust as she parked the bike, then extended an arm for her to take as they joined the flow of pretty people meandering along Lincoln Road.

"What made you decide to call me, Dez? Bored?"

Victoria was all charm and flirtation, walking slowly by Dez's side, occasionally pressing close so that other pedestrians could pass by them on the sidewalk.

"I *was* a little bored, actually. Then I thought of this cute little shop owner who probably wouldn't mind livening up my night."

She wrinkled her nose at Dez's description of her, but said nothing. Her mouth was shining and coy, inviting Dez to give into the urge to kiss her. She tasted like peach lip gloss.

"Tell me, Dez. Cute little shop owners aside, has any girl ever gotten under your skin?"

Dez didn't pause at the apparent non sequitur. With Victoria's body pressing close, she forced herself to think of long-ago women. "Yeah, Marva Kennedy in high school."

"High school doesn't even count. Especially not when you were in ninth grade."

"No, you perv. It was tenth."

Victoria laughed, just like Dez intended, grasping the tall woman's arm and pressing her breasts and scent against her.

"It was actually twelfth," she said when Victoria's chuckles died away. "She was a senior. Pretty and popular, of course. On the cheerleading squad. When I saw her do the splits, I knew I had to have her." Dez did a fair imitation of a leer that earned her a swat on the arm.

"And you never took the chance to ask her out."

"What? Are you crazy? Of course I did." She guided Victoria around a cluster of gay boys gathered around a BDSM window display, giggling at the whip-wielding mannequin in the ice-pick stilettos and cherry red strap-on dick. "The pussy was good. *I* was good. But she went back to her jock boyfriend, anyway. Looking back, I think that's what got under my skin about her, that she dumped me for some boy who couldn't even make her come. She was the last girl who did that to me."

"You left them all first, huh?"

"Damn right."

Victoria shook her head. "You are an awful woman. What am I still doing with you?"

"Because I *am* so awful. You love it. Your own bad girl on a leash."

Taking advantage of the thinning crowd, she pressed Victoria against the cool glass of a shop window and kissed her. In her tight black leather, short hair, and cock-strong attitude, she could be—to unfamiliar eyes—either a beautiful boy or a gorgeous girl, showing off her sexy date on a

Saturday night. Here on the beach, few cared if she was either, only that she not ruin their fun with any foolishness.

A hint of red behind the shorter woman caught her eye. "That would really look good on you." It was a corset. "It would set off that fantastic ass of yours to perfection. You'd look so pretty in it when I fuck your pussy from the back." Her hands slid under Victoria's blouse to tease the sensitive flesh at her spine as she kept her voice deliberately light and teasing, smiling when what she wanted to do was drop to her knees and taste Victoria's nipples, then dip lower to her wild-haired pussy and stay there all night.

Victoria turned around to look at the leather and lace confection. Her wet mouth twitched. "Then you should buy it."

Dez chuckled then dragged Victoria into the shop. Moments later, they emerged from the lingerie shop with a small pink bag, both of them giggling like teenagers.

"I thought I was going to have to pry that girl out of your dressing room."

"She was just trying to be helpful."

"Right, and get a real eyeful while she was at it. But I don't blame her. I would've done the same thing."

"No, you would have had me out of that corset and on the dressing room floor with . . . some part of your anatomy on my person."

Dez laughed. "Or, more accurately, in your person."

"Hm, even better."

They meandered away from the main drag and found a relatively quiet street with an open ice-cream shop and an uninterrupted view of the star-dotted night sky.

"Want some ice cream?" Victoria asked. "My treat."

"Sure. Uh . . . Mexican hot chocolate in a waffle cone, please."

"Whatever the lady wants."

Dez shook her head. She hadn't been called a lady in a long time. And probably never in that lightly teasing and intimate tone of voice. Victoria walked away from her, shimmying up the short ramp to the shop. A smile lingered on her mouth as she found them a bench a short distance away from where she could watch both her lover and the eclectic mix of people strolling by. The little shop had a steady business despite the slight chill in the air. Couples filed in and out of the clear glass doors, laughing and leaning closely together. Inside the store she noticed a few women—obviously dykes—checking Victoria out. They were subtle, eyeing her curves in a way that Dez had done a thousand times before. One of them separated from their group and approached her. Dez couldn't hear their words, but whatever the butch said made Victoria laugh.

She felt something cold and hard drop in the pit of her belly. Dez looked over the thick, fairly attractive woman, wondering how it would feel to pound her face in and what she would have to say to Victoria then. A part of her brain analyzed the emotion and squirmed. What the hell did she have to be jealous about? It wasn't as if the woman was a better lay than she was, or was even better-looking. At best she was more charming. Maybe even nicer and more—what was that phrase an old fuck buddy of hers always used?— emotionally available. That was it. But that didn't make the feeling go away. At least Victoria didn't give her number to the charming butch. She smiled and said something else before walking out of the store with two waffle cones in hand. The woman held the door open for her. Victoria was still smiling when she walked up to Dez.

"Here you go. A Mexican hot chocolate, plain."

She sat next to her on the bench with her own cone of rainbow-sprinkled coconut ice cream, and smiled over at Dez. The iceberg in her belly dissolved at that look and she smiled back.

With the other woman watching her and taking broad, hungry licks of her cone as she directed flirtatious glances her way, Dez managed to calm her mind to a manageable pitch. There was nothing for her to be jealous about. Victoria wasn't interested in anybody else. Dez took a bite of her dessert, savoring the cool bath of the peppery chocolate ice cream beneath her palate.

"Hey, Dez."

She couldn't stop the flinch from moving across her face. She saw it reflected in the surprise in Victoria's eyes and the soft note of query that began to shape on her lips. Dez looked away and up, knowing what she would see even before Ruben and Caitlyn appeared in her line of sight. In their matching burgundy shirts and tight jeans they could have passed for any typical heterosexual couple on the street. If Ruben hadn't said anything she wouldn't have known they were there. And her Saturday night would have continued being perfect.

She met his eyes with the winter's chill in hers. "Ruben. Caitlyn." Then she looked away, dismissing them.

"Who's your friend, Dez?" Ruben asked. "Don't be rude."

"I wasn't being rude, just trying to go on with my good time. Is it too much for me to wish you would do the same?"

Caitlyn opened her pretty red mouth to say something, but Dez shook her head. She wasn't in the mood to be nice. Not tonight. Not even with Victoria sitting so close by.

"I'm Ruben." He extended his hand under Victoria's nose, forcing her to give it a limp shake. "And this is my girlfriend, Caitlyn." For some reason it had seemed less absurd when he and Dez were seeing each other. Two queers together, that seemed right. This . . . wasn't.

"Nice to meet you." To her credit, Victoria didn't hesitate, she went on eating her ice cream while Ruben looked expectantly at her.

"Sorry about nearly running you over with my cart at the store the other day, Dez. I meant to apologize then but you were gone so fast." Caitlyn was a nice girl. Very sweet. Under different circumstances she and Dez might have become friends. Or something.

"No apology needed. What happened, happened. I've moved

on." The words fell in a monotone from her lips. "You should, too." Yes, please move on so I can get on with my date.

Ruben turned away from Victoria after it became obvious that she wasn't going to offer him anything. "So who is your new woman, Dez? You been keeping secrets from me?"

She looked at him as if he'd lost his whole damn mind. "I'm not in the mood for this, Ruben. Keep on going wherever it is you're going."

"Does she know that you do dick?" His hand drifted to his crotch. "And not just the one you probably have strapped to your pussy right now."

Dez abruptly stood up. "I guess I wasn't clear last time we spoke, Ru." Her voice was a quiet rumble deep in her chest. She wasn't even ready to look at Victoria and see what effect his little declaration had had on her. "Whenever you see me out in public, in the gay bars or wherever—and I'll show you the same courtesy—I want you to pretend I'm not there. Not a 'hello,' not a 'how's it hanging?', nothing that would indicate we'd ever had any kind of previous relationship." She looked from one pale face to the other. "Is that clear?" At her ex-lover's arch look, she actually snarled. "That means leave me the fuck alone."

People were beginning to stare. Some looked from the corners of their eyes as they walked past. Others didn't even bother to pretend that they weren't gawking.

Caitlyn noticed them, too. "Come on, Ruben." She linked her fingers with her boyfriend and tugged him toward the ice-cream shop. "Give it a rest." She glanced briefly at Dez. "Sorry."

Because Ruben was that sort, he allowed himself to be led away. But not before showing Dez all his teeth in a mocking grin. Dez turned her back to him and faced Victoria.

"Sorry about that." She cleared her throat.

"You have nothing to be sorry about." She put her ice cream on the bench beside her as Dez sat down, arranging the leaking cone on a neat pile of napkins. "Are you all right?"

"Not right now, but I will be." Dez made an abrupt noise and threw the rest of her ice cream in the trash. "You ready to go?"

"No." Victoria picked up her ice cream, and then folded the napkins into a square. Loose rainbow sprinkles escaped the paper and tumbled into her lap, but Victoria brushed them away without glancing down.

The tightness in Dez's chest worsened. They were going to have a conversation about this. And it wasn't going to go well. Victoria watched her face, slowly eating her ice cream. Her eyes seemed to take in every part of Dez—the clenched teeth, the mouth that had lost its smile somewhere along the way, even her old battered heart that was beating way too fast in her chest.

"Did you love him?"

"Yes." The answer to the unexpected question croaked past Dez's dry lips.

"Do you love him now?"

"No."

"Good." Victoria's teeth crunched into the last bite of her cone. "Now I'm ready."

They rode back to the city in silence with Victoria clutched tight against Dez's back as the bike wove through late-night traffic. The other woman's hands rested against her belly, snug underneath her jacket, keeping her warm.

Chapter 29

Victoria was beautiful. Dez could never get enough of looking at her. She made herself comfortable on the end of the high four-poster bed, adjusting the sprawl of her legs against the white cotton sheets, taking care that her special occasion thong didn't ride up too far and slip between her outer lips until she was ready. Victoria's skin really was the most luscious thing, an enticing mix of caramel and cream that made Dez's tongue beg for a taste. She hung between two poles in Dez's sparsely decorated guest bedroom. Arms and legs spread wide and tied to the poles with red velvet rope. Red definitely was her color. Except for the bed and a set of built-in shelves stocked with towels, lotions, and toys, the thick wooden poles that ran from ceiling to floor were the only furniture in the room.

It had been almost two hours. She'd teased Victoria's nipples, licked her swollen pussy and the shy puckered hole of her ass, lightly flicked the whip over every inch of her, just to make her feel the texture and the possibility of pain. Dez hadn't allowed Victoria to come. And Victoria hadn't used the safe word. Her entire body was wet and trembling and in need. She begged. Small tears escaped her eyes, wetting her cheeks and the corners of her mouth.

Impressed and damn near drowning in her own juices, Dez leaned back against the bedpost and touched herself. Her lover's head lifted, her nostrils flared at the scent of freshly aroused pussy as Dez moved her thong aside to allow a glimpse of her engorged clit and the wet lips. She held herself open and slowly slid a long index finger deep inside. Her belly tightened and she got even wetter when Victoria made a low noise of want watching each slow movement of Dez's finger. Heat flushed through her body and the nipples inside her leather bra hardened to near pain. Victoria licked her lips and moved restlessly in her bonds. Dez almost felt sorry for her. She made a full, voluptuous noise and filled herself with two fingers, then three. Her hips rose up to meet each thrust.

"Can I do that for you?" Victoria's voice rose in shy inquiry. Her eyes hungrily followed the motion of Dez's fingers.

Dez slowed her tempo but didn't stop. "You seem a little busy right now." Her free hand waved at the ropes holding Victoria captive. "And besides"—she bit off a groan as another wave of sensation flooded through her—"I like you that way. It's very inspiring."

"At least come . . . closer." Her eyes begged even more than her mouth, showing very clearly what she would do if Dez allowed her to be close and to touch.

"Hm." Dez pulled her fingers away from their cozy nest and stood. "You might be right."

She moved closer, close enough to smell the delicious sweat on her, to brush her leather-clad breasts against Victoria, then she stepped behind so that her lover couldn't see her. From the back, she was even more breathtaking, the high full swell of her ass, the hills and lulls of her back, the thick thighs and calves that tensed with anticipation. Dez slipped out of her underwear and picked up the waiting double-headed dong and its harness. The fullness of it inside her was . . . gratifying. The swirled black and white silicone head that stood out in front of her was just a little larger than the one already nestled inside her body. She hoped that Victoria could handle it. With light fingers, she stroked her lover's back. Goose pimples appeared in the wake of her touch.

"Ah, Victoria." And she slid into her.

Dez held her still with one hand just below her breasts, the other on her hip. "Is this all right?"

A deep shudder passed through Victoria's body and into her own. "Yes." Breath hitched in her throat. "Yes."

Dez's hand found her breasts, and the other slid over to caress the moist and swollen clit as she began to move her hips. A low, primal moan left Victoria's mouth, making Dez feel like she was doing something absolutely right. She was very responsive, her moans building to grunts as Dez increased her pace and forced herself to focus on the pleasure of the woman beneath her instead of on the full thick need bubbling up inside her body. Victoria's breasts were damp and hot under her hand, their tips firm and getting firmer as the slick button of her clit slid beneath Dez's fingers. Her breath burst from her throat with each controlled thrust, exploding loudly in the room.

Victoria held onto the poles to brace herself as she pushed back into Dez, her lover's name coming in deep, guttural groans. Then she started to talk. Pleas and promises tumbled from her lips, begging Dez to continue, not to tease her like last time or the time before that, or to make her beg without relief. The sound of her voice, hoarse and hot and urgent, blended with the slap of flesh against flesh, of Dez's hips against her ass, of the grunting bass of Dez's voice, the sound of her control falling to pieces. Victoria trembled as she came, her words falling away and replaced by sighs. Then Dez released herself. The orgasm brought her down hard, roaring through her body like an untamed blaze. She shouted something. Her fingers dug into Victoria's heated skin as her hips jerked spasmodically, then finally stilled. Dez panted into her hair. Her body twitched and drooped over Victoria's. The other woman moaned and sagged against her bonds at the additional weight.

"Sorry, baby."

Dez pulled back until the toy left Victoria's body with a

slow wet sound. She unbuckled the harness and tossed it toward the bed. With an economy of movement, she untied Victoria from the pole, lifted her in her arms, and took her to the bedroom at the end of the long hallway. Her bedroom. Victoria shifted against the unfamiliar sheets as Dez lay her down.

"It smells like you in here," the exhausted woman mumbled.

Dez drew her close and pulled the sheets up over them. "Hopefully that's a good thing."

A soft, contented snore was her only response. Dez smiled and kissed her lightly on the shoulder. This was new. Although Victoria didn't know the significance of being in her bedroom after almost three months of sleeping together, Dez did.

Ruben's shadow was finally gone. She settled her hand on the curve of Victoria's belly and followed her lover into sleep.

She woke up to the press of Victoria's strawberry-flavored lips against her sour mouth.

"I have to go to work." Bright-eyed and energetic, she was already dressed in a flirty little dress Dez had never seen before and high heels. "I'll call you later."

The fading echoes of her footsteps on the hardwood floors lulled Dez back to sleep. Hours later, the shrill ring of her house phone woke her up.

"Get your ass out of bed, Nichols," Rémi growled in her ear. "We have a lunch date that you absolutely don't want to miss."

She could miss it. In fact she wanted to. Dez fixed her bleary eyes on the clock. Half-past one. Victoria still sang in her blood; shit, her scent still lingered on her sheets and she wanted to lay here and savor it.

"Hurry up, Nichols. Fine ass waits for no one." She heard the sounds of jingling keys through the phone. "I'll be there to pick you up in ten minutes."

Fifteen minutes later, Rémi was at her gate and pressing the intercom button, demanding to be let in.

"Your chariot awaits, fair prince." She stopped her Escalade in Dez's circular driveway long enough for the still-sleepy woman to stumble in and buckle her seat belt.

"This shit better be the bomb," Dez said, putting on her sunglasses.

"You have *no* idea."

Rémi turned up the volume on the stereo and peeled out of the drive. The loud, bass-heavy Ragga music forced Dez out of her post-postcoital haze so by the time they made it to the restaurant, although she still looked half-asleep with her sandaled foot on the dashboard and her gaze passively taking in the scenery outside the truck's window, she was ready to face whatever it was that Rémi was about to throw her into.

But to say that she wasn't prepared was an understatement. When she walked into the restaurant, heading for their usual section on the patio with a view of the water and the passing boardwalk scenery, she immediately recognized Sage. Her friend sat at a table with three other women. She was even more animated than usual, emphasizing whatever point she was trying to make with broad, excited gestures. In deference to the warm spring day, she wore a tight white wife beater that left the muscled and tattooed arms bare. The woman on Sage's left was gorgeous. Her terra-cotta skin glowed in the sun and her thick black hair lay in a graceful fall over her shoulder and breast. Next to her sat another woman with short spiky hair and an identical face and body. And next to her was a replica of the first woman complete with the full, fuckable mouth and tilted doe eyes.

"Holy mother . . ."

Rémi chuckled. "And you're not even Catholic."

By the time she got to the table, Dez had regained her cool. "Ladies." She greeted the women with a civilized nod.

"Hey." Sage's laughing eyes met Dez's. "I thought you guys were just going to abandon me to these tigresses for the day."

"Not even in your dreams," Rémi said sitting down next to the spike-haired triplet. "Nicoletta, Matsuko, Chance, this is our friend Dez. Nichols, meet the Nakamura sisters, recently relocated from Rome."

"Georgia?"

"Not exactly," the spike-haired one, Chance, murmured with a wry twist to her mouth. Her Italian accent and gravelly voice made the words sound like an indecent proposal.

Jesus. Dez cleared her throat. "So what are we having for lunch?"

"Anything you want. We are—how you say?—treating for lunch. You're the first interesting women we've met in this city." Matsuko, who nicely filled out a pastel pink blouse and matching Capri pants, lightly touched Dez's thigh.

"So we'll bribe you into being our friends," Nicoletta finished, turning her smile on Sage. Unlike her long-haired sister, she wore jeans and a scoop necked blouse that threatened to flash the entire restaurant.

Chance took out a cigarette and offered her pack around the table. Dez shook her head in polite refusal. Thanks to Victoria, she had better things to do with her mouth these days.

"No bribes necessary, ladies," she said. "I think you'll find the three of us to be *very* friendly."

By the time the waitress came around with their meal they were all on friendly terms indeed, chatting about mutual acquaintances in Europe and the clubs they'd been to. If this had happened six months ago, Dez would be in hog heaven, lapping up the women's attentions and trying to maneuver Sage and Rémi out of whatever plans the Nakamura sisters had for later that day.

From the first rasp of Chance's gravelly voice, she knew where this lunch was leading. She didn't need Matsuko's coy touch on her thigh or the ravenous and ready look on Rémi's face to tell her. But thoughts of Victoria swam to the surface of Dez's mind and stayed there. She would never be able to touch this woman—or more accurately, *these women*—with the phantom of her lover practically sitting in her lap.

When her nose conjured the light, honey-laced scent of tangerines, she thought little of it. Then, minutes later, she heard the familiar low, carrying laugh and realized that that could not be her imagination, too. Dez turned around.

She sat three tables away with her friends, Mick and Kavi. A waiter moved efficiently around their table, serving drinks and flashing each woman a smile. He said something that made Victoria and her friends laugh. A high-pitched scream made Dez look away. A slim boy in beige Capri pants and a tight little blue shirt jerked his chair back from the table next to Dez's and stood up. His flailing hand swept a champagne glass to the floor, splattering mimosa and shards of glass all over the patio. The boy screamed again and ran out of the restaurant, ignoring his friends' raised voices and the chaos left in his wake.

"Talk about drama. Damn." Rémi coolly appraised the mess then turned back to matters at their table. Someone else was focused on them. Victoria. She saw Dez and smiled. In the next second she noticed the Italian woman with her shoulders pressed against Dez's, then the intimate arrangement of the table. Her smile froze. Dez's stomach plunged to her knees at that look. She wanted to jump up and explain, to tell her that she wasn't going to go through with it, but instead she just sat there and looked back at her. Caught. Victoria blinked and looked away.

"So, Dez . . ." Matsuko breathed an invitation in her ear. Across the table, Sage and Nicoletta already had their heads bent together, whispering. Both sets of hands were under the table doing what Dez could very well imagine.

This is so fucking unfair, the petulant part of her whined, knowing what her next words were going to be.

"As nice as that sounds, I can't."

Her friends broke off their conversation to stare at Dez.

"Are you crazy?" Rémi's thick brows nearly met in her disbelief. "This is not like you."

"Tell me about it."

Rémi frowned. "Victoria?"

"Are you punking out of this certified good time because of a woman?" Sage looked at Dez as if she'd lost her mind. When she nodded, Sage stared. "Are you high?"

"You all can go ahead without me—"

"Damn right we will. You might be crazy but we aren't."

The triplets watched their byplay with amusement. Matsuko teased Dez with her smile, lightly bumping her shoulder with her own. "I understand. It is important to be faithful to a lover, especially if she is doing the right things in bed as well as out of it, yes?"

"After today we'll see if she does anything at all."

The triplets laughed, apparently taken with the idea that Dez was so infatuated with someone that she couldn't take any or all of them to bed. Sage and Rémi fell into the spirit of the teasing, but kept sneaking strange looks at Dez. When Dez looked back over to Victoria's table, her lover and her friends were gone.

"Don't worry," Chance murmured to Dez as they all walked out of the restaurant together. "If things don't work out with your lady you can always come to us for comfort."

Looking up from her cozy cuddle with Rémi, Matsuko purred, "You can, cara mia. Anytime."

Dez drove Rémi's truck home and told her friend to call her when she needed it again. She sat in the parking lot and called Victoria. No surprise when she didn't answer her cell phone or her landline.

"I can't fucking believe this. The one time I didn't actually do anything . . ."

Dez left a message, then two. She waited until Monday night to call again. By Tuesday she was angry. Why the fuck was Victoria acting like this when their relationship was only based on sex, and not even monogamous sex? More than once, Dez lifted the phone to call Derrick and ask him if he'd seen Victoria. But she never made that call. Instead she waited. She went out with her friends as usual, drank, even watched a hot threesome with Rémi and two of their playmates. None of it made her feel better, none of it made her forget Victoria and the gnawing something in her gut that was her need to see her, to tell her that she hadn't slept with any of those women.

On Wednesday well after midnight, she took the truck and drove to Victoria's house. High in a no-moon sky a few brave stars glowed through the tattered stream of clouds. The streetlights compensated for the lack of natural light, illuminating the well-kept lawns and pretty flower waterfalls of the quiet, middle-class neighborhood.

Dez parked the truck a little ways down the road from her lover's house and, from behind the deeply tinted glass, watched the movement of light and shadow behind Victoria's windows. The television's blue-gray light flickered downstairs, then the harsh fluorescents in the kitchen. After less than half an hour, all the lights downstairs went out. Moments later, the faintest illumination on the upper level signaled Victoria's presence in the bedroom. Dez called her then. The phone rang five times before dropping her into voice mail. There was no point in leaving a message. Victoria was already sending one of her own. She waited another hour until all the lights went off. Then she drove back home.

Her brother's car sat idling outside the gates of her house as she pulled up. The truck cruised slowly past him and she glanced back to make sure that he noticed it was her. Not bothering to call out, she triggered the gate with her remote and rode up the drive. His silver convertible followed.

"What's up?" Her voice sounded drained even to her own ears.

"This and that. Can we talk?"

"Sure. Just park right here and wait while I put the bike to bed."

He looked tired but determined, not at all like she saw him last. "Is Mama okay?"

"Yeah, she's good."

She pulled around to the garage and he followed her inside, waiting patiently while she turned off the alarm. "You hungry?"

Although he said no, she led him to the kitchen anyway, walking tiredly past the stairs where Victoria had sat only a few days before, shyly asking to be topped and tied up, her legs sprawled in a little girl pose that made her too adorable to refuse.

She opened the fridge and took out the ingredients for an almond butter and grape jelly sandwich. Derrick watched silently as she made her meal, only leaned against the counter and looked curiously around at the chrome-fitted kitchen. She'd forgotten that this was his first time in her house.

Palming a long-handled knife, Dez cut the thick wheat bread sandwich in two neat triangles and put it in the microwave for fifteen seconds.

"So what's on your mind?"

"You. And Victoria."

You too, huh? She nodded, took the sandwich out of the microwave, but said nothing. Victoria was not going to like this, especially since she apparently didn't want to continue their association. Dez bit into the bread. Her inner pleasure hound woke up, groaning in pleasure at the combination of sweet, salt, and hot nutty goodness dancing across her tongue. She chewed blissfully for a few moments.

"Are you two involved?" Derrick asked.

"No."

His look told her that he wasn't a believer.

"We're fucking. Not involved." She peeled a wad of warm bread, butter, and jelly from the roof of her mouth with her tongue and slowly sucked on it. "At least we were. So you don't have to worry about it. She's not talking to me right now."

"That should make me *not* worry?" Derrick pushed himself off the counter and opened a nearby cabinet. After a few seconds of fruitless searching he asked, "Got any liquor in this kitchen?"

Dez dug out her bottle of good whiskey and a glass, then passed them to him. He took a healthy swallow of the Glen before looking back at his sister. "She came over to see me last night. At one point I mentioned you and she clammed up all of a sudden, looking like she was going to cry. A few seconds later she was fine again. I never thought I'd see the day when she lost her composure like that. And I sure as hell never thought she'd lose it over you."

Dez swallowed. "Is she all right?"

"What do you think?"

"What do I think?" She blew out a sigh. "I think that for the first time in my adult life I turned down some pussy for a woman. And look what that good deed cost me?" The savory bites of nuts from the almond butter slid deliciously between her tongue and teeth. Dez swept her tongue over her front teeth with appreciation of the small pleasure. This was all she was going to be getting for a while. "I could have slept with three very hot women on Sunday, Derrick. Three. Triplets built like Halle Berry with 'come fuck me' accents. And I said no for your precious Tori."

"Watch it, Dez. She *is* precious."

She nodded. "I've been calling her for days. I even went to her house like a fucking stalker and watched her, *watched* her ignore my phone calls." Dez looked down at the sound of breaking glass. Her cup. She'd slammed it down on the counter a bit too hard. Milk spread in a slow white stain on the cherry countertop, heading toward her denim-covered thigh. *Fuck.* She swallowed the last of her sandwich and jumped up to clean the mess.

Derrick laughed softly. "I might be worried about the wrong woman."

"Damn right." Her cloth wiped furiously at the wasted milk.

"You're obviously too far gone in love with her to think straight."

That got her attention. "What the fuck are you talking about?"

"I've been through the same thing myself. It's not very easy, is it?"

She wanted to deny it. Dez Nichols was the master of the fuck and run. Love was something she'd seen tossed back in her mother's face, something girls always claimed to feel but could never prove. It wasn't something that she did. But there was no other explanation for her feelings. It made sense. It was fucked up. But it made sense. The knowledge of it settled into her bones as she watched Derrick down his glass of scotch then reach for the bottle again.

"I should have known that she would see something in you. I could bullshit myself and say that she was looking for a female version of me, but we both know that except for this gorgeous nose the two of us look nothing alike." He lifted his glass to Dez. "Thank God."

She wanted to reach for that bottle, too, but something told her milk and whiskey weren't meant to be mixed just then.

"When I saw her five years ago I thought she was the classiest woman I'd ever seen. And pretty, too. When she told me that she was a lesbian I thought I could change her mind. When I couldn't, I resigned myself to being her friend. That was the best booby prize I've ever won. She'd been there for me in so many ways, been with me through everything." He scratched his jaw thoughtfully, as if considering his next words, wondering if he should share them with his sister. Then he shrugged. "I had an AIDS scare a few years back. She let me have it for being so damn careless. Even now I'm not sure if I wear rubbers because of the scare or because of her cussing me out." He lifted his head. "This woman means a lot to me, Dez. I love her in a way that's hard to explain, but I think even you can understand. Don't fuck up. It's obviously not over between you two."

Derrick went home and Dez stayed. She had a lot to think about. Although she didn't quite want to, the situation with Victoria kept intruding, worming its way into her forebrain until all she could do was glare at it, squirming in discomfort. She took up the bottle of whiskey her brother had abandoned and started to drink.

Dez wasn't going to look for her again. No matter how hard it was, she would not go. She had never pursued a woman before and she had already broken that rule by tracking Victoria. That was it. The first and the last. Dez walked around her empty house, deliberately prodding at her heart's ache by imagining Victoria walking with her, lovely and touchable in one of her many sundresses, tilting her bright head to listen to whatever she had to say. Dez sat finally in the empty guest room contemplating her four-times empty glass of whiskey with its pale ghost of the alcohol marring the clear crystal. Her body felt light with the stuff, but that was all. The Victoria situation still lay heavy and unpleasant on her mind. Damn her and damn Derrick for bringing her into Dez's life in the first place. The phone rang. She looked up from the glass and thought about not answering it. But it could be Claudia. It wasn't.

"Dez." The voice on the other end of the line made her heart squeeze and slow down.

"Hey, baby. You're not giving me the cold shoulder anymore?"

"I was never giving you the cold shoulder," Victoria said.

"Then what was—? Fuck it. What's on your mind?"

"You, of course."

"Of course." *Thinking of more ways to make me feel like shit?*

"I'm calling to invite you out," Victoria paused. "Are you free this weekend?"

"Maybe. What's going on?" She lay back on the bed and stared up at the high, arcing ceiling. Her head was beginning to swim.

"There's a party in the Keys this weekend. At Odette's." Her voice dropped off as if she expected Dez to say something. "Do you want to come?"

"Sure. Why not?" Odette was famous for her anything-goes, all-night girls' parties. Dez had been there several times but the one visit that stood out most in her mind was the Friday three years ago when she'd gone in and not left until Sunday afternoon. She'd ached in places she never even knew existed. It had been a *very* good time. O had lots of money, lots of coke, and lots and lots of hot women friends. Dez didn't even think that a woman like Victoria would know O, much less want to go to one of her parties.

"I'll leave your name at the door as my guest," Victoria said. Which meant they wouldn't be arriving together.

"I never went home with that woman." The words jumped out of Dez's mouth despite her determination not to say them. "Do you believe me?"

Victoria's silence was damning enough. She listened to her lover breathe on the other end of the phone, heard the soft catch in her breath that could have been anything and nothing. "You never lie, right?"

"Not about things like this."

"Okay." She paused. "So I'll see you on Saturday?"

"Yes." Dez didn't bother to ask what time. They both knew what time Odette's got started and when the giant pleasure palace closed its doors, locking its patrons inside until the morning. Dez hung up the phone before Victoria did. She didn't want to hear the finality of the disconnecting "click." She'd hear it soon enough in her lover's voice on Saturday.

Chapter 30

On the night of the party, Dez dressed with care, like she was going on a date, but sexier, taking more care with what was underneath her clothes. Her body smelled good, was clean and soft and lickable. Although the outcome of the night's activities was uncertain, she wanted to be prepared for anything. She also wanted to be irresistible to Victoria. If her lover was going to cut her loose, Dez was going to damn well show her what she would be missing. First she pulled on sheer white silk, then the leather. At eight o'clock, she rode her motorcycle down the turnpike against the flow of leftover rush-hour traffic, speeding toward the Islamorada.

It was a short ride from Highway 1 to the renovated two-story beachfront hotel. It was just after ten when she pulled the bike up to the building. The lights were dim, but as Dez drew closer she could hear the muted voices of dozens of women and, beyond them, the siren call of the ocean. She parked her bike in the parking lot facing the ocean with its thick cluster of vehicles illuminated under the half moon.

At the door, a tiny woman stood taking names and tips, smiling up at the many women who walked up to then past her. The light sea breeze ruffled her fuchsia Afro. When Dez gave her name, the woman looked fully at her.

"Desiree Nichols? No way, she left us for a boy years ago. You can't be her." Her pretty face dimpled.

"Lenny, don't be mean." She pulled the woman up from the stool and kissed her vanilla-scented throat. "The point is I came back, right?"

Lenny blushed in the light. "I guess. Don't disappear when you get inside. I want to chat with you before you get too into things."

Dez nodded. "You know where to find me." She put her motorcycle helmet in the cabinet just behind Lenny and walked into O's pleasure palace.

She sauntered past the curtained entrance where women stood scoping out newcomers for their potential as companions for the night. Her boots were quiet against the wine red carpet lining the stairs that led to the main ballroom. The decadent atmosphere sucked at her leather-covered skin, welcoming her into its heat.

Three of the pale walls flashed different images of women dancing, kissing, posing provocatively with naked backs and thighs, parted lips and sweating cleavage. The images flashed in tune to the music, giving newcomers an idea of what would happen later on in the evening if they let themselves go.

Dez looked around the cavernous room. No sight of Victoria. She straightened her jacket and headed for the bar.

"Oban. Two fingers, neat."

The bartender was back with the whiskey before Dez could settle herself properly on the stool. With a slow nod and the slip of a crisp twenty across the bar, she acknowledged the woman's promptness. She took her drink and turned to watch the show on the floor.

They were at the foreplay stage of the evening. The large ballroom was barely half-filled and the music undulated at medium speed with a deep hypnotic bass that drew a few dozen women to the dance floor, panting over their partners, sliding sensuously against them, warming up for what was to come. Despite the variety in age of the women here, they all gave off a similar energy, one of hunger and sensuality and near-danger. From heroin-thin ingénues to buxom beauties, Mrs. Robinsons and even the ripe fearlessness of women well past their fiftieth year, the ballroom was well stocked with every kind of woman, every kind of desire.

"You all alone tonight, baby?"

Dez turned from the dance floor at the sound of the provocative voice near her shoulder. She took her time looking the woman over, from her sleek cap of hair tapering down to a graceful neck, to the acres of cleavage cradled in black silk straps that barely passed for a blouse, down to the flat belly and long, long legs revealed by the matching skirt. Her eyes took an even slower trip back up. The woman allowed the scrutiny, even posing for it, turning in so the faint light gleamed on her deep brown skin and the diamond star winking from the navel. A grunt of appreciation escaped Dez's throat. But . . .

"No. Maybe some other time."

The hot girl pouted in disappointment then, after a light brush against Dez's thigh, disappeared back into the sea of women.

A chorus of disappointed groans came from some of the women seated at the bar. They could find someone else to entertain them with a public fuck session tonight. Dez took a sip of her whiskey, savoring the slow burn across her tongue and the smoky fragrance that briefly filled her nose. She spread her thighs wide against the stool, then leaned back against the bar to wait.

An hour passed and she grew nervous. Would Victoria stand her up as a punishment for failing some fidelity test on Sunday? The lump in the pit of her stomach grew in size with each passing minute. By hour two it had migrated to her throat and no amount of distraction from Lenny—who spent forty-five entertaining minutes catching Dez up on the happenings of the last two years—could get rid of it. Just as she was about to settle up with the bartender and go home, she saw the flash of ginger and copper curls at the door.

Gratitude and relief flooded her chest. In that moment, she hated Victoria. She wished that the woman had never come into her life making her feel this humiliating rush of love and lust and misery and anticipation and dread.

Victoria stalked in, lush and luscious in a honey-colored leather vest the exact shade of her skin and matching pants that sat low on her hips. The vest was cut low to show off Victoria's wealth of breast and soft skin, but she'd modestly covered up with a long piece of copper silk worn around her throat like a scarf then tucked down into the leather bodice. The silk appeared again from beneath the cropped leather top, allowing only teasing glimpses of her belly through its semi-sheer weight before flowing down, butterfly-light, to the floor and over her pants and high-heeled boots. It made Dez's hands itch to move the cloth out of the way, to feel that hidden skin. Victoria *would* make this hard for her.

You play a very cruel game, Ms. Jackson. Dez wet her lips. She knew the exact moment when Victoria saw her sitting, quiet and watchful, at the bar. Her eyes met Dez's, then slid away before coming back.

"Sorry I'm late," she said as soon as she was close enough to be heard.

"As long as you made it before they closed the doors for the night." Dez made her response deliberately noncommittal. She wouldn't let Victoria know how she had worried and was still worrying.

"So you've been here before, then?" Victoria asked.

"Yes."

"Of course." A deep breath shook her curls and brought her closer to Dez. "You airing that out for me?" she murmured as she slipped between the sprawl of Dez's thighs.

"Well, it has been a while since anybody's been in there." Dez tossed back the last of her whiskey and released an exhilarated breath, uncertain whether it was from the Oban or Victoria's smile mere inches from hers. "Dance with me." She stood up, brushing her fingers along the flowing silk over Victoria's breasts.

A Madonna oldie shook the floor as they made their way through the crowd of gyrating women.

"You look incredible." Dez traced the soft line of Victoria's back, pulling her closer as their hips moved in time to the heavy, sensual beat. "I'm glad you came."

"You thought I wouldn't?"

Dez laughed. "Let's not do this." She settled her hands on the rocking hips. "I know you didn't like what you saw at Novlette's last Sunday. I know you're angry. There's no reason for you to be. I never touched her."

"But did she touch you?"

"Ah . . . you think I'm lying by omission?"

"Isn't that one way that you 'tell the truth'?"

"Is that why you sounded so strange when I told you that I didn't take Matsuko home with me? Well, let me tell it to you like this: I didn't fuck her, she didn't fuck me, no one fucked anybody in my presence on Sunday. Is that plain enough for you?"

The music changed, becoming subtly raunchier, charging the air with sex. Even with her anger at Victoria, Dez was attuned to it. She shifted to slide her thigh between her lover's.

"Is it?" she asked again, flexing her thigh against Victoria.

"Yes. It is," Victoria murmured, arching her neck. Her hands tightened on Dez's arms as she pushed herself down on the thick muscle.

As they danced, the ceiling above them opened. They could all hear the click of the doors as the entrances were all sealed. No one would be able to get out until the morning. The moon and stars glittered down on the women, suddenly the only source of light in the room except for the gentle illumination on the floor leading to the bar. The music slowly lowered until it was background noise.

"Good evening, ladies," a provocative, female voice purred

from hidden speakers. A muted hiss rippled through the room as the velvet curtains on the glass wall were pulled closed, effectively shutting out the rest of the island. Low anticipatory laughter and conversation surged through the crowd.

"If anyone has an emergency and wants to leave before morning, please see Diana behind the bar on the first floor. Don't forget to show your appreciation to the ladies at your service tonight. In the meantime, enjoy." The heavy, hypnotic stroke of Sade's "Smooth Operator," electrified by a drumming house beat, rose as her voice drifted away.

"So what do you have in mind for us tonight, Ms. Jackson?"

Victoria moved her hands up Dez's back and pressed her face into her throat. "Something fun. Whatever you want." Then she muttered something Dez could not hear.

"What was that?"

"Nothing," Victoria said. "Just my own stupidity."

"Well, let's get that out of mind then. On to something more interesting."

Dez, deliberately provocative, dropped her jacket from her shoulders and slid it down her arms, baring the white shirt with its closely guarded flesh of firm breasts, firmer nipples, and arms that rippled with muscle and the bas-relief veins of her arousal. "How about this?"

Victoria released her breath in a surprised gasp. But not to be outdone, she ran her hands up Dez's flat stomach and over the breasts that were obviously begging to be touched. Dez arched into that touch and closed her eyes. Her arms, trapped in her jacket, tensed and rubbed against the silk-lined leather. *Yeah*, she thought lazily, *this broad really has me by the balls.*

"Would you like some help with that?" A woman appeared out of the anonymous crowd, insinuating her ocean-scented body between them. She was dressed, barely, in a wine-colored piece of cloth tied once around her waist. Gold glitter and body paint accentuated everywhere else. The girl was blade thin and gorgeous, casting her rapacious eyes boldly over Victoria.

"*Do* you need help, love?" Dez teased, eyeing the bit of candy with interest. Part of her was curious about just how far Victoria would go to prove her point, whatever it was.

Victoria squeezed her nipple through the shirt then slowly drew her hand away so the other woman could watch and hunger. "Maybe," she said. "Do you think you can handle the two of us, honey?"

The gold-dipped stranger chuckled. "The question is, can you two handle me?"

This was definitely *not* what she had in mind for the night. Just the thought of sharing her lover in this sort of scenario made Dez sick with jealousy. Victoria threaded her fingers through Dez's, then tugged the woman along with them. The threesome headed for the stairs, a daisy chain strung on the edges of the spiral staircase allowing other women to pass alongside them. Cool bodies brushed against Dez, hands squeezed her leather-covered ass, others touched the small of her back as she brought up the rear, pulled past half-opened rooms where the sounds of sex poured out like wine. The darkened hallway flickered with bright bodies, some bent over glass tables lined with blow. The music blurred conversations hissing around them, but the hard, intent bodies with hands stroking barely clothed thighs and breasts made every meaning clear. Victoria didn't belong here.

The bedroom she took them to was large and well stocked, with an assortment of whips and restraints on the walls and a mirrored ceiling.

The gold woman squealed with delight. "Oh, goody! This is one of my favorite rooms."

Dez shrugged out of her jacket then arched an eyebrow at Victoria. She was, after all, running the show.

"Do you like her, Dez?"

She shrugged. "She's all right. Nice mouth. Gorgeous tits." Dez coolly assessed their new playmate, mentally apologizing for putting her through what should have been a confrontation between Victoria and her.

Victoria turned to the girl. "Go down on her. You'll like it. Her pussy is sweet."

When the woman moved to touch Dez, the tall woman shook her head and gestured toward her lover. "She's the one who you like. Take her. Unbutton her leather and fuck her." Her head tilted as she glanced at Victoria. "That's what you want, right? A little variety?"

The gold woman sank to her knees and started undoing Victoria's pants. Her fingers were sure and practiced. They freed the soft skin from its leather prison within moments. She kissed Victoria's belly, her hip bone, and the curling sprigs of hair that crowned her pussy. Victoria stared at Dez as the stranger pulled her pants to her knees and slid her thighs apart, burrowing between her legs for wet treasure. A muscle in Dez's jaw jumped, but she didn't say anything. Instead she sat down on the bed and took it all in.

"You're not very wet, baby," the woman said. "Let me get you some lube."

"She doesn't like lube," Dez murmured, keeping her eyes on Victoria's face. "Get her wet with your mouth. Yeah, just like that."

Victoria flinched as the woman continued to paw her, lapping between her legs to generate a wetness that wouldn't come.

"Lay on the bed, baby. Your girlfriend can see you much better if you're nice and spread out."

"I'm not her girlfriend," Dez said.

With a low cry Victoria pulled herself away from the stranger. "I'm sorry." She backed away from her would-be lover, her face twisted with pain. "We shouldn't do this. I'm not ready."

The woman stood up and wiped her mouth. "No problem, baby. The night's young and there's plenty of pussy around."

She gave Dez's body a quick once-over and licked her lips. "If you change your mind, come by and see me next month." The door closed behind her with a soft click.

"I don't know why I'm trying to be like you," Victoria said. She zipped up her pants and smoothed her hands over her hips. "Obviously it's not working."

"Is that what you're doing?" Anger burned under her skin, heating her face and hands, but Dez forced her voice to stay even. "I would have never taken you to a place like this without permission. Never." She lay back against the pillows and crossed her booted ankles. "If you're angry at me about Sunday, say so. Don't fucking play games."

"I'm not playing games with you. Shit!" Victoria winced and plucked at the skin between her eyes. "I thought that things were going so well with us and that after a while that we could . . ." She cursed again. "I don't know why I expected someone who's never had to work a day in her life for anything to want to work at a relationship."

"That's a goddamn low blow. If you don't want me as I am, then say so; don't bring up inconsequential shit."

"Shit, shit, shit! I'm sorry. Let me start again." She sighed and stared hard at Dez. "I've come to care for you. A lot. But I know that doesn't change the arrangement that we have." Victoria blinked then looked away. "It didn't hit me until I saw you with that girl what this bargain really means. I don't want to . . . fuck anyone else. All I want is you and since that's obviously not possible, I'm trying to wean myself off you in the best way that I know how."

"By pushing new pussy in my face and hoping that I'll reach out and take it in front of you?" Dez snorted. "That, if you'd forgive me for saying so, is the stupidest idea I've ever heard." She stood up and walked to the thickly curtained window. Beyond the gnarled woods behind the hotel, the Caribbean Sea shimmered coolly under the moon. It was a beautiful night. "If you want, we can talk about it. We can agree to see each other exclusively. There's been no one else for a long time, anyway. You can even tell Derrick about us and get the awful secret out in the open."

Victoria looked like Dez just suggested that she wipe her face in shit. "Yeah, we do need to talk about this."

Ah, so I'm your dirty little secret, then. She pursed her lips. "After all the months of being together, all the things we've done together, do you still think that there isn't a future for us?" She recalled their conversation on the drive from Sarasota all those months ago. "Do I fit you? Do we fit together?"

"I don't know."

Well, I did ask for honesty. Dez slowly nodded.

The sound of boot heels on the floor punctuated Victoria's agitated pacing across the room. She flashed Dez a quick look. "You make me nervous. But you make me feel good, too. Most of my friends don't like you, but my mothers do. When we're in bed together everything is perfect. But I would be a fool to trust that." She stopped at the foot of the bed and looked full at Dez. "I don't want to be hasty with you. You warned me how it would be in the beginning, you told me what you could offer and although I knew you were telling me the truth, I ignored most of that. I wanted you, so I said yes. But I don't want to be your next heartbreak."

"What if I was ready to commit?" Dez folded her arms across her chest. "Would you become less uncertain?"

Breath hitched loudly in Victoria's throat. "Don't—don't tease me. I couldn't take it if you were joking."

"You really do take me for a lying asshole, don't you?" Dez shook her head. "I'm going to go and find someone who doesn't doubt every fucking thing that I say."

"Wait. I'm sorry." The press of Victoria's hand on her belly intercepted Dez's flight from the room. "I'm sorry. Sit. Please."

"No." That touch released the fear she'd had of declaring herself. "All night you've been saying that you're sorry. Stop being sorry and take some responsibility here. I want you.

I've wanted you for damn near four months now and I don't think it's going away. I want us to be together, for real, in front of Derrick and everybody. If you don't want to do it just say so. Don't use excuses, don't talk about uncertainty. Your friends aren't here. Neither are your parents. You and I are here now. Make a decision."

"You *want* me?" Victoria sat down on the bed. "Is that what you said to Ruben when you realized that you loved him?"

Dez squirmed. "You know what I mean."

"Yes, I do." She lifted a hand and reached out to Dez. She came and sat down. "That was very well put." A smile teased the corner of her mouth. "I love you, too, Desiree Nichols, although you've made it very hard."

The trembling started deep inside, vibrating low in a place she never had a reason to access before. Not even with Ruben. By the time it reached her hands, Dez had pushed Victoria into the starched sheets and buried her face in the sweet smelling throat. She nipped at the soft flesh but couldn't speak. That could wait until the morning.

Chapter 31

"Are you sure that you want to do this?"

"Are *you* sure that you want to do this?"

"Stop fucking with me." Dez squeezed Victoria's thigh under the table and tried not to look nervous. It didn't work.

Victoria giggled and leaned in close, teasing Dez with her soft scent. "I'm just making sure. It's not every day that a hot woman propositions *and* proposes to me."

"I hope not. Nobody gets to chat up that gorgeous pussy of yours but me."

Victoria giggled again. "Shhh."

But nobody was paying any attention to the two women. Chaos reigned happily on Dez's patio. The once spare, but well-landscaped space had been transformed into a lush eat-and-playground with a long, picnic-style table and matching benches set on top of a pretty stone-paved surface. A trellis veined with scented purple flowers and their vines separated the hot tub and pool from the dining area at one end and the double doors leading to the house at the other. A pair of leaf-shaped fans spun lazily overhead, adding just the right amount of tropical decadence to the newly designed back-yard.

Everyone talked at once, sipping their drinks, and eating from the huge banquet of food laid out along the table's center. It was almost too much—lobsters still in their hot, blushing shells piled high on a platter, some already missing a claw or two; summer fruits marinating in their own juices and shimmering red and orange and pink in a bowl; coconut and ginger-flavored rice; moist-looking Thai-style basil rolls; and even a large oven-roasted chicken. A bright arrangement of stir-fried vegetables and tofu sat in its platter, adding even more color to the eclectic mixture of edibles. Eden, Claudia's friend, demurely ate one of the four basil rolls on her plate, her slender fingers raised to her lips to shield their movement as she listened intently to something Rémi was saying.

A year ago, Dez didn't think that something like this would be possible—her friends, Claudia, Derrick, Victoria's family and *her* friends, all gathered around the same table enjoying one another. Happiness settled like a warm fist inside her, curling gently around her vulnerable places and keeping them safe. At her right, Claudia scooped more tofu on her plate, laughing and almost unable to wield her spoon as Sage delivered the dirty punchline to her joke.

At the far end of the table, Derrick sat between Abena and Kavi, shamelessly lapping up the attention the two women lavished on him. Even Mick showed up to make nice along with everyone else. She and Nuria exchanged small talk as they swapped the bowl of rice and the smaller one filled with melted butter between them.

"So, when are you going to tell us why we're all here?" Rémi asked.

Trust her friend to get to the point before everyone else. Dez caressed Victoria's hand laying on the table next to hers and thought about what to say.

"Could it be because of that luscious thing by your side? Is she finally going to make an honest woman out of you?"

No one was surprised by the question, but still there was a reasonable amount of silence as one or two people waited for the answer.

"I have asked," Victoria said into the relative quiet, "and she did say yes, so . . ." She held up Dez's hand. The wide platinum band with its trinity of diamonds on her promise finger sparkled impressively in the light.

"Wow! How did I miss that?" Kavi leaned in closer to get a better view of the ring. She wasn't the only one.

Dez felt her face warm as she self-consciously lowered her hand. Ever merciless, Victoria giggled.

Delia and Veronique watched all the action from their place at their daughter's side. They had been privy to most of the couple's soft-voiced conversation and knew how nervous Dez was. Just last month, Victoria had called her mothers in Canada and asked them to come down to Miami for a special dinner. They weren't told what the dinner was for, but when Victoria and Dez picked them up from the airport with both their eyes filled with love for the other, it was obvious what the big announcement was going to be.

"Ah well," Rémi said after all the excitement about the ring had died down. "I guess I'll have to go back to handling all those hot Miami babes myself."

Dez smiled, barely hiding her relief at the topic shift. "Something tells me that you're more than up for the job."

The two friends had talked the night before at a sort of "bachelors' last night out." Rémi had been in a pensive mood. "I like the girl," she said. "She's hot and she's been good for you. But I'm still going to miss you and me." Of course she meant that she'd miss their fuck runs. There was no question of Dez's faithfulness to Victoria. On a sober night a million years ago they'd talked about finding and keeping permanent partners. In their deepest of hearts, they were both monogamous women. It was just that, until now, neither of The Good Time Twins had ever found the right One to fit into the slot.

"Thanks, Rémi," Dez had murmured over their nearly empty glasses of twenty-year-old scotch. "If things work out with Victoria I'd want you to stand up with me. Is that all right?"

"You don't even have to ask. I'll be honored to be your best man. Or whatever they call it." Then they shook hands.

The two women looked at each other across the table now and smiled.

"Congratulations," Derrick said, breaking up their love-fest. He glanced first at Victoria then at Dez. "You've found a really good woman. The best." He raised his glass of wine. "To quote a classic, 'You break her heart and I'll break your legs.' "

"Come on, Derrick," Victoria muttered, giving her best friend a cutting glance even though his tone had been playful.

"I'll drink to that," Veronique said in her purring French-Canadian accent. "Although I'm sure there will be no need for that. So far Desiree seems absolutely like the kind of love Delia and I always wanted for our daughter."

At Dez's side, Victoria blushed and smiled. She squeezed Veronique's hand. "Thank you, mamá. I think."

"Another toast, then." Sage rose gracefully to her feet despite the many drinks she'd already had. "To the happy couple. May you live long and prosper"—after the laughter and groans at the Star Trek reference died away, she raised her glass of scotch and the corners of her mouth—"together."

Dez thanked her mischievous friend with an accurately tossed napkin. Sage laughed and brushed off her shirt front. A few months ago when she found out that Victoria was the woman Dez had been seeing on the sly, she almost pissed herself laughing. "Your brother's hot-ass friend, yeah?" She laughed again. "Nice."

From her seat in her girlfriend's lap, Phil had smiled devilishly at Dez. "You never take the easy route, do you?"

Nuria was far less congratulatory, but seemed determined to play nice, perhaps in hopes of using Victoria to lure Derrick into bed. At the far end of the table, she now chatted easily with her neighbors, alternately charming and seductive in her eye-catching bustier-style blouse and tight jeans.

Dez looked away from her friend as Victoria stood up from the table and walked toward the kitchen. She waited a few seconds before following.

"I knew you'd come in here," Victoria said, turning from the cupboards with a teasing smile.

"How can I resist? I haven't had you to myself all night."

"But you will later."

"True enough, but you know me and instant gratification." She dropped tiny kisses on the corners of Victoria's mouth. Her lover's hands settled on her hips, pulling her closer.

"I can't believe it's been almost a year," Victoria said.

"And I still can't get enough of you."

"That I can believe. You have the stamina of a hummingbird on speed." She squeezed Dez's butt. "And I love it."

"Good."

"Don't forget that you two have company," Rémi called out from the patio. "Let's not have a repeat of the birthday party incident." A laughing voice, Delia's, begged for a telling of that story.

Victoria blushed and tried to jump back from her lover. But Dez held her close with a low chuckle. "It wasn't anything they hadn't seen or done before," she murmured, remembering the crème fraîche tasting that had quickly escalated into heated foreplay on the kitchen counter.

"Don't be so sure." Victoria buried her hot face in Dez's neck. Only after her face cooled did she look up. "Let's get back to the table."

"What did you come in here for, anyway?" Dez asked.

A teasing smile fluttered across her mouth. "I already got it."

"You know me that well, huh?"

"Not yet, but I plan on making it part of my life's work."

And it was when she said things like that that Dez turned to fudge, melting under the sure and constant heat of her love. She playfully swatted Victoria on the ass as her lover walked out of the patio doors ahead of her. Over Victoria's head, Claudia's eyes met hers, faintly amused.

"Don't look so disappointed, darling. You'll have time enough for that later." She held out her hand. "Come, Rémi has a new dessert she wants us all to try."

"Why didn't you say so in the first place? I would have left that broad in the kitchen ages ago." She let the door swing closed behind her and walked into the welcoming embrace of her family's laughter.